"She was seen."

Like mice skittering from room to room the words spread, interrupting daily activities. Maura wasn't supposed to be seen? Why? Was there something wrong with her? Maybe it was her eyes. Papa said they were like starbursts surrounded by blue sky. That would be like Papa to make something strange seem lovely. Or maybe it was because she was a snoop, always searching for what rested in undiscovered places.

For whatever reason, Maura needed to hide. Again.

Praise for *WHEN STARS BRUSH EARTH*:

"Laurel Thomas has created a story of intrigue and danger set in a clash of supernatural powers with seventeen-year-old Maura O'Donnell at the forefront. *WHEN STARS BRUSH EARTH* will keep you reading all night and stay with you long after the final chapter."

~Robin Patchen, multi-published
author of romantic suspense
~*~

"The tapestry of Maura O'Donnell's journey in *WHEN STARS BRUSH EARTH* is woven with vivid imagery, rich characters and unexpected plot twists. Laurel Thomas is a prolific storyteller you'll want to follow for years to come."

~Melanie Hemry, nationally-known
author, speaker and mentor

When
Stars Brush Earth

by

Laurel Thomas

This is a work of fiction. Names, characters, places, and incidents are either the product of the author's imagination or are used fictitiously, and any resemblance to actual persons living or dead, business establishments, events, or locales, is entirely coincidental.

When Stars Brush Earth

COPYRIGHT © 2022 by Laurel Thomas

Cover Art by *Tina Lynn Stout*

The Wild Rose Press, Inc.
PO Box 708
Adams Basin, NY 14410-0708
Visit us at www.thewildrosepress.com

Publishing History
First Edition, 2022
Trade Paperback ISBN 978-1-5092-4441-6
Digital ISBN 978-1-5092-4442-3

Published in the United States of America

Dedication

To my sister, Nadine,
who taught me to hope in the unexpected
and believe the impossible.

Other Wild Rose Press Titles by Laurel Thomas:

River's Call

Chapter 1

The historical Magi priesthood were called alongside kings for their wisdom. What these famed astrologers discerned in the heavens was unquestioned. When the stars signaled a new generation arising, existing kingdoms were threatened. Kings bent on defying the stars had to act. Children who bore the mark of the Magi were their target.

Slate gray sky peeked through the iron lattice that covered Maura O'Donnell's bedroom window. After pulling her feet from under warm covers, she tucked a dingy handkerchief doll under her pillow, put on worn slippers, and tiptoed out of the quiet room. She crept down a granite-tiled hallway, careful not to disturb her parents. They didn't know about her journeys, stolen when no one else was awake. Her belly wiggled with the tiniest sliver of guilt. Papa had been insistent about his warning.

"You see the deer, how Papa deer searches the meadow before his family comes out to graze? Promise that you'll wait for me when you go outside. Your papa will make sure his little fawn can play in safety."

How could her mountain home be anything but the refuge she'd known and loved for as long as she could remember? She wasn't the only one here, though. Other people lived with them in the massive stone chateau.

They were mostly little ones. When Maura asked Papa about the other children's absent parents, his forehead crinkled, and he didn't say much. Only that he and Mama offered a safe place for those who had none. What that meant, she wasn't sure.

She didn't like sharing her beloved parents, who scurried about preparing and serving daily meals, patching up scraped knees, and overseeing inevitable squabbles. And they were teachers, encouraging even the youngest tongues to form words in English, foreign to many.

In the daytime, children's voices filled every available space with chatter. Maura loved early mornings, when birds greeted her with songs, and tiny pika dashed from the rocks, awake after a chilly mountain night. Everything inside Maura resisted Papa's warning. She couldn't explain how she longed to see the beginning of a new day. Her five-year-old body yearned to stretch, to run, to dance after a long night of stillness. Wouldn't Papa agree that it was important for his little Star to say good-bye to the constellations and greet the dawn?

Slipping her fingers under the wooden food safe, Maura found a familiar key, worn and nicked with years of use. She fit the key into the lock and turned it. The oaken door opened with a slight moan. The soft, damp ground of the forest surrounding the chateau soaked through her slippers. She darted among its shadows to a meadow that beckoned beyond massive trees.

Grabbing the trunk of a towering pine for balance, she skipped over a giant root extending above ground, then paused for a moment in the stillness. Blue mountain aster peeked through silver sage and rocky outcroppings in the meadow that lay before her. Autumn crocus were nearby, lovely only in appearance. Papa had warned her of their deadly poison.

She sprinted forward, then bounced with delight. The bounce became a twirl, the twirl spiraling around and around as Maura sang her own medley of nursery rhymes and psalms. On and on she danced as light appeared on the horizon.

A rustle in the brush around a grove of aspen caught her attention. Perhaps it was a marmot, emerging from his burrow. Or a chipmunk scurrying through the brush. It was time to return to the chateau anyway. No reason to be afraid. She glanced once more backward as she turned to leave.

A woman with flowing black hair, wrapped in a cloak the color of mountain ferns, stood alone on a small rise beyond the meadow. A glittering pendant around her neck reflected prisms of emerald in sunlight. She smiled at Maura, then raised one hand toward her and beckoned. Maura didn't move. Papa had warned her never to approach a stranger near the chateau. But the woman was so beautiful.

Her clear voice sounded like music. "Star. Come to me."

Only Papa called her Star. This must be someone Maura knew. Perhaps a relative who'd come to visit. Maura walked toward her, curious and drawn by her invitation. A crow cawed and Maura jumped. Soon, several of the black birds gathered around the woman, flapping their giant wings. The woman pressed her hand toward them, and they flew away. Except for one that lit upon her slender shoulder and sat as if awaiting a command.

What kind of woman commanded the birds? And not the pretty kind of birds but the scary black ones with the rough call. Maura stopped, wary. As she did, the woman smiled and motioned to her again. The emerald prism around her neck undulated on its golden cord and became a serpent's head, reaching toward her.

Maura stepped back. At least she tried. It was if a puppeteer pulled a string attached to her, drawing her forward. She pressed backward as hard as she could, but still she was pulled toward the woman. Terror rose in her throat. She was too little to resist. Not strong enough to break the power of what was pulling her closer and closer. What had Papa said to do when she was alone and afraid? It was…

"I call upon the power of the scroll!"

Her small voice rang out in the clear morning air. As it did, the strength of the invisible cord broke, and she was free. She turned and ran through the forest and across the broad lawn of the chateau, legs burning and small chest heaving. When the heavy door closed behind her with a thud, she leaned against it, her heart still hammering.

All was still inside. Until Maura heard wood scrape against stone from one corner of the kitchen. Papa rose from a chair by the blackened stove. She was caught with no escape except perhaps one drenched in tears. Opening her mouth wide, she wailed. Then peeked at Papa to view the effect of her performance. She remembered the day when Mama had opened the pantry door and found her with both hands full of cookies, cheeks stuffed, and crumbs scattered everywhere. She'd been so tired of sharing. Just once she'd hide in the pantry and eat as many cookies as she wanted.

Mama's brown eyes were stern at first, then her face had reddened. She'd averted her head and made a funny, choking noise that sounded almost like a giggle.

But these weren't cookies. Maura tried to read Papa's face through her tears, hoping he understood how truly stricken his little Star was. He wasn't one to get angry. Only once when she'd shoved a girl into a wall. Maura had wanted to talk to her mama alone. And the girl had been hogging her. Papa had pulled her into a room, plopped her on the bed beside him, and made her sit until she promised to apologize to the mean, nasty girl. The words stuck in her throat, but she'd obeyed.

Now, she stopped crying in earnest. She was surprised to see it wasn't anger that filled those blue eyes. Instead, it was tears. Why did her heart fill with such terror at the sight of them?

"Did you see anyone outside this morning?" he asked.

Maura bowed her head and spoke to the granite floor beneath her feet. "Yes, Papa." She rubbed her face with one hand and hurried to explain. "But she was very beautiful. And she knew my name."

Papa's large frame shifted, as if a strong gust of wind had blown open the heavy wooden door behind them. Her heart pounded in the silence. Would she be banned from nightly songs around the ancient piano? Or miss story times full of regal Magi priests who protected kings against sinister plots and delivered nations in certain peril? When he spoke, she'd know her punishment. He was silent, though. His chest heaved once as if resisting an invisible river inside. In the next moment, Papa held his arms out to her.

Maura ran into them, feeling their warmth against

her cool skin. She buried her head in his scratchy woolen shirt. This time her tears were full of regret.

"I won't ever…"

Papa didn't answer. His body shuddered, and when she tried to pull away, he held her closer. The top of her head grew damp. Perhaps he was praying for her, as he often did. Finally, the shaking stopped, and he set her on her feet and turned to lead the way. "Mama has prepared breakfast," he said. "We mustn't be late."

Chapter 2

The dining room filled with children coming from every direction, some skipping, some still rubbing their eyes with sleep. Mama and other women had placed large bowls of steaming oatmeal in the middle of the long oaken slab table. Pitchers of milk rested nearby alongside plates of warm bread and a large bowl of honey. It was a sight she loved every morning, especially since she was always hungry.

She ran to her mama first and grabbed her around the waist, relieved that she wasn't in trouble. One thing she knew—even through the worst of her temper tantrums and the ways she stretched the rules like a band to see if they broke, she was always loved. Mama's arms shook as she knelt and held Maura, her honey-colored hair cascading like a veil. That was odd. Her morning hugs were usually a brief, warm squeeze in between the business of feeding so many little ones. This morning, Mama held on.

When other children turned to stare, Maura tried to wiggle away. She wasn't a baby, after all. Still, Mama held her tight. When she finally released her hold, Mama stood and walked back into the kitchen. Her fluid gait was broken only by a soft bowing in her knees. Maura bounded off to her place at the table. Placing her spoon in one hand and peering up, she smiled at pretty Gwen, who plopped a generous dollop of oatmeal into her bowl.

Sometimes, Gwen played with them in the massive open library upstairs. Although she loved all the children, Maura knew Paddy was her favorite. The Paddy who beat her at every race and contest. This morning, Gwen's face was so sad it frightened her. Was she disappointed in her? A small panic rose in her heart. The oatmeal became sandy in her mouth. The other children seemed fine, talking, and arguing over the honey. Nothing had changed with them, at least.

After breakfast and morning clean-up, throughout lessons taught along the same oaken table, Maura heard adults whisper to one another. The air around the chateau buzzed like a cord pulled tight overhead. The only thing she snatched from those quiet tones were three words.

"She was seen."

Like mice skittering from room to room the words spread, interrupting daily activities. Maura wasn't supposed to be seen? Why? Was there something wrong with her? Maybe it was her eyes. Papa said they were like starbursts surrounded by blue sky. That would be like Papa to make something strange seem lovely. Or maybe it was because she was a snoop, always searching for what rested in undiscovered places.

For whatever reason, Maura needed to hide. Again. It was a familiar game to become small and disappear in the most unlikely places. She was so good at it that sometimes only the sound of Mama's tears pulled her out.

Often it was her Uncle Benjamin who scolded her. "Ye' be a tiny mite, miss. Too scrappy and persnickety for yer own good." Then he'd stomp away, muttering. He was a grumpy man but full of stories. When she couldn't get Papa to sit long enough, she'd seek out

Benjamin and plead for more. Unlike Papa's, Benjamin's stories made the hairs on her arms rise in tiny bumps, then finally settle with certain victories in the end.

Afternoon sun had begun its drift into the western sky. She peered outside through the tall windows and caught a glimpse of Benjamin's crooked brown hat, slouched over his eyes, almost covering the tangle of chestnut brown hair that sprouted out in wild shoots around his weathered face. He held the head of old Prince in his arms and pressed his head against the black mane. When he pulled away, he held on to the horse, as if for support. Why would he prepare the horses for a ride?

She'd go find out. Maura skipped down the stairs until she reached the first floor. There, she stopped mid-flight and grabbed the railing. Several adults gathered bedding in one area. Others packed dishes. Mama and other women stashed potatoes, bread, and other food stuffs into open baskets. Benjamin would have to wait until she figured out this mystery.

They'd never had picnics outside, except on quiet winter days when they'd gather in the courtyard, braced against the cold to roast apples and chestnuts. This was the season when it was most important to stay inside, Papa had warned. None of the adults acknowledged Maura's presence with more than a nod. She felt strangely at odds with this day full of unexpected preparations and no one explaining her part in them. She crept down the hallway where finally, Mama found her hidden in her favorite place in between the bed and the wall in her parents' bedroom.

"Come out, child," she said.

Maura held out her arms to her mother, who pulled her onto the bed. Mama's smile tightened into a grimace. Why had her heart stopped its progress to her lips?

Papa walked in and sat on the other side of Maura. She'd snuggled between them on the down-filled mattress every night she could remember. They'd talked to each other, to her, in a seamless flow that the three of them knew so well.

This was not bedtime, and everything about the day had been different. There was something wrong. Maura felt it. It was an interruption in the easy grace of their love and conversation. Something unspoken. Were they still angry with her? That wouldn't be like them. Although she *had* broken an important rule this morning. What was this new feeling? It buzzed in the room, entered her heart, and fluttered there as a tiny bee hovering over honeysuckle. It smelled oddly of something she despised but couldn't name. The air around them was gray, despite the sun going down in orange and rose hues. Papa gazed into her eyes as if he were memorizing them.

"It's time for an adventure, Star," he said.

Maura perked up. This wasn't so bad after all. Her senses were lying to her.

"When, Papa? When will we leave?"

"Not…Mama and I must stay here for a while. You and Benjamin will go to a place where you can run outside and play. A place where you can learn other games."

More than hide and seek? It sounded fun, except for one part. Without Papa and Mama?

"I want you and Mama to come, too."

"Of course," he said. "And we will when we can.

Now, you must listen to Benjamin. He'll take you to a safe place where you'll grow and become all that Yahweh has planned."

"Not without you."

Mama sobbed once. An almost wail began out of her mouth, then suddenly ceased. Maura watched her gulp a huge gasp and swallow.

"You must be brave," said Papa. "Remember. You carry the light of the stars. Like your mama."

Papa had repeated these words over and over as long as she could remember.

Though an enemy builds its shelters on high and sets its nests among the stars, she who carries the light of stars will find and bring them down.

Not that she understood how she and her mama were connected by an ancient prophecy. Mama's hair flowed like warm sunshine and her sapphire eyes reminded Maura of a spring day bursting out of winter's gloom. Her own eyes, on the other hand, looked more like a storm brewing. And no amount of brushing tamed the bird's nest of her brown hair.

Papa wasn't done talking. "Who you are and what you carry inside is more precious than your mama and I can explain," he said. "Our hearts are connected by a sure cord that will never be broken. It guides you even now to the unknown, but free."

Free? What did Papa mean?

Mama drew Maura into her slender arms. "You'll dance under an open sunlit sky, not only under its stars in the cover of darkness. Someday, you'll teach others how the light of the stars burns bright in the darkest of times. Even like…"

Her voice broke, and Maura thought she heard her

finish the sentence. *Even like today.*

Today, a dark time? She shook her head. The sun had shone for all it was worth through the mountain aspen, shimmering against tender leaves. If the adults hadn't been busy about the chateau in ways that didn't make sense, it would've been like any other summer day that drew her into its warmth.

Mama pulled out a small pack of clothes, the handkerchief doll, and a long cylindrical pouch with an embroidered strap. Maura took a breath of joy when she recognized the handiwork on the pouch. Mama had used her finest, most vibrant threads to shape silver, golden, and scarlet stars against its dark fabric.

"It's the Archer," said Papa. "Mama placed his constellation on this bag to cover something very precious." He pulled the scroll out from under the desk and placed it inside the embroidered masterpiece. As he did, the stars seemed to come to life and tell their story in the fabric.

"The scroll? But, Papa…"

"You'll carry it to a place of freedom. Wherever you go, it will remind you of us. Of the promise of the Magi that rests inside you."

The Magi? In her? That couldn't be right. The Magi were brave, regal warriors of faith. Not like her. Not with her tantrums and disobedience.

Mama's fragrance tickled her nose as she held her close. Sunset faded, and the horizon became dark, like a line of shadowy mountains.

"It's time," said Papa.

The three of them walked hand in hand down a dark hall to the kitchen, now dimly lit by a flickering fire along one wall. Once outside, Maura gazed up at the great arched windows, illuminated by candlelight held in many hands, old and young alike. This was her home. These were her friends. Why weren't they coming with her?

Papa kissed her, then lifted her into the back of the wagon and settled her along one side of a load of potatoes. He wrapped blankets around her, teasing in a whisper. "Hide and seek, Maura. Be very still. You know this game? And that you always win?" He tucked the scroll in its embroidered pouch beside her.

Benjamin sat on the wooden bench in front, holding the reins of the bridled horse that snuffed and blew steamy breath from its nostrils.

"She's ready, Benjamin." Papa's breath was quick and shallow, like when they chased each other down the long hallways of the chateau. Mama's face was wet with tears. Maura reached up to rub them away and grabbed her in a tight hold.

Papa pulled her away. "Mama and I will find you," he said, placing his hand over his heart like a solemn promise. He pointed to the sky overhead. "It's the Archer in the sky, waiting to lead the way." When Maura cried, he consoled her in hushed tones and lay her back down beside the lumpy potatoes.

"We aren't afraid," he said, whispering in the darkness. "For we know the One who set the stars in place—the One who keeps our lives bundled into His." The tarp settled over her head, and all was darkness, except for twinkling lights of the scroll's cover.

The wagon started in spurts, then rattled down the road. Her heart beat in quick staccatos as she struggled to breathe. This wasn't like a game she played as she settled in without a sound like a mouse. This was like times in her room when Papa appeared without a word and led her into a tiny closet hidden inside the wall.

"Be brave, little one. Not a sound," he'd say.

Brave? Even when footsteps pounded like thunder down the hallway into her room? Even when angry voices rose in darkness? She'd longed to burst out of that tiny place. But she'd seen the fear in Papa's eyes. And knew her own. One thing she'd learned from all that hiding was to listen. Listen for danger and pray that Papa's voice would soon call her out to the home she loved.

Now, all was quiet outside the wagon. She couldn't hear her uncle shift his legs or clear his throat. Papa had said to stay under the tarp. What if Benjamin was alone and afraid, though? Familiar terror rose in her gut. She tasted its burn at the back of her throat.

Suddenly, the screech of an owl dive-bombed toward certain prey. Throwing potatoes aside, she bolted out from under the tarp and scrambled up to grab Benjamin's waist.

"Get down, now." His words were a low hiss.

Splotches of ragged light tore through the dense cover of forest around the chateau. Lights became fiery swords extended by shrouded figures.

Benjamin shoved her back into the wagon and popped his whip against the horse's rump.

She struggled to stand. Papa and Mama needed them. So did their friends. The sight of the chateau disappeared as the wagon careened around a sharp bend in the road. The potatoes became hard thuds against her skin as the tarp plummeted over her once more. Maura wept soundless tears as she remembered what Papa had said.

It was time to hide. Again.

Chapter 3

Twelve years later

"Kind heart? A strong chin?" Maura rolled her eyes and forced a sigh she hoped was loud enough for Benjamin to hear.

He couldn't see her face in the darkness, except that didn't matter. He knew her every expression by heart. And how the one he ignored now could melt ice.

Maura held Nicolaus by the fingertips as he toddled toward Benjamin. They sat on a sloping hill outside their thatched-roofed cottage and peered up into the night sky. She watched the silhouette of her uncle's crooked fingers catch Nicolaus and hoist him into the air.

"All I said was there's a new footman," he said. "Came to the barn this morning. Thought you might—"

"Lucas, son of Tanner?" she asked. "He gawked at my eyes and asked if I was a witch. I told him I had better things to do than babysit an ignoramus."

Benjamin chuckled. An outline of straggly brown hair stuck out of the same aged hat he'd worn since they'd traveled here together. He was chief groundskeeper for the sprawling estate of Sir Hugh Taylor in their home of rolling hills filled with flax and cotton. The years of tilling, planting, and nurturing Sir Taylor's manicured gardens had bent his spine and caused his gait to veer right, no matter how doggedly he strode forward. She'd often doled out seedling after seedling as he burrowed a place for each one in the damp rich soil.

"See the petals circle around and around in this marigold? Symmetry. That's what it is. Patterns set in place by divine hands, like the constellations above. On earth, as it is in heaven."

Divine order.

Today was her birthday, a day that never failed to remind her of the ones she'd lost. What kind of order had separated her from Papa and Mama? Besides, even turning seventeen didn't make her fit into any blueprint she'd ever seen. After scaring off suitor after suitor, Maura had decided it was time for a job. One that didn't require dealing with people day after day.

She'd been hired as nanny for an eccentric inventor's only child, Nicolaus. She ate her meals in their upper chamber of his mansion and nodded at servants as she walked with the baby in sunlit gardens. Aside from her formal weekly reports to Sir Taylor about his son, she seldom spoke to another adult.

It was a special treat when she and Nicolaus met Benjamin at work on the grounds or had a rare evening together with the stars. Like tonight, when the baby's late afternoon nap made an evening venture possible. An early autumn breeze brushed their faces like a gentle stream as Maura held her palm to the sky. She extended her thumb and pinkie as Benjamin had taught her, measuring the distance between stars of the constellation above.

He believed the stars had been set in place as a sure guide. The earth crept in a gigantic circle around the sun itself. And because earth was willing to rotate, keeping its eye ever on the sun, constellations came into view in a never-ending but vastly comforting sameness.

"It's the bear cub peering down on you, Nicolaus. You and he have lots in common. You're built like him, strong in spirit and…well, a mite sassy."

As if on cue, Nicolaus reached up and grabbed a handful of her curls and yanked.

"Ouch!" She gently pried his chubby fingers out of her hair and set him with a firm plop on the blanket beside her.

Benjamin choked on a laugh. "Sassy, heh? Not unlike another lass I once knew?"

Maura punched him gently on the shoulder. His bones didn't take the pummeling she used to give them. But that was long ago. "I beg your pardon."

"Beg pardon nothing. Have I not the scars to prove it?"

Maura's face burned hot. "That wasn't my fault. It fell out of my hand."

They both remembered the day. The pottery hadn't slipped from her hands. She'd hurled it against the wall, and he'd been cut by an airborne shard. He'd blown out the lamp in the kitchen where she'd been tucked away in a corner, reading. Something inside had risen and spewed like smoldering oil. Stuck in darkness brought terror she couldn't explain—and a volcanic response.

This was a good time to change the subject. She combed her hair back with one hand and opened her mouth to speak, then stopped. Benjamin knew her like no one else on earth. And loved her. That was a mystery Maura was happy not to understand. She needed his wisdom now, more than ever.

"Sir Taylor is a fiend," she said, beginning with the

plain truth. She'd been afraid to tell Benjamin what she'd heard whispered in the servants' quarters of the manse. She needed her job and loved Nicolaus. Yet accounts of her employer's cruelty frightened her.

Benjamin was silent.

"You heard about the farming accident?" she asked.

He nodded.

"It was murder." Heat rose from her belly and came out in a jumble. "He murdered Nathan Turner—on his own property. Nathan didn't kill Sir Taylor's father. The horse panicked at gunfire in the distance and bucked the old man off. It wasn't Nathan's fault."

Benjamin's head bowed in the darkness.

"Any court of law would have proved his innocence," she said, her hands clasped to still their trembling. "But Sir Taylor chose his right as blood avenger. He killed a young man who was full of life and…" Maura could barely speak the next words. "And no one stopped him."

"No matter how barbaric, the law remains in place," said Benjamin, sighing deeply. "A relative may take revenge without fear. The accused is without protection." He paused and searched the night sky. "Except in the city called Sanctuary."

"In the what?" Maura jerked to face him, wishing she could read his expression that so often spoke without words.

"A city set in place to offer protection from the avenger," he said.

"Why haven't I heard of it? Is it legend, like those behind the constellations?"

Benjamin gazed into the distance, as if he saw beyond the rolling hills and pastures. "Every legend begins with a seed of truth."

"Are fugitives truly safe there?"

Benjamin turned his eyes back to the stars and said nothing.

A gentle snort came from Nicolaus, who was sound asleep. This conversation wasn't going anywhere. Maura gathered the little boy into her arms and reached out to Benjamin for a gentle hug as they stood.

"Better get him to bed." Placing a quick peck on Benjamin's cheek, she wrapped a shawl around the sleeping child and hurried back to the estate. A night watchman stood at the door with his lantern.

"It's Maura O'Donnell, sir," she said, hoping the quiver in her voice didn't betray her nervousness. "I have Nicolaus."

She offered the child's name to remind the guard who she was. Unsure of how Sir Taylor felt about her occasional jaunts to see her uncle, she felt uneasy every time they returned from a visit. But how could it matter that they were outside on a warm evening?

"Out for a bit of stargazing before bedtime," she said, offering unnecessary information to a man whose job was only to give her entrance.

"So late, miss?" he asked.

Such a simple question. Was it a reproach? Maura was glad he couldn't see the heat that traveled from her belly to the top of her head. The lantern's flame wavered in the breeze as she waited for him to unlock the massive oaken door. His hefty, cloaked frame stooped over as he fiddled with the key and glanced at her from time to time. How long could this take? Still, he was only doing his job, she reminded herself. He'd let them inside and then return to his post.

The lock opened with such a loud thwack that she jumped back. The man bowed and motioned them forward to the brightly lit foyer. Maura tucked Nicolaus more securely in her arms, nodded to the watchman, and went inside. Instead of going back to his place outside the door, the guard followed them into the room.

A shock of dark hair mottled with gray spilled out as he removed the hood that had shielded his face. Eyebrows hung like unruly paintbrushes over sharp black eyes that rested on hers too long. She fidgeted as Nicolaus grew heavy on her shoulder. Surely, their pleasantries were over. He continued to stand, leaning on one leg and then on another. He cleared his throat and came closer, keeping his gaze on her.

"Where'd you get them eyes, child?"

She reared back in anger and almost spewed her outrage. Then she remembered that she and Nicolaus were alone. Granted, her eyes were the subject of many whispered conversations and more than a few taunts. Opinions ranged from mythical ancestry to evidence of a curse. She'd plead ignorance.

"Pardon, sir?"

"Your ma? Or were it the fairy folk?" When she didn't answer, he continued. "Mebbe stars came down and rested for a sign."

Maura stared at the cold marble squares beneath her feet. How could she ignore the man's curiosity and return her small charge to the nursery?

"I'd best be putting Nicolaus to bed. Good even to you." She walked away and determined not to sprint down the hallway. Was his stare following her? When she reached the door of the nursery, she stepped inside and closed it firmly. She tucked Nicolaus into his bed after a quick kiss and whispered prayer.

Every time she entered the manse, she was reminded it wasn't home. Far from it. She remembered Sir Taylor's imposing stance during her interview for the nanny position. His fierce eyes barely deigned to glance at hers, even though he'd seen her and Benjamin often as his nearest neighbors. Most likely, his brilliant mind was filled with ideas for new machinery to produce even finer fabrics from cotton.

Those fabrics were already far beyond what home-based looms could produce. They'd brought great wealth into the country—not to mention Sir Taylor's pockets. He'd recently been appointed High Sheriff, and it was rumored that he was to be knighted. A powerful, unpleasant man, she would have thought twice about accepting the job. Then she'd met Nicolaus.

The little boy had toddled toward her on the day of the interview, his dimpled arms reaching out. She'd let him stumble twice, even though his father stepped in to set him aright each time. When the child's swagger finally met her outstretched hand, he'd grabbed her curls and stuck a wet finger into her ear. With a loud belch, he'd wrapped his arms around her neck and fallen sound asleep.

Nicolaus's touch welcomed her to a new home that day. She endured the butler's cold shoulder, ate her meals alone day after day. Most of servants avoided her, or worse, sneered at her higher station and yet obvious poverty. "Can't even afford a proper pair of shoes, can she?"

She accepted the loneliness of being neither servant nor family in that cold, stone mansion for one reason. It was Nicolaus. *Mammee* was his name for her, and that title alone was enough to keep her right where she was. Other than Nicolaus, permission to use the telescope had been the best gift in this prison of sorts. Sir Taylor had grudgingly shown her how to shift its lens until the constellations came into a focus that dazzled her senses.

When the child's breathing became rhythmic puffs, Maura scaled a narrow staircase that led to the granite-lined turret. The telescope stood in diffused moonlight as if it beckoned to her. Positioning her hands on the cool metal tube, she adjusted the eyepiece until the Great Bear constellation, Ursa Major, came into view. With another turn, she found Orion. Before long, she was lost in an adventure that called to her from an unknown land, untethered by earth.

Being alone with the stars overhead almost made up for the constant ache in her heart. She loved Nicolaus, but she wondered if this was all life held in store for her. Having a family of her own was unlikely. Who'd be interested in an awkward spinster with eyes that made people stop and stare? She loved the little boy. He was the sunlight of her very small universe, and that was fine for now.

The morning after their nighttime outing, Nicolaus woke up hot with fever. Had she been wrong to let the child play in the cool, damp grass? She shook her head. He was probably teething. All would be well. Then his fever stayed high, even after two days. Small limbs twitched as if his body fought off an impending enemy. At times, he'd awaken from a sound sleep with a cry of sudden force. She'd held his warm body against hers as the rocking chair creaked along with his whimpers.

"Take it, little one." She added bits of ginger root to cool spring water, but he turned his head and refused to drink. When he wasn't better on the third day, Maura waited until the child fell asleep, then hurried across hallways and down a flight of stairs to Sir Taylor's workshop. She rapped on the oaken door. "Sir Taylor?" A strip of light shone from under the door. "It's Maura O'Donnell. I must speak with you."

Glass clinked, but no one opened the door. She knocked again, this time louder and longer. "Sir, Nicolaus is sick."

She fought panic as she heard mumbling, then furniture skidding across the floor. The door swung open wide, and the man's hulking frame appeared. Inside the room, Maura could see flasks resting over open flames on a broad planked table.

"What do you want?" he snapped.

No *hello*, no *May I help you*. Maura was used to being treated as an underling. Even now, she wouldn't have disturbed him under any other circumstances. Surely, he had the decency to know she cared about his son. "Nicolaus is feverish and not himself. He needs to see a physician."

"Fevers are not out of the ordinary for children." Sir Taylor glanced behind at the bubbling liquids, then turned back to glare imperiously at her. She'd interrupted his work—a crime, indeed. Maura stood her ground and bent her knees slightly to still their trembling. "He won't eat or drink. I'm worried."

"Is it because you had him outside in the night air? The gatekeeper told me you were out until late. Why?"

She was being watched. It confirmed the odd sensation she'd often had in the manse, almost as if some unseen person observed her. It didn't happen often, but at times a shadow passed from a nearby hallway, or a floorboard creaked outside her room at night. She tried to ignore the signs that were almost, though not quite certain, knowing that her imagination was active enough to invent them.

"It was a lovely evening," she said, keeping her voice calm. "We were star gazing."

"Stars." Sir Taylor snorted in contempt. "I hired you to take care of my son. Surely that doesn't include taking him outside when he should be at home in bed."

Heat flooded her cheeks. "He had a long nap and was awake. It was warm outside."

"You're his nanny. And responsible for his care, are you not? Now, go. I'm busy." He turned and stomped back inside the room.

She'd been disregarded, cast away like garbage. Not only that, a servant told her that Benjamin had asked to see her this morning and had been turned away. Had Sir Taylor laid down an unwritten edict against her uncle's visits? Maura rose on her toes and pointed at the door, now slammed shut. She sputtered. "I will not be treated as your chattel."

No response. Nothing but a wooden door to answer her plea to help his own child. Later that afternoon, though, a porter arrived with medicine. When she added it to Nicolaus's bottle, he drank the sweet-smelling concoction and fell asleep. It wasn't until late that night that he stirred and cried out. Maura's feet sank into the deep plush Turkish carpet as she tiptoed into the nursery with her lantern. Heavy brocade curtains were open enough to see the crib near a rocking chair, where she'd sung to him earlier that day. Shivering pinpoints of light dotted the landscape of shepherds who guarded their flocks.

Nicolaus was quiet. Not wanting to wake him, she touched his cheek to check for fever. He was cool to touch. Too cool. She set the lantern on a bed stand and placed her hand on his tiny chest. No soft breaths lifted his chest. A low moan moved from her belly through her lips. She pulled Nicolaus into her arms and willed him to breathe, willed the warmth of her embrace to overtake his chill.

"It's Mammee, Nicki. Wake up." Maybe it was the medicine making him sleep deeply. She rocked him from side to side and sang. "One little finger, tap, tap, tap." But the fingers that had once grasped hers in a fierce hold were limp.

"Come, little one." She snuggled the sweet place under his chin, but there was no giggle in return. Long eyelashes feathered his cheeks against eyes that didn't open to her voice. She peered around the room where she already knew there was no help.

Wrapping her shawl around the child, she rushed out of the room and into the dark hallway. The servants' quarters were too far away. Which of them would help, anyway? She had to find Sir Taylor. Four rooms to the right, a corner, another three doorways, and a small flight of stairs led her to his sleeping quarters. Pounding on the door, she cried, "Sir Taylor. It's Nicolaus."

There was a shuffling sound, a thunk of furniture, and the door opened to a single flickering light. Sir Taylor held a candlestick in one hand, hair disheveled and robe askew. "What do you want?"

Maura kept the baby clutched in her arms. "I can't get him to...he isn't..."

"What?" He opened the door and peered at the child as if unsure what she was saying. He glowered down first at her, then Nicolaus.

"He's so quiet." Maura trembled. She couldn't let Nicolaus go, couldn't hand him to his father. Not until she had to.

"You woke me up before dawn to say he's..." Sir Taylor's arrogant stance moved to indignation.

Maura wanted to scream. Instead, she took a deep breath. "Please, sir. Something is wrong."

He placed the candlestick on the floor and settled a large hand first on the child's forehead, then over his chest. Maura heard a small gasp as he drew back. Was it fear in his eyes? Suddenly, he grabbed Nicolaus out of her arms, almost kicking over the candle.

"No," he muttered, holding the child out, then embracing him. "It can't be." In the next second, he turned on Maura and exploded. "This is your fault!"

"I couldn't. I would never..." An image came to Maura's mind of a young man lying face down in the grass, legs sprawled, and arms extended. Blood seeped from a gash in his head. Nathan Turner, the young man Sir Taylor had killed in the name of vengeance.

There would be no mercy for her.

"She murdered my son!" Sir Taylor shouted the words, Nicolaus in his arms.

Maura turned and ran down the granite hallway, hearing doors open and then footsteps. Her only escape was the walnut staircase that led to the front door. She hurried down the steps by the light of hanging lanterns and made a dash through the foyer. She tugged on the oaken door with both hands until it burst open with a rush of frigid air.

Cold slashed through her cotton dress and woolen shawl. What happened to the early spring warmth only days before? The watchman's bobbing light appeared around a curve in the driveway. Maura closed the door firmly and walked down the circular driveway. What could she say to explain her sudden flight? It was still dark and too early for a morning walk.

"Miss?" The watchman stood like a grizzly specter in the flickering light.

Maura gathered the shawl around her neck and searched for words. "Sir. I must see…"

The man stood in the middle of the pathway with a pepperbox revolver tucked in his belt. There would be no quick escape. She'd have to explain why she was leaving the manse.

"An early morning meteor shower." She pointed upward. "I'll return after dawn."

"A what?" he asked, peering into the sky.

She didn't have time to give him a treatise on meteor showers. "They're…like stars. Stars falling from the sky."

"Aye, 'tis a sign, indeed." He nodded and pointed at her eyes. A crease formed between the man's brows. "And ye' be the one to carry their message."

What was he talking about? She decided to ignore the comment. "Yes, well, I must go. Good day, sir." She walked briskly away.

As she was past, he protested. "It be dark. And very cold, miss. Ye'll be catchin' your death without yer woolens."

She waved as she glanced back. "I'll be fine. Thank you." She strode down the cobblestoned driveway without another word. Light from the man's lantern followed, then fell behind as she picked up her pace.

Only a few moments had passed before voices

sounded from the manor. She had to find Benjamin. Hiking up her skirt, she zigzagged through an orchard, dry grass crunching under her feet. The wind was an icy blast as she searched for the cottage. Dawn would expose her before long. She ran full tilt, her dress and shawl flapping behind her like a frightened goose. When she reached the back door of the cottage, she grasped the latch and pulled. It was locked.

"Benjamin," she cried out in a whisper, searching frantically around the cottage. Pinpoints of light approached in the darkness. Was it the night watchman? She hid behind the cover of a dwarf willow until she recognized the man's off-kilter gait. Dashing out, she almost knocked Benjamin over with her embrace.

"Follow me," he said in a low voice. Maura longed to sprint ahead, but Benjamin's legs would never survive the battering.

He pointed a long cylinder into the path. Lights of a constellation shone through broken limbs and exposed tree roots. Stars at their feet? It was the scroll, wrapped in the pouch Mama had so carefully stitched, as if she'd known another night would require the light of those stars.

A large hedge loomed in their way, dense and impenetrable.

Cries behind them grew louder. Torches filled the darkness beyond the woods. Her pursuers, too, could see the pinpoints of light that led her and Benjamin.

Sir Taylor knew the law. In the terrible moment of discovering his son's death, he'd received the right as blood avenger. Only one thing would satisfy him.

Maura O'Donnell's execution.

Chapter 4

Benjamin extended the scroll toward the hedge. An arch formed, as if an invisible knife carved a half circle above and straight lines below. "I'll come for you as soon as I can." He pushed his weight against the outline, and an entrance gave way. Placing the strap of the scroll over her shoulder, he pushed her into the opening. "Go!"

"But—"

"Remember, you carry the light of the stars."

Guards rushed in their direction.

She couldn't leave Benjamin. Maura held out the scroll toward him, but he made no move to take it. She wanted to step back to him, maybe to pull him with her, except the thatch of tangled branches closed and blocked her return. Tangled branches formed a tight prison around her. Whatever light she had was gone, eclipsed by the hedge that held her tight.

A rush of heat flooded her body, despite the cold around her. She couldn't breathe, couldn't scream. She could only thrash against the leafy web that held her. Ragged twigs and branches tore her clothing and ripped at her skin as the hedge became more impassable. She tried to jab the scroll against the tangle, but nothing happened.

She'd claw her way out, no matter how hard it was. When she jabbed the scroll into the belt of her gown, a passageway opened on the other side of the hedge and spit her out onto a patch of damp grass. Maura fell into a crumpled heap and squinted in mid-morning sunlight. What had happened to the frosty pre-dawn?

The rat-a-tat of a woodpecker sounded in a pine tree overhead. The sun warmed her body as she took long, deep breaths of the fresh air. A sparrow chirped nearby, and a gentle breeze stroked her exhausted body. With no strength to protest, she fell into a sound sleep on the soft ground, sheltered by the towering hedge that had finally released her.

Maura woke to a rustle in the grass beside her. A red fox peered at her, then slipped away. Branches stirred in one of the trees overhead. Enormous wings extended from an eagle, that swooped low to the ground, hovered, then rose to take flight. Quickly gathering altitude, it soared away into a cloudless sky.

Creeping out of the copse of trees, she saw the hedge extended for miles in both directions. A road across from the dense foliage offered easy access to anyone else who'd been spewed from its leafy tangle. A small hamlet peeked out through a stand of dense forest in front of her, and a narrow stream gurgled to her right. Something skittered nearby, and she jumped back, almost losing her balance. She sighed as a cotton-tailed rabbit bounced away.

A faint noise brought her attention back to the road, where a carriage had stopped near the hedge, hundreds of feet away. A flash of emerald reflected in morning light as someone stood with arms extended. Moments later, whoever it was reentered the carriage, which turned around and drove away. Maura didn't know whether to be disappointed or relieved she hadn't been seen.

A figure appeared through the hedge and walked

toward her. Gripping her skirt in one hand she jogged in that direction, hoping it was Benjamin. Until she recognized Sir Taylor's scarlet cloak, the one that emulated a hopeful rise to royalty. Maura bolted toward a willow grove by the stream and hid its shelter, heart pounding. What should she do? A quiet swish stirred in the bushes nearby. Dense river grass waved slightly with careful, deliberate movement.

A child's lilting tune interrupted the stillness. "*Shine bright, O star of the morning, through me, your bonny lass. For you have come among us, our dear Gad El Glas.*"

A woman stooped over a thicket laden with blackberries as the little girl skipped and sang ahead of her.

"Bonnie, stay near," the woman called out. "Help gather these berries for our pie."

The child danced toward the road while her mother combed the bushes for fruit.

A narrow wave in the grass shifted in their direction. Sinewy muscles and tawny coat hid from their eyes. The animal crouched first, then inched toward the woman and her child. It was a mountain lion stalking its prey.

Maura searched the ground and picked up a large rock. Aiming at the lion, she threw it as hard as she could in its direction and shouted. "Go!"

The animal turned to stare at her. River stones were strewn on the ground nearby. She gathered a handful and yelled louder.

The woman and her child stood frozen by the road.

"Walk slowly backward," Maura said, calling to the woman. "Don't run."

The mother grabbed her daughter's hand and backed

into the forest. The lion bounded in one leap into the road where the child had been playing.

Maura ran toward it, extending her gown in her outstretched arms, the scroll flapping at her side. "I said. Go. Now." Her voice was low and commanding.

With a deep snarl, the massive cat perused her as if sizing up unexpected prey.

She grabbed the biggest rock she could find and hurled it. It landed on the animal's forehead hard enough that it jumped backwards. Only for a moment. It stood again and crept toward her, its eyes never wavering from hers.

Maura willed her body to stop shaking and kept waving her arms. The lion padded in careful steps toward her as she reached down for more rocks but found none. Suddenly, a noisy clatter sounded down the road. A carriage rounded a bend and hurtled toward them, horses galloping with mouths frothing. They sped so near that she had to jump back to keep from being run over. The mountain lion bounded away.

Horses neighed, and the driver called *Whoa* as the carriage turned back in her direction. Sir Taylor had recognized her, of course, and charged forward. He was almost in striking distance when the driver pulled to a stop in front of her. Which was worse? A known avenger bent on killing her or an unknown idiot who drove his horses with senseless abandon, nearly mowing her down.

Maura held her chin up and straightened her shoulders as a young man dressed from top to toe in a crimson uniform with spangles on each arm stepped down from the driver's seat. Auburn curls spewed out from under the burnished helmet.

He walked toward Maura and Sir Taylor and stood

between them. He turned first to Sir Taylor and then to her, as if sizing up the situation.

Maura scanned the scruffy driver who was hardly older than she. If he was supposed to represent royalty, he'd failed. For one thing, when he should have been assessing the situation, he stared at her with open curiosity. She crossed her arms. Her eyes. Yes. They were strange. And still he stared as if she were a freak. Now, right in the middle of a crisis. Who'd hired this buffoon? If only she could throw a volley of rocks at him too. Instead, she curtsied.

"I've come for...for..." Maura had no idea why or how she'd arrived in this unknown place. Her voice trembled, but only once. She pointed at Sir Taylor. "This man has come to avenge his deceased son." She stopped and grabbed a breath. "He'll kill me unless you stop him."

"You've come for refuge?" The young man's eyes glazed in unashamed wonder. He moved closer.

As he did, Sir Taylor took a step forward, and they formed a tight, smoldering circle.

Did the young soldier think she needed tea? What could she say? Refuge from being impaled by the sword of her enemy?

"Yes," she said.

"Ah, well, that's a good thing. Aiden Garrett, here." The young man rubbed his hands. "I mean, good because you're here, in the city called Sanctuary. The one set apart to protect those accused of murder, to offer them fair trial and to forfeit the right of the blood avenger to take immediate...action. So to speak."

She'd stumbled upon the city Benjamin had mentioned that night with Nicolaus. He'd only mentioned it in passing, although maybe he knew she'd need its refuge one day. That still didn't answer the question of how she'd gotten here.

Sir Taylor shook his fist in the young man's face and jabbed in Maura's direction. "This is *not* the city. She is mine. I *will* exercise my rights as blood avenger."

The young attendant positioned himself between them. He straightened his shoulders and put a hand to his blade. "This woman has come for shelter and shelter she will have."

"She hasn't arrived at the Hall." Sir Taylor pulled the sword from his belt.

Curls bobbed under Aiden's helmet as he struggled to pull his sword out of a brazen scabbard. He yanked it harder. Finally, it burst out in a flash of metal. He pointed at Sir Taylor's chest. "As emissary of the High Council itself, I'm here and will escort her."

Sir Taylor drew back at the mention of the Council.

The two men faced each other, neither backing down. The older man's hulking figure towered over the carriage driver, only their breath meeting in the narrow space between them. Aiden didn't waver.

"And if I stop you?" Sir Taylor's voice boomed.

Maura trembled at the intimidating roar of his voice.

Aiden, however, only tightened the grasp on his sword.

Sir Taylor's sword met the young attendant's blade before he realized he'd been thwarted. In the next moment, his sword fell to the ground, and the tip of Aiden's sword rested against his throat.

"You will leave." Aiden spoke in a commanding voice. "Now."

Sir Taylor backed away and tried to reach for his

weapon. The young man's boot secured it to the ground. Sputtering with rage, he ranted. "She's mine. I'll make you pay. You'll see."

"I said. Go. Now." Aiden remained calm and resolute.

"I need my sword." The older man bent again to retrieve the sword, but Aiden's boot refused to budge.

"You will go. Without the sword."

Sir Taylor shook with anger. He glared at Maura, then turned, stumbled once, and walked down the road with a small slump in his shoulders.

She understood. Rage was a cover for grief that didn't have words.

Aiden bowed before her, then placed Sir Taylor's sword into his belt." He held his arm out. "May I escort you to the carriage? And ask what it is that you hold against your side?"

Maura studied the scroll's case, somehow still tucked into her belt. She pulled it out and placed it over her shoulder with its strap. The softness of Mama's velvet pouch at her side comforted her. How could she describe it to this man who'd come to her rescue?

"A scroll. From my uncle," she said, noticing that he studied the pouch with the same intensity he'd searched her eyes. No matter how timely a rescuer, he was a nosy man. He finally stopped staring and helped her inside the carriage. Maura leaned back into the quiet space and sighed. Maybe she was safe, if only for a moment.

A command sounded from outside, and the horses lurched as they moved forward.

Maura adjusted the scroll against plush upholstery beneath her. She hadn't thought about using it to command the lion. After all, the cursed hedge had held her tight, even when she'd jabbed the scroll in Benjamin's direction. Instead, its branches opened to this land of mountain lions and the same determined blood avenger who'd pursued her on the other side. Maura remembered the terror of touching Nicki's cold little form. The revenge-fueled chase. And losing Benjamin. She had to find a way to reach him.

They'd been traveling for what felt like hours when she pushed aside the curtains and peered outside. A golden-domed building with a granite colonnade at its base loomed in the distance. Long narrow windows around its perimeter glistened in the sunlight. She strained her neck to see what appeared to be gold that flowed from a statue at the top. The carriage jolted as the pavement changed to bricks and they approached a city ahead. If she could position her head just right, she could study what towered like a mighty overseer from its perch on the dome.

The carriage descended a small hill and blocked her view. Finally, they came to a rise where Maura realized the stream of gold on the dome was a gown on the statute of a magnificent woman. She wore a gleaming breastplate alive with movement and held a shield in one hand so large that it reached from one hip to the base of her gown.

Up, up the carriage ascended to this city set on a hill. As they did, Maura craned her neck out the window and saw something behind the statue's shield. An enormous brazen coil lay there, like a snake positioned to strike. In a moment, she understood. This wasn't just any woman. It was Athena, goddess of war.

Why would a goddess of war be lifted high over a city known for its refuge? The closer the carriage approached, the more foreboding settled over her. The shield that appeared alive was engraved with writhing snakes. Her body quivered with disgust, and she pulled her head back into the safety of the carriage.

Years ago, Maura had been escaping afternoon chores in the barn, lying on the hay, and enjoying a moment all to herself. A movement had sounded at her side. A viper with its distinctive zigzagged pattern had lifted its head from a coil. Black eyes keyed upon her, and a serpentine tongue whipped in and out.

Maura had frozen. Their gazes locked in one breathless moment until, with a slow roll, Maura rotated her body over and over until the hay underneath became the damp earth of the barn. She felt its coolness and kept rolling until she was far from the hay, then stood and dashed out the door. Benjamin had run to her screams and responded in his usual taciturn way. He killed the viper with his hoe, then turned to her still quivering self.

"Best stay on task, Star."

Maura ran her fingers through mangled curls, now free of the pins that had held them. Star. That's what her uncle had called her when she needed a reminder that she was an obedient, not willful, child.

Stay on task. Now, she could only think of one. Stay alive long enough to find out what had happened to Nicolaus. His illness had been bad, but not deadly. Yet, something had taken the innocent child's life.

Her heart was broken, but she'd find answers. Somehow, somewhere. She missed Benjamin terribly. How would he find her in a city he'd never visited? Surely, he'd find a way.

****

SIR TAYLOR

I was so close. I could've ended this with one slash of my sword. Instead, I was forced to retreat, to walk away as if powerless.

What had the red-haired hayseed rambled on about? Swearing to bring the woman to the refuge of Sanctuary, my eye. His head will roll if I have anything to do with it. And of course, I do. I say the word in Sanctuary, and it is accomplished.

I can have anything I want.

Except my family back. Sweet Abigail, dead only moments after setting eyes on the child she'd given everything to bring into the world.

Now, Nicolaus, dead at the hands of that…that murderess. If she didn't kill my son on purpose, her poor care did the job. Either way, Maura O'Donnell will pay.

Chapter 5

The carriage stopped on a wide boulevard outside the stately domed building. Marble columns with ornamental capitals stood like sentinels. A fountain spewed in the middle of a circular pool, which cascaded into twelve smaller pools in a gentle flow of clear blue water. A towering flight of granite steps led to bronze doors that stood two stories high and as wide as the side of their barn at home.

Through the window, Maura watched as Aiden climbed down and handed a uniformed sentry a note. He unlatched the carriage door and held out one arm. Maura accepted it, intending to take a dainty step out of the carriage. Instead, first one foot, then the other collapsed into an ungainly plop on pavement.

Aiden kept his eyes on a spot over her shoulder and offered a gloved hand to hers, his chin upright and gaze professional.

She took his hand. Blue eyes and a kind smile from a young man who'd kept sneaking glimpses when he didn't think she noticed.

Aiden carefully helped her up. He waited as she straightened her ruined gown and frowned at the towering edifice.

Taking a deep breath, Maura took the first step toward the mountain of stairs. Aiden came alongside her and together, they scaled the steep incline. At the top, two uniformed guards opened the massive double doors. She hesitated for a moment, then walked into a marble foyer.

Arched doorways lined each side of a broad hallway. Bronze octagons etched with sunbeams overlaid the ceiling like a golden beehive. Right angles of stairs in ivory and obsidian extended upward as far as Maura could see. Rich tapestries hung from walls, and prisms of light glittered from chandeliers. Elegantly dressed women and genteel men came and went.

Aiden knocked and then entered one of the doors, which had the name *Tobias Fitch* engraved on a silver plaque.

Left in the hallway, Maura took in the grandeur feeling like a pauper invited to a coronation. She stood, torn between longing for a place to hide and searching for other refugees. None of the people she saw appeared fresh out of a tangle with a mountain lion and a blood avenger. A tapestry hung nearby of a towering griffin that hovered over tiny soldiers, who cowered in its shadow. She and Benjamin had read about the mythical beast with the wingspan the size of a grown man, razor-sharp talons, and a lion's body. At least *her* enemy was human.

Aiden reappeared at the office door and motioned her inside. Maura checked his face for any clues of what to expect, but he bowed and left her standing at the door. She pulled a stray curl behind one ear and stepped across the threshold.

A tall, finely dressed man whose face appeared chiseled in ivory stood from a mahogany desk. His skin was flawless except for a finely etched scar that began at his temple and stopped half-way down one cheek. He motioned for her to take a seat, then rifled through a stack of papers.

Maura sat carefully on the chair's rich fabric embroidered with wild roses. Folding her skirt over a smear of mud on one side, she straightened her shoulders and tried to be attentive. Her stomach growled so loudly that its rumble broke the silence.

The man glanced up, then resumed searching through the papers.

The wall clock ticked, ticked. One minute, two…When he finally lifted his head, his eyes widened. Had he forgotten she was there? "Forgive me. My name is Tobias Fitch. Miss Maura O'Donnell. I understand you've come to seek refuge for the accused murder of a young child, Nicolaus Taylor."

Maura wasn't sure how he knew her case already, although the note Aiden had given the sentry may have revealed her name and accusation.

Tobias barely acknowledged her nod. "There are certain guidelines as a refugee you must be aware of. May I inform you?" he asked.

Surely, he didn't need her permission, but she nodded again.

Tobias picked through the papers again. Finally, he placed one on the top of the pile. How many refugees did this handsome man interview every day?

"Excellent," he said, peering at her from across the desk. "We have much to cover in a brief time. Each refugee has five days to prepare for trial with an assigned advocate. Your trial will take place on the morning of the sixth day. While there are many advocates, also called guardians, I've been assigned to your case. A series of interviews will help me understand how to defend you against your accuser, Sir Hugh Taylor, before the High Council."

Tobias checked the clock as it chimed at half-past the hour. Was there a time limit on this interview? He cleared his throat. "The Council is an assembly of twelve tribunes who form the governing body over Sanctuary." He was reading from a sheet of paper and barely taking a breath. "They'll determine your innocence or guilt. If you're judged innocent, you're free to return to your home without fear of vengeance. If guilty, your sentence is execution." He recited the words as if he'd repeated them many times with only a slightly raised eyebrow at the word *execution*.

A pit formed in Maura's stomach. Five days to find out what had happened to Nicolaus. Five days to decide her life or death. She searched the man's face, but his eyes were expressionless. He didn't appear to care, much less demonstrate the support of an advocate. One so manicured, so proper in every way, probably avoided getting dirty with other people's accused crimes. Taking a long breath, she spoke, measuring her words. "I need to see my uncle."

Tobias Fitch glanced at her, then lowered his eyes again to study the paper. "Each refugee is sequestered in the city, although approved family members may visit."

How could a family member be anything but approved? Unless they interfered with the proceedings. "I only have one. He's my Uncle Benjamin."

"I understand the nature of this time is difficult. Still, our assignment is critical. I must add that no one may stand with you during the trial."

She hadn't asked about anyone standing with her. Evidently, he wasn't listening to anything other than his prepared speech. Having Benjamin beside her would be a comfort, though.

"Except for me as your advocate, that is," he added.

Precious comfort he'd be. He'd have to stop and comb his hair between arguments. Maybe he carried a hand mirror for that very purpose. Could this man possibly care less about her fate?

Tobias continued his speech, despite the war Maura fought in her own thoughts. Not that he noticed. "If for any reason you choose to leave the city, you forfeit protection from the blood avenger."

The man kept talking, seeming not to care that she offered no response. Her life tottered in the distracted hands of a politely detached stranger. Tottered? Careening out of control was more like it. She was alone and without Benjamin for the first time in her life. At least in the life she remembered.

He took a breath, and she jumped in to speak before he began another recitation. "Where will I stay? Will I be imprisoned?"

Again, Tobias glanced up from his papers. "It is our custom to provide a host family for every refugee. Their assignment is to shelter you while you rest and prepare for the trial. You'll meet Anton and Lilith Gunter after our meeting this morning."

Maura noticed the hem of her dress, which was now shredded. "I don't have extra clothing, or…anything."

"Each home is furnished to supply what you need." Tobias stood and turned to search a bookcase behind his desk. "May I speak freely," he asked, pulling down a book but keeping his back to her.

This condescending stranger's formality was strangling. She'd dealt with a meddlesome carriage driver, faced down a wild animal and the man who wanted her dead. And now, the one assigned to defend her found everything around him more important than her presence.

She was a mess. She might as well be one Tobias Fitch couldn't ignore. Holding her skirt in one hand, she climbed onto the upholstered chair and shouted. "May *I* speak freely?"

She thought about lowering her voice, but then again, she was standing on a chair. "I'm discussing my impending execution with a disinterested stranger who doesn't care that a man wants me dead for a crime I didn't commit."

Tobias spun around to stare at Maura, his eyes wide. An unidentifiable expression simmered in his eyes. Her cursed temper. Would she be promptly carted off for a speedy end? She'd offended, on purpose, the only one sworn to help.

His placid expression cracked. A smile took over. His belly shook with a chuckle that bubbled from so deep, she wasn't sure even Tobias recognized it. He leaned over in his impeccable suit and held his belly as a deep, guttural laugh bubbled up with a joyful roar.

Maura suddenly felt small, her filthy shoes on the lovely fabric. She ventured a glance to Tobias who struggled to contain himself. So much for her proper advocate. She'd cracked his façade. She wasn't sure which was worse, detached decorum or a man who practically rolled in the ground laughing—at her.

Would people in the hallway wonder what was going on in this staid gentleman's office? She was too shocked to do anything but stand like an uncertain statue on top of the man's furniture.

Finally, her advocate wiped his face with a silk handkerchief and straightened his jacket. He walked to Maura's perch and held out a manicured hand.

Maura hesitated before she took it, surprised by the strength of his grasp, which helped her to the floor as if she were a misplaced china doll.

Tobias held his gaze and her hand long enough that Maura squirmed. The scent of evergreen overtook her senses and made her sneeze. On him.

He didn't turn away. "You may speak freely." Then with a grin he added. "And I will hear you."

Maura gathered her skirt to sit primly on the chair where she'd just stood.

Tobias took a seat across from her, keeping his gaze locked on hers. She'd shocked him senseless.

"I'm accused of a murder against a child I …loved." Her voice hitched on the words. "The circumstances of his death don't make sense. I must find answers." Maura hurried to speak before tears overwhelmed her. "I refuse to be a powerless victim. I do need help, though. Are you the one willing to do so?"

Tobias studied his hands and shook his head. "Powerless isn't a word I'd use to describe you." He held one hand up, as if taking an oath. "My vow is to build the best defense I can, and together we'll discover what happened to Nicolaus."

Maura relaxed a bit against the soft chair.

"Our legal process," he continued, "has been in place for generations. It isn't complicated but is unusual because of what we offer as a city."

"Are there other refugees? I mean, other than me?" she asked.

Clasping his hands, Tobias leaned toward her. "We

offer true refuge to all, Miss O'Donnell. People come from all over the region seeking protection. All have been accused of murder. It is the mission of our city to offer a safe place for each person to prepare for a fair trial. And yes, your adversary will also prepare.

"At the end of five days, the Council will hear and judge the evidence. Ours is a civil system that has been set in place for generations. Very little has changed. Most people who seek our help are unfamiliar with our procedures. For that reason, we ask that each refugee not only learns, but also cooperates with, the process."

Tobias took a breath and wiped his brow. "Obviously, we can't write the end of every story, but our history of just decrees and judgments is unparalleled. You're in good hands. In fact, the best, if I do say so." He smiled and bowed. "I'm happy to defend you, Maura O'Donnell."

Maura thought he was finished until he took a breath and spoke again. "One more question. Will you take my hand when it's extended?"

"What?"

Tobias cleared his throat and paused before he explained. "My job is to ask difficult questions, to prepare you for the unexpected. I'll do my best to carry out what for me is a generational legacy as guardian. But whether or not you choose to receive my assistance is your decision."

"I'm accused of murder. My blood avenger is happy to end this process with one swipe of his sword. And I have to find out what happened to Nicolaus. What part of that can I do alone?"

"Perhaps I misspoke. I'm here to support you in your case, but our relationship is two-sided. You're on trial for your life. I'm here to make sure you get home at the end of this week. Will you trust me in the process?"

Before she could answer, a knock sounded. "Pardon me." Tobias went to the door and opened it slightly. "No, we're finished. Proceed," he said to someone. Then he turned and bowed to Maura. "Good day, Miss O'Donnell. I'll contact you for our next interview."

And with that, they were done. Tobias resumed his professional demeanor and returned to his desk. Maura glanced at her advocate, curtsied, and walked to the door. She stopped for a moment to take a deep breath. Struggling to merely breathe morphed into a shudder that quaked her exhausted body. So ended yet another bizarre event in a day that felt far from over.

Maura was almost out of the room when Tobias cleared his throat. She stopped and turned back, wondering if he had more to say. The man spoke so quietly, she strained to hear him.

"Trust me."

****

SIR TAYLOR

I found her. I knew a way into the city, one long forgotten but still accessible. I pursued her without delay. She thought she was so special. But I knew. Knew there was something wild in those eyes. How could I have trusted her?

And now my Nicolaus is gone.

Maura O'Donnell—speaking her name is difficult—is positioned for certain judgment. Tobias Fitch was assigned as her advocate. An intelligent, faithful and above all, compliant man.

She'll stay at the Gunter home. The woman won't recognize the honor of living in that esteemed company.

No matter. Her presence in that house is an unfortunate necessity. As a so-called refuge city, it is important to maintain appearances. They must have their trial, which they assure me will serve as a platform to affirm her guilt to all.

The Council has its own agenda, of course. Our desires serve one another. Textiles from my factories line their pockets, while I require justice only they have the authority to offer.

I can't stay at the manor any longer. The memories scream. First Abigail. Now, Nicolaus. There's nothing left for me there.

Vengeance is a terrible fuel, but it drives me forward. She must pay the price of my loss. That goal alone keeps me upright.

Chapter 6

Maura peered out arched windows that lined one end of the marble hallway. Sunlight glittered on a waterfall that plummeted in the distance. She imagined standing on its brink, hearing its roar like a storm approaching on the horizon. One push, and she'd plunge into its wildness. Sir Taylor planned to make sure she did just that.

A great amphitheater sprawled outside the building with circle after circle of seats lining its cavernous hole. An ornate dais of carved stone stood in the center, surrounded by upholstered thrones in rich fabrics and silken banners. Someone cleared his throat behind her. Maura turned to see her carriage driver, Aiden.

"Miss O'Donnell," Aiden said, bowing. He extended his elbow to receive her hand. "To light, miss."

Maura was too tired to ask what he meant. She placed her hand on his elbow, and they walked back to the front door, which opened by the hands of uniformed sentries. She and Aiden descended the long flight of stairs to the waiting carriage. She managed not to stumble as she climbed in. And he'd stopped staring at her eyes. Progress, she decided.

The carriage traveled along city streets where magnificent Grecian buildings and graceful water fountains in the middle of manicured gardens lined the streets. The scenery changed to row after row of brick homes, smaller than Sir Taylor's castle but statuesque with lush green lawns and potted flowers that spilled over onto broad verandas.

Finally, the carriage jerked to a stop at a house that was set apart from the others in its size and grandeur. Aiden unlatched her door, and Maura stepped out, wishing she were home and not there, ready to meet more strangers in an even stranger city. They walked to a wide veranda with rocking chairs and wisteria streaming down its white columns.

A woman dressed in a simple black dress and a starched apron opened the front door. Her green eyes studied them without wavering. Something about her unforced elegance made Maura wonder if she'd traveled from an ancient Celtic tribe, far from the land of her birth. More likely, Maura was drawn to a place of rest in the woman's kind gaze. She didn't know whether to curtsy or offer her hand.

The woman stepped aside to allow her inside the house. Maura steeled herself for one more step into the unknown.

Unlike Sir Taylor's manse, light flooded the Gunter home, and fresh flowers filled the air with their fragrance. Once again, Maura pulled on her tattered gown, ashamed. She needed clean clothes and a bath. And food. Hunger pangs were unrelenting now.

A blond, Germanic man walked toward them from an oak-lined library on one side of the foyer. Despite his tailored silk suit and the atmosphere around him, he looked like a battle-scarred warrior. Or aged bulldog.

"My name is Anton Gunter." He bowed and gestured to a woman who appeared from a hallway and stood at his side. "And this is my wife, Lilith."

Maura wanted to melt with embarrassment. The woman was dressed in a gown that appeared to be something between lace and cloud. A stunning emerald pendant graced her slender neck. Unlike her husband, she approached Maura with an invitation.

"Welcome to our home." She led the way into a parlor, where tufted silk chairs and embroidered settees were set in small groupings around the room. A mahogany grand piano stood as a centerpiece. Lilith invited Maura to sit on an armchair upholstered in thick velvet. "We require tea, Nona," she said.

Maura felt like a stray puppy that had wandered into a fine mansion. Her dress hung in an odd angle from where she'd stepped on its hem, causing it to tear from the rest of the skirt. She perched with her back straight and hands folded in her lap. Her stomach growled.

Anton sat beside his wife across from Maura. They sat in silence until, a few moments later, Nona returned with a cart that held a silver teapot and gilded china cups. Small biscuits and a bowl of lemon curd sat on one side.

Maura's stomach growled again. This time louder.

Lilith dismissed Nona with a wave of her hand. "Sugar, dear?" she asked.

Maura pushed the scroll behind one arm and took two cubes as Lilith offered a tiny bowl with an equally tiny silver spoon. Maura took a sip, relishing its sweet warmth. Reaching for a biscuit, she willed herself to take a delicate bite. When she did, the biscuit crumbled in her hands. As much as she longed to upend the contents into her mouth, she slipped it back on the plate.

"What a lovely pouch. What is it?" Lilith asked, peering at the scroll tucked behind Maura's back. "I haven't seen anything so beautifully crafted for years."

"It belongs to my…uncle." Maura didn't know how to describe the scroll or its covering. "It's a family heirloom."

Lilith rested her teacup on the saucer. Her eyes never left the embroidered pouch as she rose and walked toward Maura.

Instinctively, Maura pulled the scroll from behind her back and held it close under one arm.

Lilith stood over her in flowing elegance, her eyes still trained upon the scroll. Suddenly, she knelt at Maura's feet.

Maura pressed her back against the chair, wishing she could disappear into its softness.

"May I see it?" Lilith searched Maura's eyes with a gentle plea.

Maura's thoughts were in a flurry. She couldn't think of any rules of etiquette that would allow her to refuse her hostess. And yet, the woman's hungry gaze unnerved her. She glanced at Anton, who sat ramrod straight against the settee. A faint glimmer of something Maura couldn't name dashed across his face before she could study it.

Maura pulled the scroll from under her arm and placed it in her lap. She stopped short of offering it to the woman. Lilith took her gesture as a yes. Still on her knees, she touched the velvet with one finger and stroked it lightly. Then, almost as if she'd gathered courage, she placed a slender hand over the silver thread of stars that formed the Archer.

Maura sat, frozen in place, unable to move and uncertain how to. Lilith carefully lifted the scroll in its pouch from Maura's lap and held it in both hands. A minute passed. Then another. Silence filled the room, once bustling with the activity of her welcome. A smile played on Lilith's face. She handed the scroll back to Maura, stood, and straightened her gown, assuming her graceful carriage, as if it were perfectly natural to fall on her knees before an unknown stranger.

"Oh, my. I was transfixed with the beauty of that handiwork," Lilith said, resuming a light tone of voice. "Surely that of an artist. Possibly a woman? Those stitches, that design. It's a masterpiece, indeed. The work of one who sees."

Maura took a deep breath. She tried to release it slowly, but it came out in a huff of relief. Lilith didn't appear to notice. Maura pulled the scroll back under her arm and tried to smile. Was the woman also a seamstress? Surely not. Still, Lilith's home was evidence that she loved beauty. Everything around her was an exquisite expression of color and texture. Prisms from the window reflected dancing streams of light on the designs of an Oriental rug at their feet. It was hard to believe the woman had been overtaken by the pouch, bunched, and battered by warfare as it was. Maura felt deeply honored by Lilith's appreciation. Her mother would've been proud.

Anton straightened his vest and pulled on his necktie. Clearly, it was time for business, and he was taking charge. "So, Mona."

"Maura, sir."

"I'll explain our role in your stay here," he continued, leaning against the chair with an imperious air. "We're a refuge home within the city and are pleased to provide you with clothing, food, and company as your case is being prepared. We're here to serve you. Your part is to receive our hospitality, keep your appointments at the Hall, and ready yourself for the trial.

"We are not to know the particulars of your flight into our city, so refrain from trying to explain. We *are* here to help, as are the people of our fine city and the ruling Council responsible for the abundant goodness we enjoy. Any questions?"

All she had were questions. Anton Gunter wouldn't be the one to hear them, though. The teacup trembled in her hand until Lilith gracefully retrieved it.

"Our guest is exhausted, Anton." She nodded to Nona, who stood at attention by the parlor door. "Escort Miss O'Donnell to her apartment, please."

Sunset hues of rose and blue peeked through heavy curtains, and the space was dim in fading light when Maura entered the bedroom that was to be hers.

Nona curtsied, then exited through another door at the back of the room.

Maura missed her immediately. Her chamber was splendid, larger than the entire cottage she and Benjamin had shared. Oil paintings of refined ladies and pastoral fields graced the walls.

One of the paintings pictured a hunt with gentlemen riding handsome steeds. A rider bent over his horse, as if to dodge a tree limb. Another held a riding crop in his hand, positioned to spur on the chase. It was a fox hunt in progress. Maura had seen several and hated them. The events she'd observed were made up of men who fancied themselves hunters. Sadly, they were only dressed to appear sporting as half-starved hounds chased a lone fox and tore it into bits when they finally caught it. It was a massacre, not a hunt.

The object of this hunt wasn't a fox. Instead, it appeared to have wings and was unlike any prey Maura had seen. Muscles in its enormous body strained to mount up and fly away. As she studied the winged beast pursued by determined hunters, she noticed a small hole drilled into the wall beside the ornate frame. Placing one finger to the frame, she shifted it away to see that it was covered with glass. Had it been drilled by an insect in the fine wooden paneling, then filled with glass instead of plaster?

She shook her head, suddenly exhausted and longing to crawl into the downy comfort of the bed. She glanced down at her own tattered clothes and slippers, then unhooked the scroll from around her neck and placed it on a small table by the bed. Memories of Nicolaus and what had brought her to this place rushed back without warning. Even amid all this beauty, nothing had changed. Nicolaus was dead. And she was accused of his murder.

A knock sounded, and Nona appeared again, this time with fluffy towels, a tray of soaps, and pitcher of water. Maura wasn't sure how to address this lovely woman with thick chestnut hair and sturdy arms.

"I'm sorry. I don't know what to call you," Maura said. "It's strange to be waited upon. In my home, I was the one who did the serving. This has all been…I've been accused of…I loved the child." Maura wiped her eyes with one sleeve, adding tears to the grime of her day.

The woman nodded in sympathy. "Aye, tis a hard lot, miss. Nona here to help ye, child."

She led the way to a spacious bathroom with a claw-foot tub full of water dotted with rose petals. Maura'd never seen such loveliness. Nona placed the towels and soap on a marble vanity and left the room, and Maura wasted no time peeling off her stinky clothes and slipping into the curved tub.

Warmth surrounded her. Taking a breath, she ducked under the water and let her hair float like a mermaid's. And quieted her mind to think. Five days. She had to figure out some way to check on Benjamin. Tobias Fitch seemed vague about approved family members being allowed to visit. Surely it wouldn't be difficult to bring an old man to her side. She missed him, and his quiet wisdom that seemed effortless. He'd know how to unravel this knot that became more tangled with every moment.

When the water cooled, Maura pulled herself out of the tub and into a fresh cotton robe that hung from a stand nearby. She wrapped a towel around her head and stepped back into the bedroom.

Nona was setting a tray of bread and bowl of soft butter on a small vanity. She poured milk into a crystal glass. "Thought ye might need a mite more than tea and biscuits."

Maura almost wept with joy over the simple meal. "Thank you, Nona. So much." After slathering the butter on bread still warm from the oven, Maura took a bite, then another, and tried not to gulp the cool milk.

While she ate, Nona pressed through a closet the size of Maura's room at Sir Taylor's. Inside were gown after gown in fabrics and hues she'd never seen or thought possible.

"Ye'll be attending the Gunters' dinner party tonight." Nona bustled around the room gathering shoes from one cabinet, undergarments from another, and placing items either at Maura's feet or on the bed.

War broke out in Maura's heart. She forced herself to swallow a bite of the delicious bread. "I can't." Seen by countless eyes, judged, and declared guilty in their hearts? There must be a mistake. She wasn't a guest. She was a refugee.

"Ye have no choice, wain."

Appearing before strangers and parading around like a peacock must be part of an unseen prison sentence in this lovely home. It didn't make sense that her attendance was required at a party where she wouldn't know anyone and worse, was accused of murder. "Can you tell me about the Gunter's?" she asked Nona.

"They be leaders in this community."

"You mean in the government?"

"Mr. Gunter is a leading magistrate for the High Council. Mrs. Gunter is, well, much like a first lady of Sanctuary."

Maura wondered how she'd ended up in this home. She'd expected to barely get by while she waited for whatever refuge the city offered. Instead, she was lavished in comforts. She stuffed another bite of the bread in her mouth, then forced herself to chew and swallow like a lady instead of starving harvest hand.

Nona busied herself around the room while Maura finished the glass of milk. "Do the Gunter's have children? I didn't see any when I arrived."

"One daughter named Alessandra. A wee thing, she is. Off to boarding school."

Maura sighed, and her shoulders relaxed. She could ask Nona the questions she'd been too scared or embarrassed to ask others. She finished the last bite of bread as Nona pulled out a gown the color of a rain-washed sky. On the floor were supple leather shoes with tiny eyehooks.

Wiping her mouth with a napkin, she stood as Nona

held out a stay and undergarments. What was she supposed to do? No one had helped her dress since she was a child. She lowered her head and blushed.

" 'Tis is a complicated business. May I offer ye' a hand?" Nona handed Maura the underclothes and turned away for a moment while she put them on. Picking up the stay, she laced it against Maura's back with deft hands, careful to leave breathing room. A starchy petticoat came next, then another and one more flounced in place. Finally, Nona lifted the silky dress over her head and let it cascade over the layers. It settled to the floor just above her toes.

"How do all these clothes fit me? The dress, the shoes?"

Nona paused before she spoke. "We're told each home is kept in readiness."

"What about the other refugees? Are they all treated like this?"

"If there are others in the city, they're cared for. For now, ye be the task at hand."

Maura's hair was still damp, but she brushed out the tangles while Nona placed an assortment of cosmetics, brushes, and ornamental combs on a gilded tray. She motioned for Maura to sit, then took the brush from her hands and pulled it through Maura's hair.

Tension crept away with every stroke. When her hair fell in soft curls around her neck, Nona gathered it up and placed a gem-studded comb into an upsweep. As the woman stood back and admired her work, Maura ventured the question she'd been waiting to ask.

"There must be many refugees who've come to this city for shelter. Are they assured of a fair trial?"

Nona positioned a stray curl over Maura's ear. "Yes,

many have come. Each case is its own."

"And if…the case isn't won?"

Nona's dark eyes met hers in the mirror. "Execution, at the behest of the Council."

****

SIR TAYLOR

The woman sought out my telescope on clear nights, and now, a similar mechanism is in place to monitor her in a way she'd never suspect. An intricate web has been laid, and she will not escape.

Perhaps she'll try to pull on the sympathies of the unsuspecting. After all, she's an orphan with only a poor, broken uncle to call her own. I don't feel sorry for her. The Black Death stole my parents when I was only five. If the Community of St. Mary hadn't taken me in, I would've starved. I'll never forget the arms of those women who embraced me, such a pitiful child.

No one pities me anymore.

Sister Catherine took me as her own. Even she didn't understand the grit that formed inside me. *Not enough* shouted in my young heart. I had no family line, no significance, and certainly no money. That lack spurred ambition, and even creative thought. I saw the spinning frame in my mind and labored day and night until it became a reality. I imagined textiles no longer produced by hand but created in factories that employed many. Families had to leave cottage industries, of course. They were far better off working and living in the cities.

Orphans? My factory employs them, even offers a place to live. They can earn their keep and learn a trade at the same time. I offer them a future.

Abigail. I'm grateful you aren't here. Losing our child would have been more than your young heart could bear.

Chapter 7

A knock at the door startled Maura. It opened, and Lilith stood clothed in a jewel-encrusted gown the color of lilies, her raven hair twined around a delicate tiara. She still wore the emerald pendant as her only jewelry. Something about her smile awakened the trace of a memory in Maura. Would her mother approve of how she'd grown?

"Nona, you're dismissed," said Lilith.

Nona curtsied and left through the same door she'd entered, which must be the servant's entrance.

"Let me answer any questions you have," Lilith said once they were alone. "I can help guide you through this evening."

"I don't want to be…impertinent. Or ungrateful," Maura said, beginning slowly. "May I ask why my presence at a dinner party is requested?" She didn't mention that Nona had said required, not requested. "I have much to do in these five days, and I'm unsure of what's expected of me," she said, concluding as politely as she could.

The soft chatter of people being greeted at the front door and entering the spacious foyer drifted up the stairs.

"I understand." Lilith's tone was warm. "I'm aware that you're new to our city and unfamiliar with our culture. This evening will educate you. Sanctuary, I'm happy to say, represents community, friendship, and protection. Our home exemplifies its heart. You have nothing to fear."

So much for begging out of the evening's ceremony. Maura took one last glance into the mirror on her vanity and followed Lilith down a hallway that overlooked a grand ballroom filling with guests. A string quartet played in one corner of the room while people chatted in small groups. She longed to rush back into the shelter of her bedroom. Instead, Lilith grasped her elbow and glided down the stairs as indisputable queen of this universe, with Maura her unwilling satellite.

Tobias Fitch stood near the bottom of the stairs in the middle of an intense conversation with Anton Gunter. Anton gestured wildly around the room, in character for a man who appeared to prefer command to conversation.

Tobias stood a head taller than Anton. His black hair was glossy against a finely milled tweed coat and high-collared shirt.

Women glanced away from conversations in his direction. Maura wasn't the only one to admire this attractive man who held her defense in his hands.

"Excuse me, dear. One moment, please." Lilith left her alone to greet a man dressed in a ceremonial garb of black with red satin trim.

Maura stood alone feeling awkward and out of place. Tobias's back was toward her. She stepped closer, then stopped when she heard Anton speak.

"You were instructed…" Her host spoke in a loud hiss.

"She's been informed." Tobias spoke with calm, measured words.

"Is it too difficult…?" The rest of his words were

too muffled, though the contempt was clear.

Tobias' demeanor changed. A musky scent touched the atmosphere around them, then dissipated. Even from behind, Maura saw his body tense. He was done with whatever conversation—or diatribe—Anton offered. Tobias turned abruptly. When he noticed her, he bowed, his face unreadable.

Lilith returned from her conversation and placed a slender hand on Tobias's arm, smiling with the detached air of a hostess with better things to do than take care of a refugee. "Tobias. Be a dear and escort Miss O'Donnell to dinner?"

Tobias extended his arm. "My pleasure. Miss O'Donnell, will you do me the honor?" He leaned close, and Maura's senses filled with the scent of a meadow, freshly mown. "In lieu of my favorite chair, will you take my hand?"

Maura straightened her shoulders and lifted her chin. She placed her fingers lightly on his sleeve and felt his muscular forearm. Then met his gaze with a challenge. "As long as you lead me where I want to go."

"Follow me then, my young charge," Tobias said, the frozen reserve melting away in a smile. He walked her through the crowd and greeted guest after guest, introducing her as Maura O'Donnell, not refugee and possible criminal. Beautiful women positioned themselves to get closer to him. Too bad for them he was evidently required to stay by her side.

"You have many admirers, Tobias Fitch. Are you not married?"

"I am not. And this isn't the time to be distracted." He nodded to an elderly couple who angled through the room, intent on apprehending them. "Shark approaching on port side. With mate in tow. Prepare for cross-examination."

"Sir Franklin," Tobias said, as the couple arrived with a triumphant bow. "And Mrs. Franklin. May I introduce Miss Maura O'Donnell?"

Sir Franklin's smile boosted a wiry moustache that met equally wiry and unruly nose hair. Mrs. Franklin resembled an aging peacock with purple corkscrew curls that sprang loose in unruly abandon. She breathed in short puffs and peered into Maura's eyes. "Forgive me, dear. What is wrong with your…"

Maura grimaced before she could control her face. Some things never changed, regardless of the social status of those around her.

In the meantime, Mr. Franklin bowed to Maura and shouted, "How do you do?"

Perhaps remembering her manners, Mrs. Franklin leaned in closer at the same time, muttering like a conspirator. "Pardon me, dear. I adore your lovely eyes."

"Bubbly dies?" Sir Franklin protested. "What *are* you talking about, Mildred?

"I said LOVELY EYES."

Several guests turned in their direction.

"And what brings you to the party this evening?" Mrs. Franklin asked.

Tobias stepped in, thank heavens. "Miss O'Donnell is a refugee in our fine city, Mrs. Franklin." His tone was casual, as if she'd been on her way to another engagement and happened to stop by.

"A refugee. Oh. Dear." Mrs. Franklin grabbed her husband's arm and yanked. "A refugee," she said, sputtering. She about-faced and swung her husband around with her. If it hadn't been for another guest's large behind presenting an abrupt stop, Mr. Franklin would've spiraled off into the nearest wall. He tottered, then glared at his wife, who led him away.

Maura grinned sheepishly at Tobias. "This doesn't bode well for the society column."

"A column that would be much improved by your presence. It's time to enter the dining room." They joined a long procession to the dining room where footmen escorted people to chairs around a table that stretched from one end of the room to the other. Crystal, silver, and fine china were set in perfect alignment.

Nona stood by an ornately carved buffet, her green eyes overseeing activity in the massive dining room. She smiled and ducked her head at Maura's gaze.

Anton and Lilith appeared at the head of the table. Anton took his seat with a flourish of his arms, inviting each guest to join him. Tobias led her to one of the elegant, upholstered chairs as uniformed footmen arrived carrying tureens of soup. A young soldier appeared behind Tobias and waited for his attention. Tobias stood, with his hand on her chair. "A pressing need. I'll return."

Maura wanted to follow Tobias out the door. She suddenly felt exposed. Fitting in was impossible. She settled for studying the dinner guests who were seated beside and across from her. A man dressed in military regalia sat to her left with his wife, whose eyes darted everywhere except in Maura's direction. "Your name, miss?" he asked.

"Maura O'Donnell."

"Of the Barrett O'Donnells?"

"I don't think so, sir. I don't live here. I'm a refugee and new to the city."

The man's eyes lit up. "A refugee! A tribunal

judgment on the horizon. I do so love a good trial." His wife jabbed him in the side, and he yelped. "What? You enjoy them also, Gwyneth. Don't lie."

The woman harrumphed and turned her back to her husband.

"I apologize, my dear," he said to Maura with the graciousness to do so with a red face. "We'll start over. I'm Colonel Reginald Perry. My wife, although she chooses to disregard you and your predicament, is Angela. She isn't unkind. Only…"

Afraid? Maura wanted to ask. Embarrassed? She understood both. At least the colonel was honest.

"What brought you to the refuge of our fine city?" he asked.

Maura thought she saw a glimmer of compassion in his eyes. She returned his gaze without flinching. Even though she was an accused murderer, she refused the shame that had tried to settle in like a woolen cloak. "I'm accused of…I was a nanny. My young charge died after a fever."

"Ah. Medicine was provided?"

"Yes, but—"

"Perhaps an herbal remedy. Arguably a blessing or a curse, depending on who you ask. I know a woman near the tenements." He lowered his voice and glanced at his wife, who continued to ignore them. "Her name is Hildegard Brennan. A remarkable woman, schooled in the art of healing. She's mocked by local physicians. Her intervention saved our son when he lay dying, though. He's a father himself now. I'll never forget the mercies of meeting that woman."

Maura was taken aback. She'd found an unexpected friend at the very event she'd dreaded. "Do you know where I can find her? Her shop?" she asked.

"Why do you ask?"

"Maybe she…can help me understand what was prescribed for Nicolaus."

"Indeed. Well, her home and her shop are one and the same. Don't go any farther into the tenements than her home, though. They're very dangerous."

Maura wanted to ask in what way they were threatening but decided to get on with the question she most needed answered. "How do you get there?"

"The main road—the one that ascends to the Hall of Justice? Go the other way. Make a steep descent. Her shop is on the outskirts of an area banned for the citizens of Sanctuary. You must not enter. Believe me, a young woman as lovely as you would be an open target. Hildegard's an odd woman, but immensely gifted. Some believe she's a witch. Not me, though. You can judge for yourself."

Maura would find that woman the next day and investigate the potion given to Nicolaus. "Thank you for your kindness, Colonel Perry."

"Not to worry. You'll find friends here—once you overlook those who see you as potential diversion instead of a human being on trial." The colonel turned his attention to a group of men clad in black ceremonial robes who sat at the end of the table near Anton and Lilith. "Members of the Council."

Anton had told her at their first meeting that the Council was responsible for the abundance they enjoyed. All Maura remembered were Nona's words. *Execution at the behest of the Council.* These men would determine whether she lived or died.

Tobias returned to his seat as the colonel's wife

required her husband's attention. Footmen returned to serve course after course of a magnificent meal. Somewhere in the middle of the feast Maura gave herself permission to breathe. She wasn't being hurtled into a rushing river any longer. Thanks to the colonel, she had a plan. At least the first step of one.

Footmen arrived to remove plates and serve coffee. Finished, they stood against the wall of the dining room as Anton rose to his feet. "My dear friends, Lilith and I welcome you. We recognize the presence of our beloved Council members."

As if on cue, the four men at the head of the table stood and bowed to the gusty applause of the otherwise staid dinner guests. Everyone's eyes were focused on them.

"As I said," continued Anton. "We praise the members of our ruling Council for their benevolence. Their protection. Their compassion for our fine community." He bowed low in their direction.

"Be praised, O Council. Be praised." The guests stood and murmured in response. "Be praised, O Council. Be praised."

Tobias rose with everyone else, tugging at Maura's elbow to stand with him.

Maura's eyes blurred with fatigue as she stood at Tobias' side. With a full belly, everything in her body longed for sleep. Yet, the odd ceremonial acclaim droned on and on.

"Be praised, O Council, for the prosperity we know," one of the guests intoned.

"Be praised, O Council, for the safety we enjoy," said another.

A man added, "Be praised, O Council, for the justice

we enjoy. For the sanctuary you offer to us and to others."

The air felt thick around Maura, and she wished she could free her waist from the corset that had become a vise. She shouldn't have eaten everything in sight. And yet the rote tributes continued. Everyone else stood at attention as she wobbled.

Tobias steadied her with one hand on her elbow. Anton was bowing toward her. What was he saying?

Tobias nudged her arm. "Anton Gunter is introducing you."

She wasn't sure how she was supposed to respond. She tried to curtsy, but one foot caught the tablecloth. Maura wrested it free, but not until she tottered and fell to the floor. Along with remnants of dessert, crystal glasses of wine and delicate cups of coffee splashed and shattered around her, surprising dinner guests who jumped out of the way.

She peered up from the floor. Was Tobias stifling a grin? Her proper advocate with impeccable manners?

Colonel Perry, his wife, and others around them, stared, mouths open.

Anton didn't hide his irritation.

"I'm…" Maura's voice was much too loud in the shocked silence.

"A mess," Tobias whispered with a small wink as he bent to help her up. "You, Maura O'Donnell, are a delightful mess."

****

SIR TAYLOR

She didn't see me at the dinner party. No reason to draw attention to my presence. I watched and listened— skills that've made me who I am today. She didn't escape my scrutiny at the manse. I wouldn't leave my son with anyone without oversight. No. I had my helpers. They kept me informed.

I have people here, also. Not that anyone would recognize them. A few servants. Anton Gunter. Several others scattered throughout the crowd. The accursed woman sat by Colonel Perry, a foolish man for someone from his station in life.

I shivered with pride when the Council members stood to attention as the entire group of dignitaries, some real, some not, acknowledged their authority. They're a cut above the rest, something that became clear the first time I met them. Men of ambition, of vision and purpose. Shrewd enough to make sure no one hinders their plan.

They summoned me, you know. I didn't have to beat on their doors. They recognized genius, even sought it out. They, unlike others, recognize my contribution to the cause as a worthy one.

I've kept my days full but cannot escape the night. In those lonely hours, I hear Nic's laugh and see his brown eyes dash with mischief, so much like Abigail's. The way he cocked his head and jutted out his chin at a new discovery. Just like Abigail when she listened to one of my ideas for a new machine. Tension always melted with the sweetness of his arms around my neck.

I remember the first time I saw him in Abigail's arms. He wriggled with such vigor against her gentle embrace. How could one moment contain such joy and such sadness? For her life ebbed away as my son's had only begun.

How different our lives would have been with her presence. Meals together, walks on summer evenings. Probably Abigail would've pulled me out of the laboratory more often. As it was, family became Nicolaus and me.

I've ached for her since she died. And now, without Nicolaus, I'm shattered and without a compass. I must defend his life that could've been. And hope that at some point, sleep will come.

Chapter 8

A knock on the door startled Maura the next morning. It could've been Nona arriving to prepare her for the day, except it didn't come from the servants' entrance. Running hands through her hair, Maura shot a quick peek into the mirror. Tangled curls twisted around her shoulders, and her nightgown—a satiny one Nona found for her in the bureau—was askew. Maura grabbed a woolen shawl, tempted to drape it over her head like the gypsy vendors at the village's open-air market. When she finally opened the door, she found Lilith waiting, dressed in a morning gown, and holding a cup of tea.

The woman extended the cup and smiled. "I couldn't wait. Would you like…? Do you have time for an outing? We can shop. I know a charming sidewalk café for lunch. We could…" Lilith seemed uncertain. "This is your first day. I've asked the Council to offer this as a day of rest. Perhaps one is in order?"

Maura stood at the door, struggling to find a way to answer her hostess, who wore a winsome smile. Maura needed to find the apothecary and Tobias had said something about contacting her for another interview. She couldn't go shopping when all she could think about was the stream of events that had pushed her to this place. But she'd tried to refuse her hostess's invitation the night before, and that hadn't worked. Maybe this unwelcome diversion was more of the same protocol that required her to appear at a dinner party. And pretend to be sociable when it was obvious she was an outcast and spectacle.

Maura shifted from one foot to the other. "What a lovely offer." She'd try polite and see if that worked. "I'd better stay here, though, to prepare for my trial."

To her surprise, Lilith walked past her and into her room.

Maura hurried to pull the coverlet over her tussled bedding, but Lilith acted as though she didn't notice. Instead, she strode to the walk-in wardrobe and rifled through its contents.

Unsure of what to do, Maura positioned herself nearby, anticipating Lilith's next invitation—or command.

Lilith fingered each gown, pulling one aside, moving on to the next as if she were on a specific mission. Finally, she landed on a rose-colored one. "Try this one. Join me downstairs for breakfast before we head out for our adventure." Then, she added, as if an afterthought, "Take your time, Maura. Tobias will be here tomorrow morning. We have the day to enjoy."

The last thing Maura wanted to do was traipse around a store, even though she'd never been to one and couldn't guess what it would be like. Back in the village, her clothing came from a dressmaker whose cottage was two fields down the road and one to the right. Maura sighed, washed her face, and prepared for a day that promised to contain yet another string of unknown events.

When she was ready, she started to head out the door to the main hallway. Curiosity overcame her, though, and she chose the door Nona had used to come in and out of her bedroom. Maura wondered why the servants needed a separate hallway. Nona appeared and disappeared so seamlessly that it was as if only her service mattered. Who she was as a person was tucked away out of sight. A dimly lit narrow corridor turned right at a sharp angle. Maura took the turn and saw a stairway, where a closed oaken door stood at the bottom. A shrill voice from the other side of the door broke the silence.

"I'll take this cleaver to yer neck! Get out of my kitchen or be damned!"

Maura gathered up her dress in one hand and charged back up the stairs, around the corner and down the hallway. As much as she'd wanted to investigate the Gunter home, she entered the shelter of her room with a giant sigh of relief. What room had she almost entered, where a knife-wielding fiend threatened?

When she opened the door of her room, a young housemaid stood over the vanity, pawing through a basket of ornamental hair combs. She jerked her hands away when she saw Maura. Contempt seemed to flash across her face before it turned to fear. She clenched her hands in a tight fist against her starched apron and curtsied.

Maura stood, unsure of how to respond.

The housemaid straightened her shoulders and spoke in a loud voice. "Me mistress invites you to breakfast. In the sunroom." She turned and led the way down the main hall, listing slightly from one side to another as she walked down the grand stairway with Maura close behind.

The breakfast room was full of windows on one side that opened to a manicured garden. Maura took in the expertly trimmed hedges and variety of roses with a sudden pang of homesickness. Benjamin would love to see this beauty. And she longed to see him.

Lilith sat at a table set with china and silver tea service and patted the arm of the chair beside her. Maura took a seat, careful to avoid the lace tablecloth that dangled to the polished hard-wood floor.

The young maid brought fresh fruit, buttered toast, and hot black coffee to the table. Maura noticed a flush in her cheeks, which otherwise were thin and sallow.

"Pretty Adele," Lilith said. "She won't be in our service long. Some handsome man will whisk her away, and we'll be seeking someone else just like her."

Maura couldn't help wondering how long the girl would last in a household filled with such bounty. Could she resist filching here and there?

Adele's hands trembled as she poured fragrant coffee into their cups, then offered Maura warm cream. Lilith chattered on about their day, naming shops and charting their course. Even the delicious meal couldn't dispel the angst in Maura's heart, though. She'd never shopped. Or had lunch at a sidewalk café. Her life had been a sequestered one for so long. It was strange to be cared for in a gracious home with a kind hostess when she'd expected a prison.

Lilith led Maura through Sanctuary's business district, which was bathed in sunlight with the mountains as a backdrop. Exquisitely dressed women walked on the broad sidewalks or played with children on a grassy patch of manicured lawn that marked a city park. The streets were clean cobblestone, and the air filled with sound of courteous greetings and pleasant conversation.

Maura followed Lilith into a shop filled with table

after table of fabrics. Upholstered settees arranged in cozy circles were ready for potential customers. A woman dressed in a simple tailored gown curtsied and led them to a sitting room upstairs, where several bolts of fabric had already been placed on a round table near their seats.

"Each dress is made to order," Lilith explained. "Choose a fabric that you love."

Maura was in awe of yard goods she'd never known existed.

A young assistant stood poised over the bolts. Lilith nodded her head toward a bolt of creamy yellow fabric. The clerk pulled it out and carried it to Maura, holding it as if offering a gift.

It was too beautiful to touch. There might still be jelly on her hands from the toast she'd enjoyed that morning.

Lilith smiled as if she understood her uncertainty. "You won't hurt it, Maura. Tell us what you think."

Maura placed one finger on the bolt and jerked it back. Then reached to touch it again, this time with a lingering caress. It felt like Nic's cheek, soft and warm. And like sunlight on her face as she lay in meadow grass after a long day of work in the garden. Tears rushed to her eyes.

Pulling a dainty handkerchief from a miniature purse, Lilith pressed it into Maura's hand and spoke to the clerk. "We'll take this one. I saw some lace downstairs. Perhaps it would be nice around the bodice?"

The woman curtsied and left. When she returned, she carried the lace in one hand and a tape measure in the other.

Maura studied the plush carpeting, suddenly

embarrassed.

"Not to worry," Lilith said, rushing to explain. "Monica will take your measurements and craft a dress as lovely as the pouch for your scroll."

Maura stood and let the woman fuss until every inch of Maura's body had been measured and noted in the small binder.

"I have no money, no means to pay for such a fine dress."

"Allow Anton and me this small joy," Lilith said. "You will, after all, need appropriate clothes. And will be the loveliest of lovely when it comes time for the trial." Lilith turned to study another bolt of fabric. "Today is for enjoying."

Maura's heart melted with Lilith's generosity. Her gowns had always been the serviceable variety in various shades of brown or gray. Even though finding out what had happened to Nicolaus never left her mind, this dress was a reminder that, no matter how she was accused, she'd straighten her shoulders and face whatever lay ahead. Lilith's kindness was truly a refuge.

Lilith bought the gorgeous fabrics and left her address for later delivery. Not that they didn't know where to find her. Everyone bowed and scraped when Lilith walked into the store. Croissants at an outdoor café came next, then they sat on a park bench and ate chocolate as they watched children play on the grassy lawn.

A young woman who wore a flower-strewn bonnet walked past them with a baby carriage. Despite the broad brim of her hat, she and Lilith made eye contact. Maura was sure they'd stop and chat like other small groups of friends who enjoyed this day.

Instead, the young woman picked up her pace.

Lilith stood quickly and caught up with her.

Maura didn't know what to do, so she followed her hostess to meet the pleasant young woman. Perhaps she was an acquaintance. Except, the mother seemed to hold her breath. She tugged slightly at the carriage handle, despite Lilith's light touch on its side.

"What a sweet baby," Lilith said, cooing and reaching to caress the infant's cheek. "And so sleepy. Wake, little one. Let me see you."

Maura was confused. No one in her experience awakened a sleeping baby. The little one stirred and opened his eyes. Sunbursts of golden in the middle of sky blue peered up at Lilith. Startled, Maura took a breath. The baby boy had eyes just like hers.

Without warning, the mother snatched the baby to her breast and ran, leaving the carriage behind. A pale yellow blanket followed them like a small banner, then plummeted on the ground.

Maura turned to Lilith, hoping she'd explain the woman's strange behavior. But her hostess had walked over to offer a little girl in the park a bit of chocolate as if nothing unusual happened.

The young mother ran full tilt. She swerved around people who stood in her path, still clenching the baby to her chest. Ladies dropped parcels and steadied carriages as she careened by.

Soon, a group of uniformed men gathered from several directions. They spread out into clusters, blocking the woman at every turn.

The mother stopped, searching frantically for a way of escape. She cried out in fear, holding tight to the now wailing child. She dashed into a side street, out of sight.

She screamed, "No!"

"Only our security at work. Never fear," Lilith answered calmly.

Security? A woman with a baby? Maura tried to shake the terror she'd seen on the woman's face. "I don't understand. How could a mother with her child be a threat?"

"I'm confused too. Did I frighten her?" Lilith acted like the woman was somehow at fault. She saw Maura's confusion and explained. "She was guilty of something. Laws here are set in place for our own safety. No one who lives here is ignorant of them. A class of rebels fly in the face of our time-honored traditions. They live here as usurpers, doing what they wish, bending the laws, yet still enjoying the prosperity of our city. This woman must be one of them. They're a dangerous people, hiding among our faithful."

Maura wondered what qualified citizens as faithful. "What kind of rule could she have broken?" There hadn't been anything suspect in the young woman's behavior, other than her sudden flight after Lilith woke the child.

Instead of answering, Lilith turned to leave.

Maura joined her, and they walked down the even sidewalks they'd traveled that morning. Lilith waved and offered best wishes to others as if a lone woman and her child hadn't just been apprehended by uniformed men for no apparent reason.

Maura remembered from her carriage ride that the city was set on a hill. From this perspective, she could see they were near the top, where the stately Hall of Justice stood as a sentinel. Where would Maura find answers in this city that seemed to defy conclusions? What she'd seen was intriguing, but a gauzy veil descended any time she peered in more closely.

After their shopping trip, Maura joined Lilith and Anton for dinner, then dessert in the parlor. She retreated to her room that night, changed into a simple linen nightgown, and settled under the covers. Thinking overcame sleep. She couldn't escape the image of the young mother who'd grasped her child and run in such terror. Had the guards separated her from the baby? The thought of a son forced out of his mother's arms took Maura's breath away.

A familiar ache returned as a pain that rarely went away. Her memory of her own mother was dim. Images she'd conjured over the years were mostly imagination and not much reality. Benjamin had secured her heart in the eternity of the stars and creation in the tiniest details. And in his everyday love.

Papa had been her unspoken favorite. Mama had understood. At least she seemed to. After all, Maura had needed her daddy's stories. To say nothing of the firm set of his jaw when rules hindered her freedom. Her mother's presence had been like the sunlight, only missed when obscured by clouds and rain. Or longed for in the darkness. Her quiet ways had kept their universe in sync. Maura hadn't noticed until she'd grown up without her. She was sorry for what she'd never said, even as a child.

Tossing against the downy comforter, she remembered Nicolaus. Sorrow would have swallowed her if hope hadn't arrived in Colonel Reginald Perry. He'd given her a lead on a local apothecary. She'd find the woman tomorrow after her appointment with Tobias and investigate the medicine Nicolaus had taken. After that, she'd find the road back to the hedge. She couldn't leave the city, but surely Benjamin was on his way.

Light from a full moon shone through an opening in the curtains. She pulled the fabric aside and studied the night sky. There was Orion, the Hunter. Or as Benjamin had told her, Orion the Warrior, with one foot poised over the head of a serpent.

Maura was hunted by Sir Taylor. That she knew. Had Nicolaus's death been accidental? Surely there wasn't any other explanation. Settling back into bed, she finally drifted into a deep sleep and a vivid dream.

In the dream, she perched on the back of an ebony horse. His muscular haunches tensed, ready to spring forward. Clouds rushed across the moon as she bent low. A tall, robed figure placed a cylinder of parchment into her hand. Overhead, the constellation Orion extended its starry arm as if ready for battle. Behind them, white sand sprayed in puffs from hooves pulsing in relentless pursuit.

She whispered to the man standing beside her. "What if I—?"

"Go in the strength of the Almighty," the man commanded. He held the horse's face in his hands. "Nageed, flee with your rider. Protect the scroll!"

Maura felt her body tilt backward. She grabbed the lush black mane and held on as the horse reared as if in assent.

A flaming arrow plummeted into the sand beside them.

She lowered herself against the horse's warm, musty scent and held on with all her strength.

The clank of amulets against brazen armor approached. One command rose from behind her, ever closer, closer to their prey.

"Retrieve the scroll. Or die."

Maura saw the precious parchment under her arm. It was the one Papa had laid beside her in the wagon many years ago. The one she and Benjamin had read from since she was a child. The one now in the room where she lay.

The ground shook, and a multitude of hooves drew near. Suddenly, the scroll leaped from under her arm and wrapped itself around her, encasing her body until they became one. Together, they shone in the darkness. She heard cries from the horsemen. "There! In the light."

Hooves pawed the ground, and bows were drawn as an army of horsemen surrounded her and her horse. A cry burst through the night. It was a shout of triumph. The scroll had been taken, and now she was theirs, too.

Chapter 9

Maura woke with a start, breathing hard, skin clammy. Reaching for a tangled mane, she found a blanket twisted around her body.

A knock sounded at the servant's passageway. She glanced at the table by her bed and saw the scroll, undisturbed. Sunlight streamed through the windows. It was the morning of the second day.

Nona entered, carrying a tray of tea and toast. Maura tried to comb her hair with her fingers and straighten the covers. She hovered between two worlds, one from her dream and one of reality—morning at the Gunter's with a servant appearing to help her get ready. Maura wasn't sure which world was stranger.

Nona frowned at the mass of covers and Maura tangled inside. "So, was it a bear ye wrestled, wain?" She placed the tray beside Maura, then busied herself around the room. She chose the new yellow gown from the closet and placed it on the bed. Then poured warm water into a basin and put a clean towel nearby.

Maura watched, too exhausted to be polite or even climb out of bed. "I'm so tired."

"'Tis all right, my dear. Don't I know ye is in quandary? But you'll never plow a field by turning it over in your mind. You'll rise to a new day. Never fear."

Nona had appeared at Maura's side after the dinner fiasco like a gentle breeze, placing broken plates and shattered glasses on a cart. Maura had jumped up to help, which appeared to be just as shocking to the guests as taking the tablecloth and all its contents with her to the floor. How could she let Nona clean up her mess without helping?

"Peace, lass," Nona had said.

Day two in the count to five as Nona helped Maura get dressed for an interview with Tobias that had been set for this morning. She'd placed a final comb in Maura's hair when someone pounded on the servants' entrance. Nona opened it, and Adele tumbled into the room, trembling and out of breath.

"What hissy has provoked ye?" asked Nona.

The young girl panted the words between gasps for breath. "There's been an accident at the factory."

Nona turned white and ran to the door, then stopped and spun once around the room.

"Go," said Adele. "I'll take care of the young miss."

Nona gathered her skirt and ran out the door.

"Accident?" asked Maura when she was gone.

Adele closed the distance between them and whispered, "Her grandson Rory works at the factory."

Nona had a grandson? Compassion welled up in Maura. "May I help in some way?"

Adele didn't answer. The young maid who'd toppled in unannounced stood frozen in place, gaze beyond Maura.

Maura turned to see Lilith standing imperiously at the entrance of the room. Someone was in trouble. Perhaps she hadn't heard what happened to Nona's grandson.

"Mr. Tobias Fitch has arrived, Maura," Lilith said, examining the room. "He's waiting downstairs." She glanced at the young servant with open irritation. "Adele, take your place in the kitchen."

"Yes, ma'am." Adele curtsied and slipped out the servants' passageway.

Lilith stood like a Roman goddess, carved in stone, with her black hair pulled into long ringlets against her shoulders. Gone was the gracious matriarch. Her porcelain features were frozen in place. The Lilith who'd taken her shopping the day before had vanished, replaced by this cold, angry version.

Maura felt she needed to make an appeal. "Nona's grandson has been injured. Adele delivered the news."

Lilith's countenance softened. "You aren't acquainted with how we run our home, which is understandable. We have an assignment to carry out, and it requires the help of many. You were to be ready for an interview with your guardian this morning—one to prepare your defense. Because of the confusion, you're late."

Late? Maura was already dressed, thanks to Nona's help. Lilith's barely contained outrage didn't make sense. Something else had offended her, but Maura didn't know what.

"This is the second day of your stay, and each day is critical to prepare for your trial," Lilith said with lifted eyebrows. "I have an appointment and must leave now. Adele will serve tea in the parlor."

Maura took another look in the mirror and adjusted a simple golden strand around her neck. Thanks to Nona she was prepared for any social event of the day. And looked far better than she'd ever managed on her own. She had no idea how a disaster with Nona's grandson had become a breach in protocol, as well as a reminder of what she already knew. She was on borrowed time.

Adele had seated Tobias and stood nearby with the tea service when Maura arrived downstairs. The fabric of the young maid's apron wiggled as her knees shook, like a frightened gazelle.

Tobias stood and bowed when Maura entered the room. Maura took a seat near him as Adele served them.

She searched his eyes, wondering how his attitude toward her had changed since the formal dinner. She'd shattered all kinds of social conventions—along with everything on the table. Tobias appeared to be his usual picture of composure, though. He took papers out of a leather case and placed them in a neat stack on his lap.

She remembered her dream from the night before. Something about her advocate reminded her of a picture she'd seen once of Orion. Before he'd become a constellation, anyway. Orion was so handsome, so loved by the goddess Artemis that she'd carried his body to join the stars.

This was a strange time to remember Greek myths.

He met her gaze, seeming oddly immune to her strange eyes. How had a man who had never worked a plow or dug in a garden gotten that scar?

He lifted his gaze to hers. "Tell me about your flight as a child."

Maura pressed her back against the chair, shocked at this opening statement. "How do you know about that? Have you spoken to Benjamin?"

Tobias scrutinized her intently. "I've been studying your case, Maura. We can't afford surprises during the trial."

"Then you also know, Mr. Fitch, that I was very young. I don't remember much. Only that Benjamin and

I left and settled in the village near Sir Taylor's estate."

"You don't know why you left?"

"This information can't matter. I'm on trial for the death of Nicolaus Taylor, not an event that happened to me as a child."

"Of course."

What happened to sweet, funny Tobias? This was the man she'd met the first day, all business. What had it meant to take his hand?

"The prosecutor, Sir Hugh Taylor, will offer any incriminating evidence he can find," he said. "I need to know as much about you as I can."

Maura took a sip of tea and placed it back on the saucer with careful hands, stalling for a moment to gather her thoughts.

"Uncle Benjamin raised me," she said as her mind rushed through the snatches of what she knew and how Benjamin had filled in the gaps. She swiped at tears that ran down her face without permission.

Tobias pulled a silken handkerchief from his pocket and handed it to her. She dabbed her cheeks, unsure of how to return it soaked in tears and a runny nose.

"I understand this isn't easy," he said.

"Benjamin...I need to know if he's safe. That he isn't paying the price for my escape here." Maura hugged her arms, suddenly chilled.

Tobias peered out a towering window that warmed the room, then turned back to her. Maura thought she saw a glint of darkness brush across those brown eyes. "Our lives here are sequestered, in a way. We aren't privy to information about the world outside, unless it pertains to Sanctuary, of course. But I'll pursue information regarding your uncle."

"I was forced to leave my parents as a child," she said, staring at a fleck of dust on the carpet. "They promised to follow me later, but they never did. Benjamin is the only family I've known since." She shoved a strand of hair back into what she hoped was its place. As if in answer, the ornamental comb fell into her lap. Carefully styled locks now streamed out of place, unrestrained. Like the emotions she fought to control.

Tobias leaned closer. "Tell me about the night Nicolaus Taylor died."

Maura took a deep breath and blew it out. "He'd been feverish for several days. When I tried to talk to Sir Taylor, he sent me away and told me not to worry. A potion was delivered later that afternoon. I gave Nicolaus the medicine, except he only grew weaker.

"When I heard the child cry out, I went to him. He wasn't breathing. I ran to Sir Taylor immediately, hoping maybe he could do something. He's so smart, and he has all those machines and… I wasn't thinking, wasn't willing to accept the truth.

"Sir Taylor accused me of murder." Maura swallowed a sob, her throat tight. "I wouldn't have hurt Nicolaus. You must believe me."

Tobias was taking notes. He glanced up. "What did you do then?"

"I ran…to Benjamin."

"How did you find our city?"

"My uncle somehow knew…the way." She couldn't tell Tobias about the hedge without sounding crazy. "Aiden Garrett saw me on the road to Sanctuary. He escorted me to the city by carriage."

"Before Sir Taylor exacted revenge?" Tobias jotted notes on his paper without bothering to notice the expression on Maura's face.

"How did you know?" she asked.

"There are many paths into the city," he said. "We're aware when a person seeks refuge, as well as when the blood avenger pursues."

"The hedge extends for miles. It's hard to believe that every entrance is watched." Especially the unlikely ones like hers.

"We have a responsibility to steward our refugees. A host of creatures, trained for that very purpose, live alongside the wilderness hedge. Perhaps you saw a bird of some kind after your arrival?"

Maura had seen the great wings of a bird when she'd landed on the outskirts of Sanctuary. "The eagle was a spy?"

Tobias shook his head. "Not exactly. He's a sentinel and one of our finest. His name is Maximillian. You had nothing to fear from him, formidable as he appeared. He was noting your entrance and alerting us to your circumstances."

"If the carriage driver hadn't arrived, Sir Taylor would've killed me," she said, reminding him of what he supposedly already knew.

"True. Although legally you were within the boundaries of Sanctuary. And the carriage did arrive with timely help, did it not?"

Maura thought about Aiden's open curiosity and how he'd appeared to bumble her defense. And then how he'd wielded his sword so skillfully. Strange. But he'd done his job.

"You'll find mysteries in this city that have existed for many years," continued Tobias. "Your days here will unveil a multitude of ways we honor our time-honored calling to provide refuge for the accused, until a fair trial can be arranged."

"I don't understand—not exactly—how I made it to this city. It seemed almost magical. The time, the weather, and the terrain here are entirely different, but my journey from home was brief. How could that be?"

Tobias shook his head. "Whatever path you took, I'm glad it led here."

To safety? Or to him?

Tobias reached for a sheet of paper from the stack on his lap. "Now. About the trial. The entire city will gather at our city amphitheater. You'll face the Council, Sir Taylor, and me at the base of the arena. I'll find a way to communicate with you. Keep your eyes on me. The crowd will be noisy. Our community regards their participation as a right and a duty. It won't be a quiet gathering."

"Like a real amphitheater? Will there be lions? Wild beasts?"

"No lions. Sir Taylor will be the first to bring his case before the Council."

"Sir Taylor murdered a young man in cold blood before Nicolaus died. One who had no opportunity to run to the shelter of this city. Certainly, you're aware of this."

"He's a man of great influence and will use his standing in this region to leverage his case. He'll malign your motives in any way he can. I cannot speak to Sir Taylor's behavior. My concern is for you and your case. For that reason, I must ask. Is there anything hidden that, if discovered, would seal his arguments against you?"

"How can I know?" She glanced out the window. A day like this one had convinced her to bring Nicolaus for an evening visit with Benjamin. A cloudless sky became a perfect night to share their favorite constellations. She took a deep breath. "Sir Taylor accused me of neglect when I took Nicolaus out one evening to visit Benjamin. He'd napped long that afternoon, and the weather was balmy. Nothing to suggest it was a dangerous venture."

"Yet you fear he'll accuse you of causing the boy's illness."

"I'm afraid so. And there is one other thing. The medicine that was sent had an odd scent. It wasn't like any medicine I'd given Nicolaus before."

Tobias took furious notes. "When you took him outside at night—was that routine?"

"It wasn't routine, but neither was it forbidden. I was often lonely. I would never have put the child's health in jeopardy."

"What else?"

"What else about me that could incriminate my motives? My parents are…gone. Sir Taylor's wife died in childbirth. That fact only drew my heart to Nicolaus."

Tobias nodded. "It's clear that you loved the child. One more question. What is the mystery behind your eyes?"

So, he *had* noticed. She lifted her chin and straightened the soft fabric of her new dress with one hand. "My father once told me I carried the light of the stars. Are you implying I may be accused as a witch who enchanted a small child only to poison him?" She gathered herself up in a huff, resisting the urge to run back up the stairs to the safety of her room. Instead, she stood with one hand on a hip and the other pointed at her advocate.

"It's true that I'm odd and alone." She hated the way

her voice wobbled and curls dangled into her eyes. "I have no friends other than an aging uncle and a young child who died unexpectedly. If you view these speculations as incriminating, I may as well lay my head against the executioner's axe right now."

Tobias stood and bowed. He held up a hand as if to stop her words. "I'm here as guardian and advocate, not adversary. I must be sure you won't bow to accusations I'm certain will come. Sir Taylor will do all in his power to prove you guilty. Are you confident in who you are? Will you stand, knowing the truth about yourself despite lies?"

There was a mystery behind this man, her advocate. His face was usually the picture of undisturbed poise. Now, though, and certainly at the dinner party, something in his form betrayed that composure. What did his body say that his face would not?

"One thing I know," she said, straightening her shoulders. "I'm innocent of the death of Nicolaus Taylor."

"Excellent. How else can I help you?"

"I remember the smell of the medicine sent for Nicolaus. It seemed familiar in some way, but I couldn't place it. There's an apothecary nearby that I'd like to visit in hopes of identifying it."

"I'll send an escort."

"That won't be necessary. I'll go and return without delay. You'll check on my Uncle Benjamin?"

Adele hurried in to bring Tobias his coat and hat.

"Tell him how to find me."

"Wait for an escort." Tobias's words were more command than request. "We'll meet again, and I'll give you an update at our meeting. Two o'clock tomorrow afternoon."

Chapter 10

After Tobias left, it was time for Maura's mission. Find Hildegard, the apothecary. She didn't need an escort. Colonel Perry's directions were simple enough. She thought about bringing a shawl, but it was too warm to need one. At home, they had cloudy days and rain, especially since it was late fall there. Not in Sanctuary. The weather hadn't changed in the days she'd been there—temperate with only a light breeze.

The road she and Aiden had taken to the Gunter's stretched out before her. Colonel Perry had told her to turn left instead of right toward the Hall of Justice. She peered across the street, dodged a driver and his wooden cart full of vegetables and took off at a brisk pace on a sidewalk that extended beside the busy road. Mothers strolled with baby carriages. Others gathered in small groups near the park, where children played, and dogs jumped for balls in games of catch.

Pulling in a long breath, Maura felt the warmth of the day relax tension that had settled into her muscles. A robin bounced from the sidewalk to a nearby tree, while a woman lifted her spade from her planting and waved at Maura. The road wound slightly around neighborhoods much like the ones that held her host home. After several minutes of walking, its cobbled stones became a steep descent.

A rutted path moved in a steep hill away from the

lovely homes behind her. A faint stream of smoke from a factory wafted in the distance. Maura wondered if it was the one where Nona's grandson had been injured. The neighborhood below the Gunters' home was filled with smaller structures, and the one beyond those even tinier dwellings with tidy patches of grass along the road. As Maura continued down the hill, a group of narrow timbered buildings appeared. Surely, they were the tenements, supposedly too dangerous to enter.

A thatched cottage stood at the entrance of a maze of alleys and ill-kept yards. She walked to door, where a signed carved in teakwood declared APOTHECARY.

Suddenly, a ruckus ensued behind the door.

"Fie! Back ye! Out of this shop."

The door flew open, and a tiny woman rushed out brandishing a broom, shouting at a crow that ducked low, then circled as if it mocked her. "Oi. Blasted bird."

When the woman noticed Maura, she lowered the broom and gestured toward the door. "Come, come, my dear. 'Tis Hildegard, here. Quite harmless, I am, unless ye be crow in disguise." She settled the broom in a crook beside the door and offered a grin showing off sporadic teeth. Maura stood, unsure that this diminutive, crow-chasing woman was the one Colonel Perry recommended.

The little woman cackled with joy, as if she understood Maura's thoughts. "Come, ye. Won't do to scare away me payin' customers. I'll fix ye a cuppa, quick as a wink."

Maura ducked her head into the shop, where an orderly universe of flasks on rows of open shelves greeted her. A ladder rested against the wall, the only way to reach wooden pestles and bowls that lined an upper sill. Dried herbs hung upside down in bunches. Scents of peppermint, basil, oregano, and something else she couldn't name lingered—some in quiet whispers, others in loud shouts. It was a world of warmth and industry. Mystery and comfort.

A miniature in an aged shell, Hildegard's frame cloaked what appeared to be the energy of an eternal spring. Her eyes were sharp and black against a shock of white hair that drifted over one side of her face. She pushed it away like an unnecessary hindrance. Much like she handled the bird—in no uncertain terms. A shawl, intricately embroidered in the rich colors of a tree of life, covered her shoulders and drooped near the stone-tiled floor. "Who may ye be, my pretty lass?"

"My name is Maura. Maura O'Donnell."

"Ah, tis a fine Celtic name. I'm not recognizin' ye, though."

"I'm a refugee. I arrived two days ago."

Sudden tears sprang to Hildegard's eyes. She flitted a handful of tea leaves into an ancient china pot. "Sit, dear. Talk to an old woman, longing for company. Sugar?"

Maura nodded as she seated herself on a wooden stool.

Hildegard placed sugar cubes in a teacup and brought it to her. She poured herself a cup and sat across from Maura. "Where ye be hailing from?"

"A village near here. I don't know exactly where it is, though." How could she explain what she didn't understand?

"That hedge…"

"You know about the hedge?"

Hildegard's answer shook her entire body. "That I

do, that I do."

"I can't explain how time, weather, climate—all changed on the other side."

"Sanctuary tis a conundrum, indeed. With a fair bit of magic thrown in. Set in place when I was a wee lass by a kind and wise regent. Once five cities, now only one. In days past, a step into its borders offered true refuge. Today, it be far from perfect…Still, we be grateful for those like yerself who find us."

Maura felt peace despite the chaos of smells and clutter of this and that stored in every inch of the little shop. "I fell asleep right after I arrived. It was the strangest thing. I'd just been pursued by a man determined to kill me and didn't even know where I was."

Hildegard listened without questions. Maura's words spilled out with unexpected tears. "The blood avenger was my employer. It was his son I cared for who died that night."

"I be sorry. Truly."

"The medicine sent for him smelled odd." Maura studied the wizened face with faded blue eyes that brimmed with tears once again. "A man at the Gunters' dinner party told me about you. The medicine I gave Nicolaus didn't seem right. He died several hours after I gave it to him." Maura noticed vial after vial of unknown concoctions on the shelves. "Could it have been poison?"

"Oi. Such sadness," Hildegard said in a soft voice. "Drink ye tea while I be thinkin' what be poison in the wrong hands." She scurried up the rickety ladder with a youthful spring. Her dark eyes perused bottle after bottle. After gathering several, she placed them into a pocket on her apron, and descended with one hand lightly on each rung.

"Here. This one—belladonna. Nightshade, foxglove, and autumn crocus. Not too close," she said, pulling out each one and placing it on a small table. She firmly nudged Maura away from the vials.

"Autumn crocus?" Maura said. "My father warned me never to touch it."

"Aye, he were a wise one. It be poison. Egyptians used it. Let's see, which book were that in?" She pulled out an ancient tome from a nearby shelf and fingered aged parchment. "Egypt. 1550. Mebbe to knock off one of them tetchy pharaohs. Jilted lover."

Hildegard carefully replaced the book and turned to Maura. "Autumn crocus be a lily, not a crocus. The flowers, they bloom in early fall—when the garden 'tis ready for winter sleep. Treats gout in just the right dose." She opened a blue flask of white powder. "Don't touch."

Maura leaned from her perch to sniff. "Sweetness. I recognize that scent from the powder I put in Nic's bottle. The porter, James…" She struggled to remember his last name. He'd delivered medicine from time to time at the manse. A pale, scraggly-haired youth, he skulked around like he wished he was anywhere, doing anything other than making deliveries for the old apothecary, Mr. Perkins. It was an odd name, like a biscuit. "Honeycutt. That's it. James Honeycutt. But how can I get any information from him? I can't go back to the village. I'll lose my protection as a refugee."

"You'll be findin' a way, dear one. Mebbe a way where there is no way." Hildegard sat on a stool across from Maura and extended her hands. "Now, let's be lookin' at ye. There be no cures for a broken heart in these bottles. I'll be prayin' instead."

"How?" Maura backed up.

The woman chortled with glee. "No potions of toads and pulverized snakeskin here. Only light from the Father of lights. The One who keeps our lives bundled into His."

Maura was silent for a moment. "My papa said that."

"And he be at home, awaitin' ye?"

"No. Only my Uncle Benjamin. He hasn't come, even though he promised."

"Sadness, indeed. Living One of light and hope, we call upon Ye. Protect this child. Swallow that pain with Yer goodness." She hadn't bowed her head, hadn't lifted her hands, or adjusted the tone of her voice as if addressing a distant, somewhat deaf deity. She spoke simply, as if to a friend.

Maura stood, dumbfounded. "I feel…"

"Better? Then ye must promise to visit agin." Hildegard slipped the shawl from her shoulders and draped it over Maura's. "Ye'll be needin' this."

Maura tried to refuse it, but her new friend's face was so crestfallen, she thought the better of it. "It's too…lovely."

"It be yours." Hildegard's words to her were as unadorned as her prayer. She kissed Maura's cheek with a leathery peck. The scent of sandalwood filled the air around them as Hildegard walked Maura to the door. She waved as Maura stepped from the threshold of that gentle cosmos.

If she could find the hedge, maybe she could get a message to the village apothecary. He'd know what kind of medicine had been sent. Mountains loomed farther away than she'd recalled from the carriage drive, beyond the tenements Colonel Perry had warned her about.

She'd hurry and at least chart a path for the next day.

Timbered buildings she'd seen earlier that day blocked the sunlight. This world was dirty, unkempt, and dark, a stark contrast to the world of Hildegard's shop. Boys tossed a rag back and forth, shouting and tussling each other. A man dressed in a coarse tunic slumped against a curb, head in his hands near a sewage-filled gutter.

She quickened her steps only to slip and fall hard on the damp pavement. She tottered upright and rubbed her hip, in pain and thoroughly lost.

There was an alley through a livery stable and barn, where a glimpse of water flowed in the distance. If this water was connected to the river she'd seen near the hedge, it would take her there. She stood, and made her way through winding alleys to the sound of rushing water.

Suddenly, darkness parted, and acre after acre of cultivated fields sprawled in front of her. Fear disappeared, replaced by relief. It was almost like home. Barges drifted by on the stream that had become a broad river carrying bales of cotton and flax. Several two-story rectangular brick buildings extended at one end of a massive property. Windows spaced evenly from each floor were like cloudy portals.

A few minutes of walking brought her close enough to one of the buildings that she could see into its windows. Showers of lint defused sunlight and suspended in the air, like soft flakes of snow that somehow never descended. She covered her ears against the din of machines that roared louder the closer she came. Some unknown army worked inside, running machines that were so deafening that her ears pounded.

The lint alone would fill their lungs and dash any wish for fresh air. When she reached the building, she climbed grimy steps and grasped the handle to open an entrance door. The handle didn't budge against her grasp.

Maura piled several logs against a wall and climbed them to get a glimpse through a window. Rubbing away its grime, she peeked inside. What she saw made her stumble as one after another, the logs rolled away, leaving her collapsed on the ground. She ran to the door and pounded, shouting, "Let me in!"

No one answered. She ran back to the window and rattled its wooden panes, her hands aching and scraped. This was no army. These were children. Children hunched over rotating spools of thread, little ones gathering scraps from the floor, older ones stationed at the giant looms. They filled the room, manning every station as cotton turned first to thread and then into fabric with dizzying speed.

A man's face filled the window. His pocked visage sported gray hairs that stuck out of large ears and brows that grew in one shaggy line against a dirty forehead. He opened the door and stepped a narrow shoe outside, then pulled it back in. Maura charged over to confront him face to face. "What do you want?" he asked.

"I want to...I need to see...Why was the door locked?"

"Who are you? This is a place of business, ma'am."

"But..." Maura was intimidated but determined to speak. Why were those children trapped in a haze of swirling dust and unrelenting machines?

"Go your way." He stood at the door as though he guarded the work going on inside. A few of the children glanced at her, but most kept working. One child crawled under the slats of an operating loom, sweeping stray lint and cotton dust with a long brush. Line after line of children leaned over the whirling machines. A spindle nipped one boy's finger when he turned to offer Maura a shy smile. He yanked it back and whimpered in pain, his blood dribbling to the floor. None of the children stopped their work to help him.

"He's hurt and must be attended to," Maura said, demanding the man's attention.

"You distracted him," said the overseer. "It's your fault. Now, leave, before I send for the authorities."

The child held his hand to one side and went back to work as the man stalked toward him. He raised a rod over the child's head. The little boy hiccupped, dried his eyes, and returned to work.

She'd heard the servants at Sir Taylor's speak of massive looms that were powered by water mills. This was greed at work. Had these children been conscripted from orphanages? Surely loving parents wouldn't allow a child to work in these conditions unless they were so poor, they had no choice.

Lilith had said the city promoted friendship and protection of the community. Apparently, that protection didn't extend to the most vulnerable. This was a city that enslaved its children. Maura had told the woman that Rory, Nona's grandson, had been injured at a factory. Maybe she believed he was an adult, instead of a child. She couldn't be aware of this. She'd find Tobias. He'd know what to do.

Chapter 11

Maura avoided the tenements and ran alongside the river until a glimpse of the dome of the Hall of Justice finally appeared. It felt like late afternoon. She'd lost track of time as she wandered lost through the tenements, and worse, found the factory filled with child laborers.

She kept her eye on the dome, determined not to get lost again. The sun was setting on the horizon, becoming an iridescent scarlet drape over the stately pinnacle of the city. The streets were quiet. Lights flickered inside the homes as she walked past the flowing pools of water.

Taking a breath and holding her gown in one hand, she trudged up the steps to the bronze doors, where the same two uniformed guards stood at attention. They seemed unfazed by her wild eyes and wrecked appearance. She cleared her throat and determined to be calm. And authoritative.

"Please. Tobias Fitch is my guardian. I must see him."

They opened the doors without a word.

The grand foyer was quiet. People must've gone home for the day. She wasn't certain if Tobias was still there. Maura took a moment to smooth her dress and comb through her hair before charging to Tobias's office and pounding on its heavy door. No one answered. Maura whirled around in panic. What did Tobias do when he wasn't representing her case? She hadn't considered that she was barging into a place of business instead of pleading for a friend's help. She turned to leave and ran into him.

He held her hands for a moment, and a fresh scent filled her senses. "Maura. Come into my office."

She followed him into the elegant room. As soon as he closed the door behind her, she blurted out her words in a tumbling heap. "I saw children working in a textile factory. One child was hurt. There was no one to help."

"Children?" He motioned for her to sit, as she paced the room, back and forth across the plush carpet.

He stood with the cautious unease of one peering over a cliff and wondering if another was planning to jump. Maura stopped pacing and sat in the chair where she'd once stood and ranted. She arranged her skirt and took a breath. "There are children working in a factory. They're locked inside and working in terrible conditions."

"Past the tenements? Near the river? What were you doing there? That's unsafe. I asked you not to go without an escort."

"I told you I needed information about medicine sent for Nicolaus. It wasn't hard to find the apothecary's shop. I got lost afterwards and stumbled onto a factory." She'd leave out the part about trying to find the hedge for now. "Yes, it was one by the river." Her words came out in a jumble, though surely Tobias understood.

"Of course. The apprentices." Tobias appeared relieved. "A Council-funded project. Most of the children are orphans who'd been in workhouses before they came to Sanctuary. They come from all over the region."

"They were very young. Certainly, Sanctuary

doesn't approve of businesses that employ small children, especially with locked doors and no freedom to play outside. The overseer was a beastly man. One of the boys was injured. He ignored the child's pain and sent him back to work. No comfort. No medical care. I've never seen anything like it."

"Ah, well, you're from the country, of course. Far from cities that manufacture the textiles that run our economy. These children are used to working. Their families need all the income they can get. Their living conditions are much better than they would be without work in the factories."

"Where I'm from isn't the point. This isn't the Sanctuary I heard praised at the Gunter's dinner party."

Tobias seemed lost in thought. Maura didn't know if he was only distracted or considering the children's plight.

"What were you doing by a factory? The textile industries are miles from here."

His words were like an afterthought, far from the heart of what she'd been trying to say. Did she need to defend her actions—and her response to what she'd seen? "I went to Hildegard Brennan, an apothecary. Colonel Perry told me about her. I told you I was going."

"I planned to send an escort."

She remembered his plan, though chosen to ignore it. "Hildegard showed me several different poisons. I smelled one much like the so-called medicine sent for Nicolaus. It may be the evidence we need."

"That doesn't explain why you were near the factory."

"Are my movements scrutinized? Surely you want as much information about my case as possible." Maura felt her chest tighten and cheeks flush. Tobias stared at her as if she were an errant child. "If you must know, I was trying to find the hedge when I lost my bearings. There was nothing wrong with my quest."

"Why would you go there?" Tobias asked, his voice grim.

"I wanted to send a message to our village apothecary. To find out what kind of medicine was sent for Nicolaus. What's wrong with that?" This interview was quickly turning into a prosecution, instead of defense.

Tobias brows wrinkled. "You were told to avoid the tenements. Did you consider that you were close to our borders and therefore unprotected from retribution from Sir Taylor?" There was no hiding the anger brewing in Tobias' face. His lips thinned into a line, and his shoulders tightened. When he spoke again, his voice was several decibels higher—and louder. "To say nothing of the fact that the area around the hedge is an ungoverned wilderness."

"You don't need to yell at me. The prowling lion I faced paled in comparison to what I saw at the factory. Besides, *you* said there were creatures who protected refugees there."

"I said there were creatures who *informed* us. *Why* would you push the limits of our protection?" he asked, now shouting.

"I didn't mean to… Don't you understand?" She was the one bellowing now. Her words spewed with anger and hurt. "I have to know if Nicolaus was poisoned." Her body shook with frustration. She wanted to explain, but he wasn't hearing. "I loved that child. I thought if I got close to the hedge, I could send a message." She held out the vial of powdered autumn crocus in one hand. "I found this at the apothecary. It smells like the medicine sent for Nicolaus." She jabbed the vial into one hand and turned to stalk out of the room. "Never mind, though. I'll keep it."

"Wait!" Tobias plopped down at the desk with his hands folded so tightly that his knuckles turned white. He finally peered up at Maura, fire still lingering in his eyes. "Perhaps you think I'm not doing my job."

"What? I came to talk to you about children I saw. How is this discussion suddenly about me? Of course, you're doing your job. I told you about Hildegard and that I was going to her shop."

Tobias stood and paced behind his desk, hands clenched behind his back, staring at the ground. His voice rose another set of decibels. "Do you not trust that I know this city better than you do? That I understand how it works?" A musky scent filled the room. Maura pulled back as a shadow rose on the wall behind Tobias. His shoulders seemed to expand. The effect was there and gone in an instant as he let out a breath. "Your fearlessness could've gotten you killed." His voice was lower, dead serious. "No need to worry about Sir Taylor."

Maura drew back, almost afraid, but mostly confused. They stood facing each other. Tobias had become a stone wall. His fingers pressed against the desk like talons, his glare heating her skin. Enough of this impasse. There was nothing left to do or say. She placed the vial of powder on his desk, turned, and walked away. Closing the door behind her, she trudged down the quiet hallway, exhausted.

A flash of red caught her eye near the entrance of

the Hall. Sir Taylor stalked toward her.

The hallway was deserted. Maura searched for a way to duck around the man and exit the building unhindered. There was no way to keep their paths from intersecting. She twirled around to call for Tobias but remembered that she'd closed the door to his office.

In moments, Sir Taylor stood in front of her, clenching and unclenching his large fists. She braced herself for an assault. Then, exhausted and, frankly, tired of it all, she planted her feet and stood tall. She'd done all she could to save Nicolaus. The law was clear. She was safe here, at least until her trial. Why should she cower in this man's presence or wait for him to pummel her with his huge fists? She willed herself not to flinch.

There was a tiny change in his eyes.

"Maura O'Donnell." The air seemed to still. Where was everyone in this normally busy hallway?

"Sir Taylor."

"Your trial approaches."

Maura nodded and curtsied slightly. Her breathing was shallow enough that she wasn't sure she wouldn't pass out. She hadn't eaten all day and had faced down a bully in the form of the overseer. Sir Taylor was another just like him. She was done bowing.

"I'll see you punished," Sir Taylor said in a low growl. "You'll pay for murdering my child."

Maura wondered what kind of payment she could offer, even if she were guilty. What would be enough to compensate for the loss of Nicolaus? Indeed, what could either of them offer for his precious life? Nothing.

"The final judgment is in the Council's hands," she said, mustering a calm voice. "Perhaps I'll pay with my life. Or go free. One thing is certain. I'll never be free from the death of Nicolaus."

Sir Taylor's gaze shifted toward approaching footsteps.

"Sir Taylor." Tobias stopped beside her and bowed to the man. "May I help you?"

"Come to the side of truth and declare this woman guilty before all. She doesn't deserve to live."

A bitter taste filled Maura's mouth.

Tobias bowed low again, then extended one arm toward offices that lined the hallway. "To justice."

Sir Taylor shot her a malevolent stare and strode down the hall, where he rapped on a door beyond Tobias's.

Tobias only glanced at her before he returned to his office and closed the door with a firm thud.

Maura shuddered, thinking of Sir Taylor's words. Declare this woman guilty? No one had introduced Tobias to Sir Taylor and yet, he'd known he was her advocate. What kind of dealings had the man already had with Tobias? Perhaps enough to understand that her advocate had the power to convict as well as defend. Suddenly, her position as refugee and her relationship with Tobias became tenuous. How would her cooperation—or lack of it—affect his defense? Would he become prosecutor instead of advocate?

She forced her legs to move toward the entrance, tears streaming down her face. An attendant led her to a carriage that stood at the bottom of the stairs. Leaning her head against the cushioned seat, she longed for a magical path back home to Benjamin, back to the life she'd shared with Nicolaus only days before. She peered outside and saw the sun had faded into dusk. When she arrived at the Gunter's sprawling porch, Lilith met her at the door.

"I was worried about you." Lilith rested a slender hand on Maura's shoulder as she led the way to the parlor. She motioned her toward a plush settee and ordered tea from the ever-hovering Adele.

Maura pulled a sweaty strand of hair behind one ear. The ornamental comb was long gone. Her curls hadn't seen a brush since that morning, and her belly was empty. She glanced down at the bottom of her lovely dress, its hem lined with mud and street grime. It looked like she felt, as if it had barely survived the day.

Lilith appeared sympathetic, unlike the cold statue she'd been that morning. "What happened?" The woman leaned forward as Maura slumped into the couch.

"It has been a terrible day," Maura said, unsure where to begin or exactly what to say. Shadows formed in the spacious room from lamps on tables and sconces against the patterned walls. Night had come.

"You were gone such a long time."

"I got lost." Maura stopped short of telling Lilith about Hildegard or her plan to find the hedge. "There were children working in a factory. It reminded me that Nona's grandson was injured in one. Do you know how he's doing? The children I saw were very young. How could that be?" She rattled off questions, suddenly nervous.

"You must have seen a part of the city very unlike ours. May Anton and I be of help?

An unexpected sigh came from Maura's belly. "Would you inquire after Nona's grandchild?"

"Of course. Nona has been an excellent employee. We're happy to do so."

"Thank you." Maura wanted to hug her neck, but she

was far too dirty to do anything but smile. "I'm so weary. And I need a bath."

Lilith stood, dismissing her. "You can join us for dinner. I have a special meal prepared for the family."

For the family. And Maura was included.

A glimpse of light in the darkness that had descended over Sanctuary.

Chapter 12

It was day three. Surely, Benjamin would arrive soon. He'd help her investigate and maybe even intercede with Tobias. His wise ways that didn't scream for attention never failed to bring peace amid chaos. Maura hopped out of bed and stuck her head out the window. A carriage rattled by in the early light. Somehow, a view outside every morning grounded her in reality—at least one that, unlike the city, didn't shift on a regular basis.

Adele, entered from the servant's corridor to prepare her for the day. She bobbed around the room like a nervous colt

"Good morning, Adele."

The young housemaid's fingers shook as she handed Maura a tray of breakfast. Hot water spilled out of the tea pot and drenched the napkins beside it. The young woman scurried around the room, filling a basin with water, and arranging a stack of towels nearby. Unlike Nona, who had cared for her with seamless grace, Adele appeared ready to bolt at any minute.

"Adele, sit with me, please."

"Oh, no, miss. No."

"Something's wrong. Can I help?"

"Not a'tall."

Maura sat down to take a quick bite of toast and sip of tea while Adele dashed to the closet and pulled out a winter gown of deep green velvet. Maura set her tea to one side and went to the closet for another. "Perhaps this one, instead." She settled on a peach-colored satin and laid it on the bed. "Have you heard anything from Nona?"

Adele jerked, as though Maura's words were buckshot. "I couldn't say, miss."

"You don't know or can't tell me?"

Adele's face lost color. Her hands trembled as she tried to help Maura get dressed. For some reason Adele had been forced into a role far beyond her skills. Either that or she was ashamed of something she'd done. Was she truly a thief?

Adele fumbled with the last button at the back of Maura's dress, then ran out of the room, disappearing through the servant's corridor.

Maura missed the warmth of Nona's presence. Adele avoided Maura's eyes, and worse, ran when they met unexpectedly in the house. Nervous energy teemed all around her. Although Maura felt compelled to reassure her in some way, Adele dodged her as if she carried a virulent plague. She couldn't help but wonder why it was Adele, not Nona, who'd come to help this morning. Maybe Nona was taking care of her grandson.

The hall clock chimed seven times, hours before Tobias would arrive. Maura wandered around the quiet house, seeking out Nona. The servants either ignored her or shook their heads when she asked about her. Finally, she tried the kitchen.

Sunlight wavered through a tiny, grease-filmed window at one end of the large room. The door at the back of the kitchen opened, and a footman appeared, dressed and ready to serve breakfast.

A sudden explosion of wrath sounded from the sink, where a stocky woman with muscular forearms and gnarled hands towered over a chicken carcass, cleaver in hand.

The footman tentatively placed one perfectly polished shoe into the kitchen.

"I sed, out with ye!" she said, her command breaking the early morning stillness.

"Mrs. Ransbottom. I need…" The man was practically begging for entrance.

So, this was the knife-wielding woman whose voice Maura had heard earlier. As if in proof, the woman lifted the cleaver into the air and shouted, "Be gone, ye buzzard!"

The footman backed out of the room, almost tripping in a speedy exit. Evidently, he knew obedience to the kitchen's tyrant was a wise choice.

Maura wondered who would finally be allowed in to serve breakfast.

If anyone would know what had happened to Nona, the burly kitchen manager would. Mrs. Ransbottom obviously didn't mince words like timid Adele. Maura had to know if Nona and her grandson were all right, even if it meant bearing the woman's wrath. Taking a breath, she knocked on the open door but remained standing at the threshold. "Good morning," she said, keeping a careful distance. "I wondered…"

Whack. "Speak up, child. Can't hear ye." Another whack, and the chicken's head tumbled into the sink, blood spurting.

"Um…Nona. Is she all right?"

Whack. The wooden cutting board shook as the chicken splayed, split down the middle. Maura backed up a little more. Maybe she should leave and hope that she fared better than the poultry. When Mrs. Ransbottom did speak, her words spewed into the air. "Her quit," she snarled. "Wit no notice. None a'tall."

"That can't be true." Maura spoke without thinking.

Mrs. Ransbottom gaze was so withering, Maura drew back into the hallway.

Nothing in Nona's honest ways made Maura believe she'd leave without saying good-bye. Somehow, she had to try another appeal to the commander of the kitchen. Taking a small step over the threshold, she held out one hand for emphasis.

"Where can I find her? It's important."

"No need to be beggin'." The woman pointed the bloody cleaver toward to the back door of the kitchen. "'Tis her cottage by the river."

Maura blew out a deep breath. Not only had Mrs. Ransbottom pointed the way, but she'd also granted a speedy exit. "Thank you. Thank you so much," Maura repeated the words, as if she uttered a mantra to release her from a dragon's lair. She dashed through the room, leaving a wide berth between her and the cook, grateful to escape with head still intact.

Maura wrapped Hildegard's shawl around her shoulders and walked to the main road. She had plenty of time to find Nona, and maybe even figure out where the factory was. This time, she skirted the tenements and headed to the river, where several thatched cottages stood on the outskirts of the city. Any or none of them could be Nona's. A woman came out of one, pulled down a sheet hanging to dry, and went back inside. Maura scurried down the hill to get a better view.

How could she knock on a door and hope the house

belonged to Nona? The woman hanging laundry had long, chestnut hair the same color as Nona's, that shifted in a breeze. Maura couldn't be sure it was her, though. She stood for a moment at the woman's house.

The door opened a crack and a small, bandaged hand appeared. Maura squatted at the opening and saw a pair of bright eyes gazing back at her as the door opened wider. Like hers, they were miniature starbursts lined with blue. A little boy, maybe only four or five years old, scrutinized her, as if she were a peculiar adornment on a fierce dragon, terrifying, but fascinating. One arm was bandaged around a wooden splint.

Maura smiled and held her hand out. Instead of shaking it, he placed a shiny piece of coal in her palm with the healthy hand. She wrapped her fingers around it, then covered her eyes and peered through her fingers.

Mimicking her, the child covered his eyes also. She hid the coal behind her back, then held up her empty hand. He grinned through sparse teeth and reached behind her with a quick grasp, pulling out the coal in triumph. In a moment, he'd covered his eyes again, motioning for her to do the same.

She watched him through one hand as he hid the coal under a thatched rug by the front door. When he was done, she shrugged, and held out her hands in dismay. Then he pulled the coal from under the rug and held it up like a trophy as Maura applauded.

Their game broke the silence. When Maura searched beyond him at the darkened room, little heads popped up from pallets that lined each side. Some sat up and leaned on one arm, others had turned their bodies and lay peering over with large eyes. They were all children. And were all broken in one way or another. A bandaged arm or hand. A splint that supported a small leg.

This wasn't only a home. It was a hospital. Maura wanted to go to each child, to see if she could bring a smile to their serious gazes. She hadn't been invited inside, except by this handsome boy who kept his eyes on her as if he hoped for another game.

Maura heard the rustle of a gown. A woman approached, wiping her hands on an apron. As she came closer, Maura knew she'd found the right place. They were Nona's strong arms, straight shoulders, and kind eyes. Before Maura could explain, the older woman pulled the child to her side. "Hush now, Rory."

Maura rushed to explain. "This must be your grandson. I've been trying to find you."

"Thanks, milady. We appreciate your concern." Nona backed away slightly and taking the child with her.

Surely, Nona understood that she'd searched her out because she cared. "I miss you and hoped for Rory's speedy recovery. It will be wonderful to see you back at the Gunter's."

Nona shook her head. "They'll not be requirin' me services."

"You aren't coming back?"

"Please, miss. 'Tis not a concern. We be fine."

Nona took another step back with Rory. The boy turned to his grandmother, then to Maura, as if he'd hoped his new friend would stay. Nona didn't feel the same way. She stood at the door, blocking the entrance into their home, and waiting for Maura's exit.

"I don't understand." Tears prickled behind Maura's eyes.

The woman's expression never changed. Nona held the door with one hand and turned to Rory.

"Go now, child." She curtsied to Maura. "'Tis lovely to see ye. Good day, then."

Fighting sadness, Maura stepped outside and stood on the threshold as the door closed. Nona's coolness didn't make sense. She'd been a bright spot in the Gunter home, the one servant Maura trusted to ask questions when she was confused. Not here, though. For whatever reason, Nona's heart and door had closed firmly in Maura's face.

What should she do now? She'd gotten her question answered. Two questions, really. Both answers proved Lilith Gunter had lied. She and Anton hadn't helped Nona as she promised. Not only that, but they'd also fired the kind, competent woman. Maura hadn't seen any evidence of neglect in her work, no basis for terminating her job. Nona's work had been timely and excellent. Lilith certainly hadn't promoted a better employee in Adele, who was an inept, untrustworthy replacement. More puzzles in a city that kept her peering through grimy windows, struggling to see inside.

The area around the other homes was quiet. There were no people milling around, no sounds of life. Unlike the Gunter's neighborhood, where children played and mothers, or at least nannies, stood nearby, there were no families in sight, no laughter or scents of meals simmering by a fire.

Sighing, Maura started back toward the Gunters'. As she walked, a man with spiraling red curls approached from the opposite direction. It was Aiden's familiar lanky frame.

Maura let out a puff of relief, lifted her skirt, and rushed to him as if she feared he might run in the opposite direction. She didn't have to worry. He seemed happy, as well as curiously unsurprised, to see her. When she reached him, her words spewed without a greeting. "You're the one who brought me here. You protected me from Sir Taylor."

"Indeed, I am. And how are you faring in our fine city?"

"I came here to find a woman I met at the Gunters' named Nona. Do you know her? She cared for me with such kindness. I heard that her grandson had been injured in a factory accident, so came to see how they were doing."

Guileless blue eyes peered into hers. Suddenly she wanted to pour her heart out to one she'd considered merely a country bumpkin. "I hadn't seen Nona at work and missed her," she said, feeling her brows crinkle into a worry line. "When I found her, she wouldn't talk to me." Maura longed to hide a sudden rush of grief. "Why would she leave the Gunter's without a word?"

Aiden spoke simply. "Mrs. Gunter fired her for leaving work."

"No. I mean, what?"

"She was fired because she left the Gunter home."

"But her grandson was injured."

"Correct." Aiden's face was as impassive as if they'd just been discussing the weather.

"I mean." Maura backed up a little, confused. "Lilith said she and Anton would help."

Aiden held out his arm for Maura. "Come with me. We'll talk."

Despite Aiden's grasp on her arm, Maura struggled to keep up with his stride as he maneuvered through the narrow streets, recognizing every shift and turn. The final block opened into the fields of maize and wheat she recognized from the day before. Aiden slowed down near the river.

"Let's sit," Aiden said, heading to an area of sandy shoreline where a willow extended its feathery fingers into the water. Aiden cleared away a few twigs and patted the ground beside him.

Maura sat, wishing she was wearing one of her simple gowns from home. The petticoat under the dress she'd chosen that morning billowed around her like a satiny balloon. Finally tucking it under her legs, she pulled in a deep breath of the fresh, clean air. A family of otters slipped in and out the water in playful succession, as unforced as the river's flow. Her breathing gradually evened out from the sharp staccatos she'd known since she'd arrived in Sanctuary. This felt like a little bit of home.

Hugging knees to her chest, Maura rested for a moment. "I don't understand, sir." She was so tired she could've curled up and slept. Except somehow, she knew there were questions only Aiden could answer. "The death of a child I loved brought me here." She stopped for a moment to watch the otters. She didn't know where to go from the awful reality that never changed.

Aiden stretched out his legs but kept his attention on her.

"You came to my rescue at the beginning," she said, realizing she'd never thanked him. "I stood by the hedge and watched my blood avenger approach with sword in hand. I'd be dead now if you hadn't arrived. Thank you. You were a true refuge for me." She glanced into his freckled face, remembering how she'd wondered if he'd be any help at all.

"You're welcome." His face lit into a sweet grin that

flashed a dimple she hadn't noticed.

Maura brushed away an ant that scurried over her peachy pillow of a gown and tried to regather her thoughts. She studied a swirling current, determined not to be distracted by that smile. "Sanctuary is full of contradictions. For one, there are two worlds here. One at the Gunter's. Another here. Are they connected? I mean, Lilith promised to help Nona. Instead, she fired her."

"You don't need to call me sir. My name is Aiden." He leaned back, resting his palms against the sand. "Not every offer for help is a refuge," he said quietly.

"You sound like Benjamin," Maura said, peering at him. "Why were there so many children at Nona's house?"

Aiden picked up a rock and skipped it across the flowing stream, careful to avoid the otters, who'd moved downstream with their game. "Nona cares for them. Their parents and siblings all work. Every member of the family has to contribute to survive."

"The children I saw were hurt. Her home was a hospital."

"They've all been injured in the factories."

"Are they getting medical attention? Is anyone other than Nona helping?"

"Not really. She's gifted with children, though. A benefit for our little ones since she isn't working for the Gunter's anymore. The parents will pool their wages to pay her."

Maura gazed at the tenements behind them. "There are so many buildings here, but no people. Where is everyone?"

"All working. Twelve to fourteen hours a day."

"I wouldn't have found the factory, never would have ventured there unless I was trying to get information about a medicine I gave the child in my care."

"Did you hear that the tenements were dangerous, that you should avoid them?"

"Colonel Perry, a man I met at one of the Gunter's dinner parties said that. So did Tobias, my advocate."

"And what have you discovered?" Aiden's gaze was as unperturbed as a mirror glaze over a lake.

"Not threatening as much as deserted. Why would he warn me about this area?"

"Maybe so you won't enter it."

"I don't understand."

"Some believe it's filled with people who threaten Sanctuary—its people, its refuge."

"Certainly not Nona." Maura remembered the woman and child she'd seen on her shopping trip with Lilith. "I...I was near a park by the Gunter home. Lilith stopped a young woman who walked by with a sleeping baby. She woke the child. On purpose. Suddenly, the mother picked up the baby and ran. Guards chased them." She shuddered with the memory. "Lilith said there was caste of people who ignored their customs. Are there people like that here?"

"Come back this evening. People work from before dawn to almost dusk, but I can introduce you to some of them. You can judge for yourself if they're a threat."

"I'll be ready."

****

SIR TAYLOR

The problem of the tenements, they call it. Not an issue for me, at all. Those people streamed into

Sanctuary, seeking the refuge it promised, and found work. Should they complain now that they discovered what they sought? Honest work. I even solved the orphan question with the Scarborough House. The children are fed an evening meal, offered schoolwork in the evening, and a bed. To say nothing of learning a trade that offers a future. It's so much more than they had before.

What could make more sense? A booming textile industry driven by children whose families are happy to receive additional income. Critics who assume those children suffer are enemies of progress. Utter nonsense.

I saw Maura O'Donnell yesterday at the Hall. Rage swept over me. I had no weapon in my hand, but my wrath didn't require one. I knew that. Tobias appeared before I could strike.

Anger has been a familiar friend since I was a child at the abbey. I learned its power to control then, as a powerless child. Adults drew back. Even Sister Catherine pulled away. As a grown man, I discovered that strategically placed fury propelled me through barriers of opposition. I was heard. I was obeyed.

Now, it consumes every waking moment. I'm too tired to know if I am its master or if it has become mine.

Chapter 13

Maura waited until the sun drifted low in the sky. She'd met with Tobias, eaten with the Gunters, and retired for an early bedtime without a word of her plans for that evening. She was afraid that anything she shared about this venture would be thwarted. And she needed answers. Who were these people who supposedly endangered Sanctuary?

Maura pulled on a hooded cloak, crept through the servants' corridor, and slipped out the kitchen door. A quiet call signaled, and Aiden appeared at her side. Together, they walked past Hildegard's shop and down the steep road toward the tenements.

A group of boys tossed a wadded piece of cloth back and forth, swerving in and out of the narrow streets at the edge of the neighborhood. Firelight shimmered in windows, and the smell of porridge wafted into the air. Aiden stopped her before she stepped into a puddle of raw sewage. He gave her a minute to redirect before they trudged toward an open fire pit where a crowd gathered in a village square ahead.

Voices got louder as they neared men who stood around the fire in small groups. Maura wanted to slink back into the shadows, but Aiden kept a grip on her arm and led her toward them. Muscular arms bulged through torn and ragged shirts. Soot smudged faces were hard to read in wavering firelight. An older man refused acknowledge her presence. One of the men cursed loudly. Most stopped talking as she and Aiden walked through the crowd and stopped at the fire pit. Their shoulders slumped along with the rest of their bodies that appeared weary beyond words.

"This is Maura O'Donnell," Aiden said. There were short grunts of hello. Beyond that, the men only glanced in Maura's direction. They returned to pipes or stared into fire that blazed in the center of their gathering. "She's a refugee. The one staying with the Gunter's."

A few of the men reacted with a start.

"She wants to know more about our city. I've brought her here, at the end of a day, to feel its heartbeat—you, the fathers and the sons who work long hours to feed your families. For the wives and children, you rarely see, the ones who work as hard as you do."

At this, the men exchanged glances.

"She won't understand," Aiden said, scanning Maura and then turning back to the men. "She wants to, though. She's accused of a crime she didn't commit. And is at the mercy of the Council."

An aged face crinkled with dust, and deep ruts on weathered skin searched her face and nodded.

"These men were artisans not so many years ago. Some were farmers." Aiden pointed to a young man who stood at the back of the group of men. "Jonathan. What craft were you and your family known for?"

The young man paused, lifting his knife from a piece of wood he'd been carving. It looked like a caricature much like the factory overseer, unruly eyebrows, and all. The man's face was boyish, ruddy under the ever-present layer of dirt. His fingers were long and slender as if they'd been created to play concertos on a grand piano.

The fourth finger on his right hand was only a nub. "Weavers, we were. Had been for generations."

"And now?"

"I keep the belts of the spinning machines oiled, tip-top shape. This job don't end. The belts be twirlin' from the wee hours of morning to the last light of day." He coughed against one arm. Maura remembered the windows that had been sealed shut and the lint suspended in the stale air. And children's faces flushed with afternoon heat.

"Dangerous work?" Aiden asked.

"Aye. Me mate lost a hand last week."

"His family?"

"We be helpin'. Live in the same flat, 'cause rent be high." Jonathan shrugged and stared in the direction of the tenements. "Miss me family around the kitchen table after work. There'll be no going back. Our land is sold. The future is here, or so we were told."

In her own village, families spent time together for countless mundane reasons. There were pubs where neighbors gathered to celebrate the end of a week's work. Harvest time required long days of work, of course. It ended, though, with a week of festivities when children competed in games, artisans displayed their wares, and families strolled through an open field of scents and sounds of community.

Aiden thanked the men and led Maura away. The men's voices became a deep rumble, indistinct but certain as a train rumbling in the distance. Despite their weariness, they were a force. An angry one. These men were attached to families. Families separated by an industry bringing wealth into the country, fueling its economy. Making everyone except them rich.

She and Aiden approached the river for the second time that day. Flaming hues of orange reflected sunset in its muddy flow. Pools of gold twirled, carrying snatches of wood and fuzzy swatches of cotton downstream toward the factory. An owl circled overhead in wide arcs, searching for prey.

"What do you do, Aiden? I mean, other than rescuing me. Everyone seems to work all day. Yet, I saw you in the middle of the afternoon."

Aiden searched the sky as last bits of sunset moved quickly into dusk. "I work for the Council as an attendant. My job is to bring refugees safely into the city, as well as to the Hall of Justice where each one is assigned an advocate."

"Before a blood avenger can strike."

"Yes. That's where my sword comes in. Other than that, it's an enviable job. Especially because it gives me time that others who work in the factories don't have."

"It sounded like people who work here were kept against their will. Why do they stay? I can't imagine a job that kept me from seeing my family."

Aiden's face twisted into a frown. "It isn't that simple. They came here for refuge willingly. They weren't expecting the city to become a prison, instead."

"How are they held here?"

"By poverty. They have barely enough pay to keep their families fed." Aiden rubbed his thumb against a calloused palm. "It's dangerous for Nona to be seen with you," he said. "Especially now."

"Why?"

"There have been…events, in the past. Children could be at risk. At least those in the tenements."

"Explain."

Aiden's eyes were so searching, she was embarrassed. And relieved when he finally turned his attention to rooftops of homes beyond the tenements. "The children carry treasure that's contended for."

"Another riddle." Maura smelled the earthy scent of the river, felt damp grass around them, and longed for home. "I told Tobias about the factory. He said that it was a Council-funded orphanage that offers homeless children a place to live and work. Even an education."

Aiden was silent.

"Tell me what you know about it," she said, straightening her shoulders. Aiden had been an enigma from the beginning. One thing she was sure of. He knew more about the city than he'd told her. "What about the peace the city has enjoyed—all the praise I heard at the Gunter dinner party the first night I arrived?"

Aiden leaned in to face her. "The factory operates under the guise of helping children who have no future, no hope of pursuing the gifts they've been given."

"What kinds of gifts?"

"Abilities to create, to solve problems. Factory work keeps them out of school, where they would surely excel. They aren't allowed to meet children above the tenements. Their parents, aunts, and uncles can serve as lady's maids, housekeepers, and household staff. Their role is only to serve. Yet these are people destined to lead, to take places of influence in civil government. They are banned from those places because of their race."

"Who are they? Where did they come from?"

"They're a people from the east, a people known for their wisdom. Counselors of kings and famed astrologers."

"Like the Magi? Benjamin told me about them. These people came to Sanctuary because they needed refuge? What happened?"

Aiden glanced at the darkening sky. "It's time to go."

Maura turned to face him with arms crossed against her chest. "Answer my question first."

Aiden offered his hand, and she took it. He helped Maura to her feet and faced her, silent for a moment. "The original intent of the city was refuge," he said. "It's been corrupted."

His words rang with clarity. If what he said was true, it shattered what she'd been told about Sanctuary. And put her own trial in question. "Why hasn't something been done? I'll bring the children and their plight to the attention of the Gunters. They must be unaware."

"Your job is to stay alive and be proven innocent."

Together, they walked a path that eventually intersected with the road that led to the Gunters' neighborhood. Streetlamps were lit, and glimmered against dark streets. Maura wanted more time with Aiden, but he seemed intent to get her back to her host home. His presence was like the river, calm and with deep undercurrents of something Maura couldn't name. "By the way, I met an apothecary named Hildegard. Perhaps you know her."

"She's a healer. Censured by the authorities but loved by those who've been helped by her knowledge of healing remedies. And prayers."

"She prayed for me," Maura said.

"And?"

How could she put what she'd experienced into words? "I felt...the universe. Or I don't know. I don't have words for it. Peace, mostly. But more. Like my fingers touched an ocean." She glanced at Aiden to see if he was laughing at her. He wasn't. "I guess I do have words, after all."

He gripped her arm tighter as they walked up the final incline to the Gunter home. "Ah, well, that would be Hildegard's prayers. She has an unusual connection with heaven."

"She also understands herbs and medicines. She showed me a poison that smelled much like the powder prescribed for Nicolaus. I went to find the hedge after I left her shop, hoping to get a message to the young porter who delivered the medicine. That's how I got lost and found the factory." She had a sudden thought. Aiden had picked her up at the hedge. Surely, he could take her back. "I…You could you take me there. It won't take long."

"Without leaving the city?"

"Right. Sir Taylor would love that. He'd be free to take his sword to my neck without delay."

Aiden didn't respond right away. When he did speak, his words were measured. "Here's what I think. Cooperate with your defender. First, and above all. If you can't find the evidence in any other way, I'll take you to the hedge."

"There's something you're not telling me."

"You're a visitor here."

Maura felt outrage rise in her belly. "What does that have to do with helping me find out what happened to Nicolaus? Don't you understand how important that is? Especially as an attendant for the Council. Humph. I'll appeal to the Gunters, instead."

"I didn't say I wouldn't help." Aiden bowed slightly

131

as they approached the Gunters' back door. He turned and walked into the darkness without another word.

Maura was so aggravated, she didn't even say good-bye. Slipping back into the kitchen, she hurried through the servant's corridor and to her room. She fell asleep hoping that as sure as the stars watched overhead, Benjamin was on his way. He knew their village apothecary. If no one else could help, he would.

Chapter 14

The next afternoon Lilith appeared at her door. "You had a late evening." Her tone was pointed. Almost accusing. She was most likely concerned about Maura's absence, especially since it was the fourth day in Sanctuary.

Maura felt like a young truant returning from an illegal adventure. "I stepped outside to speak to the young attendant who drives me to the Hall."

"The one with the wild curls. A bit of a hooligan dressed in uniform." Lilith smiled with a mix of maternal protection and…something else.

Maura wasn't sure what it was. She attempted a smile. "Yes, he's the one. I was checking on…" She stopped, feeling the oddest descent into the sticky trap of a spider's web. Nona had been fired, she reminded herself. Lilith either knew what happened and lied about it, or Anton had fired their servant without her knowledge. The evidence was clear.

Lilith led her to the parlor. "Sit with me. We'll have tea."

Maura studied the woman's face. Nothing seemed to hide behind her clear eyes and gracious smile. Aiden had introduced her to the men who only appeared to their families at the end of the day, if that often. They were hidden ones whose lives were far from the reality of the Gunters and their neighbors. It was time to find out what

Lilith knew.

"I found children working in a factory," Maura said, taking a sip of tea, deciding to carefully lay out the information she'd discovered. "The conditions weren't suitable for children. The overseer was harsh, so harsh that the children seemed afraid. The little ones were exhausted and overworked."

"The only children's home I'm aware of is the Scarborough House," said Lilith, responding after a thoughtful moment. "It was founded by a compassionate entrepreneur who wanted to bring children out of workhouses. It offers experience in skilled labor as well as room and board. Even an education. It doesn't sound like the same place."

"Nona's grandson was injured in an accident at a factory. Was it the same one?"

"I can't be sure. Many families request that their children work at Scarborough. The home gives them a much-needed opportunity to become productive citizens of this community."

Adele came around the corner, carrying the tea service. She kept her eyes focused on serving and didn't acknowledge Maura other than to nod when she thanked her.

"Are all the refugees treated like I've been?" Maura asked. "With such generosity?"

"You're wondering why you're here in our home," said Lilith.

That was exactly what Maura wondered. "The beauty of your home, your kindness. It's all far more than I expected when I came to Sanctuary for refuge."

Lilith leaned toward Maura and spoke with a quiet intensity. "That's easy to explain." There was hunger in the woman's voice, like the craving she'd seen in her eyes when Lilith first touched the scroll. "You are here to be protected, for you are a pearl of great price."

Maura drew back. "Pardon me. I don't understand."

"There is a greater battle waging for you than you understand. More is at stake than you know. Tobias is a fine guardian, but I'm happy to help as well."

"I never expected my life to be at stake, Lilith. Or to be here in Sanctuary, away from my home. I do appreciate your help. As well as Tobias and his expertise in my defense."

Lilith's eyes filled with passion.

Maura tried to reason away a sudden clench of fear in her belly. Surely, the woman only cared that Maura was well represented and proven innocent. Her feet bounced up and down against the soft carpet with nervous energy, unlike Lilith's elegant composure. Shadows grew longer through the great windows of the parlor. Why was Tobias so late for their appointment?

Lilith finished her tea and wiped her mouth on a dainty napkin. She stood and held her hand toward the stairs. "Come. Let me show you something."

Maura couldn't shake a sense of dread at this lightly veiled command. Still, she followed her hostess up the staircase and into Maura's room.

Lilith went to her closet as if she already knew her mission. She pulled out a milky chiffon dress. "White is best." She draped it over Maura's shoulders and peered with a critical eye. After placing the dress on the bed, she turned back to her. "This is more important than how you're dressed. Refuse to bow your head. Face your interrogator and keep your poise. Don't be shaken. By anything."

135

Lilith walked closer. The emerald pendant she always wore, no matter what occasion, caught a beam of light and cast a prism on the wall.

Maura wished she could politely leave. No exit presented itself, though.

Lilith straightened Maura's shoulders and placed a light hand under her chin. "Did your mother teach you to hold your head high, and never to cower?"

Maura cleared her throat and drew in a strangled breath. She gathered her strength to ask the question that had hovered under the surface of their conversation. "I haven't seen Nona in the house."

"Are you wondering why I fired her?"

Maura was caught off guard, surprised at Lilith's direct response. She'd be equally pointed. "I wasn't sure what happened."

Lilith stepped away and studied Maura for a moment before she spoke. "Our home isn't an ordinary one. We have responsibilities that affect the city and beyond, which can't be undermined by impulsive decisions. Nona was hired for a job. She violated it by leaving without notifying us."

"She was concerned for her grandson. How could that be grounds for dismissal?"

"As I said, our home has been set apart for a special cause. Anyone who chooses to work here understands its uniqueness."

"It would help if I understood how your home is unusual."

A knock sounded on her door. Adele entered and curtsied. "Mr. Tobias Fitch is here to see Miss O'Donnell."

Maura tried not to blow out a breath she hadn't

known she was holding. She almost tripped as she took several steps away from Lilith.

Lilith walked to the door. "Anton and I are attending a Council event this evening. We'll discuss your concerns. Adele will bring supper after your interview."

Maura hurried to the mirror to comb her hair and saw her own confusion. Lilith's omission itself was a lie. She hadn't skirted the issue of Nona but refused to tell Maura the truth until she asked. Would the factory really become an object of Council discussion this evening?

By the time Maura descended the long flight of stairs, Tobias waited in the foyer, pacing. He bowed and walked with her into the parlor.

They sat on the settee she and Lilith had just left. The last time they'd been together, he'd been so angry she wasn't sure he hadn't decided to fire her as his client. Or become prosecutor instead of advocate. Best address this head-on.

"Are you still mad?" she asked, waiting for his eyes to connect with hers.

Tobias shuffled and reshuffled the ever-present papers, then shoved a lock of hair that dangled over one eye in place. His normally upright stance relaxed a bit against the seat. An almost grin appeared on his face. "I'm not. You?"

"Me neither. I'm sorry. You've been an excellent advocate." Maura hesitated for a moment. "And friend."

Another smile brushed his face. Then, getting back to business, he cleared his throat and pushed away the stray hair again. "Unfortunately, we don't have much time."

Tobias was silent for a moment. He gazed at the papers on his lap, as if they held an answer. "I went to the village apothecary but found no record of the medicine prescribed for Nicolaus.

"How is that possible? It makes no sense at all. What about Benjamin? He could help you find the porter. He knows everyone in the village."

Tobias studied his hands as if they somehow held an answer. "I went to his house. The doors were locked. The yard was overgrown, and the cottage deserted."

Maura took in a sharp gasp of breath. She sprang from the settee to face Tobias. "Benjamin would never let the yard go untended. A neighbor—someone—must know where he is." She spun around as images of Benjamin injured, alone, or even captive hurtled through her imagination. "You don't think someone hurt him? Why wasn't he protected?"

"We're bound by conventions of the city that don't apply elsewhere. You're our primary concern."

Maura strode back and forth across the parlor and finally stopped in front of Tobias. "I have to find him. I'm going back to the village. There's still plenty of light. I'll find a way. Somehow."

Tobias jumped to his feet and came to her side. "You can't. Sir Taylor will find out immediately. You have no protection against him there. You know that."

"I don't have a choice. Benjamin is...my family. It was my fault that he was taken. Release me, Tobias. You have no part in this."

"Please. Let me do my job as your advocate. When you're acquitted—in two days—I'll help you find Benjamin." Tobias extended his hand. "Stay here, in the safety of this home, Maura. I beg you."

Had Sir Taylor done something malicious, knowing how she loved Benjamin? He was an easy target.

Tobias moved closer. His hand wavered as he kept it stretched out toward her. "Don't leave," he said. "I'll commission soldiers to continue a search. They'll return with word as soon as they find him."

Maura studied the lovely room, as well as the look of anguish on her advocate's face. And knew. She was cornered again. This time not by a hungry mountain lion but by circumstances beyond her control. When she faced Tobias, his eyes hadn't wavered from hers. "How can you ask me to stay," she asked. "Benjamin is all I have."

"I ask because I want you alive. Benjamin would, too."

Tobias was no longer the detached stranger she'd met her first day in Sanctuary. But who was he, really? Suddenly, she realized she knew nothing about him outside of his profession as advocate. "What about your family, Tobias? Do they live nearby?"

Tobias stalked to the window and stood with his back to her. His body was almost motionless, except for a miniscule shudder that began at his shoulders and traveled down his back. He appeared molded instead of chiseled or even sculpted, for there were no ragged edges. Was he a god? Or more like Orion, one too perfect for earth.

The air seemed to chill.

"Forgive me. It's none of my business." The last thing she wanted was to go back to the place they'd been the day before. To offend the one sworn to help her.

Tobias pivoted in one motion. His face was a composed mask. Not a wrinkle of emotion etched his ivory skin. His voice was even when he spoke, except hardness had replaced its tenderness. "My family were guardians—of treasure."

"Do they—are they here? In Sanctuary?"

"They are not."

"I'm sorry. I know what it's like to feel alone. Unsure of who I am because a cord was cut as a child. One that would've shown me who I am. I only have a few memories of my parents." Maura felt like she was rattling on, making noise to fill silence that overwhelmed the room.

"Oh, I know about loneliness," he said. Was it rage that flashed in his eyes? "I understand what it is to lose family. And to suffer captivity that binds the heart, keeping it from flying free." Tobias kept his gaze at something just beyond Maura. His stance appeared encased in stone.

Maura moved toward him but stopped short when his body stiffened. Something around his eyes quivered. She'd accidently tread on pain so raw it resisted touch. All she could do was offer what she'd hoped was true. "Who you are, however shaped in pain, makes a difference."

Tobias stared back without a trace of emotion. "You're an innocent, Maura O'Donnell."

"I know I'm often frustrating. I *am* your friend, though. And pray that your heart will eventually fly free."

A sardonic laugh spewed out of Tobias. "That, my dear, will never happen."

Maura sucked in a breath at the sound of his bitterness. She *was* an innocent. She had no idea what kind of memories still ruled him like an unwieldly tyrant. The longer she was in this city, the more she understood the assurance of a hand extended, a friendship offered.

"I'll believe when you can't," she said, stretching out her hand.

Instead of taking it, Tobias bowed and walked to the foyer. His heels snapped against the marble floor like gunshot. Without a word or a glance behind, he left.

That night, Maura slept only in fits and starts. Her heart was at war. Grief was a thieving intruder that rose uninvited at the strangest times. Impenetrable hurt had risen in Tobias when she'd asked about his family. She understood. For years she'd peppered Benjamin for answers about her own parents.

"You'll see them again, little one," he'd said, patting the damp ground so she could plop down beside him. "It's like a tent," he'd said, gesturing overhead. "The universe spread over our lives, covering, connecting us as surely as constellations in the night sky. Like the stars, their brightness may be hidden for a moment, but they still shine."

No wonder she loved the stars. Because seen or unseen, Papa and Mama were somewhere, watching over her in the beauty and order of the heavens. Now, it was Benjamin she missed—and feared for. And she was no closer to solving the mystery of Nicki's death. Tobias wavered between supporting her and retreating into an impenetrable wall. She would threaten her own safety if she pursued the information she needed.

Maura finally fell asleep and into a vivid dream, where a narrow tunnel stretched before her. Smoke crept into her nostrils and burned her throat. Scarlet hues flickered ahead, and voices joined in muted pleas. Amber light grew in intensity and in heat as she walked toward it. Soon, her dress was drenched with sweat, and she struggled to breathe.

Great drafts of air circulated by something ahead. With the air came fear that overtook her curiosity. As she turned, thinking she'd run, the voices became more distinct. Children were calling.

"Help us."

Was it a phantom, mimicking the voices of little ones and drawing her into a trap? How could she ignore them? Maura crept forward, keeping one hand against a granite wall. A long, rasping breath sounded, and she retreated into the shadows as the serpentine tail of a dragon, luminescent in the gloom, spewed fire with each breath.

Maura drew closer to the voices until what she saw ahead made her knees buckle. Children were pinned on hooks like insects, legs dangling and arms waving on both sides of a stone wall. The dragon swung its great head back and forth as if laughing at the little ones' plight.

She had to find a way to help them. Maura bumped into an invisible barrier and fell with the impact. A clear but solid wall stood in her way. She pounded it with her fists, but it didn't budge. She took off a shoe and hammered it, but all her efforts did nothing. The dragon moved unhindered, and no one could help the suffering little ones. Maura kicked at the wall, screamed at it, and finally cried in defeat.

Chapter 15

Maura woke up gasping for breath, surprised that she wasn't still pounding on an invisible wall. It was only a nightmare. Forcing herself out of bed, she opened the window. No one stirred outside, and streetlamps flickered in the darkness. It was the morning of the fifth day, her last day to prepare for the trial. Well, not quite morning. Too early for Adele to make an appearance.

Maura washed her face and chose a gown from the closet. She brushed her hair and longed for a cup of tea as she stuck her head back out the window. An acrid stench filled the air, and muted cries sounded in the distance. The dream wasn't real, she reminded herself. Yet, the image of the factory overseer with his rod extended over a child returned. She remembered that when she'd tried to open the door, it had been locked. Like the unseen barrier in her dream.

Today was critical to her defense, especially since the trial was scheduled for tomorrow morning. They needed to pursue information about the autumn crocus further, since it was key to proving her innocence. Those who'd been commissioned to find Benjamin could also investigate the local apothecary.

Smoke wafted through the darkness outside. Maura opened the window wider to what she knew was reality. There was a fire somewhere. Grabbing Hildegard's shawl, she headed toward the door that led to the main hallway until the tiny glass-covered hole near the gilded picture frame caught her eye. Was she being watched? Making an about-face, she went out through the servant's corridor instead.

The hallway was so dim that she had to walk slowly with a hand against the wall. A muffled snore came from the tiny room where Mrs. Ransbottom sometimes slept near the kitchen. Too early for breakfast preparations. Maura entered the kitchen, skirted sacks of flour that lined one wall, and made her way to the back door. As she opened it, cool air rushed in and penetrated the shawl. She stood by the door for a moment, unsure of what to do.

Her trial was tomorrow, and the time she'd had with her advocate had been cut short when she'd asked about his family. Even Tobias seemed to waver about her case. Unlike their first meetings, when he'd been certain of her acquittal. Still, the memory of children in the lint-filled factory wouldn't leave her. Maura wrapped the embroidered shawl tighter, silently thanking Hildegard for its warmth, and walked down the dark street.

The tenements appeared in the distance like the jagged fortress of a sleeping dragon as smoke grew denser. Maura drew the shawl over her mouth and kept walking. The clatter of a carriage sounded in the darkness ahead. Instinctively, Maura ducked out of the roadway and hid along one side of a livery stable. Someone wrapped in a dark cloak ducked out of the shadows and slipped into the carriage with a flash of gold and green. A whip lashed, and carriage wheels careened over the cobblestoned roadway. Maura ran out into the street and watched as it rushed up the steep road past the Gunters' and toward Hall of Justice.

Streetlamps dotted the road in dim, wavering light. Not enough to illuminate the haze that obscured any sense of where she was or where she was going. Smoke penetrated the fabric of the shawl she'd placed over her mouth. It was odd that no one else stirred. Surely residents hadn't slept through the smoke and unnatural glow that seeped through narrow buildings.

Voices shouted in the distance, and Maura tried to follow their sound. She stumbled over a curb, righted herself, and kept going, unsure where she was in the maze of tangled streets. The voices grew louder, and an orange strip of horizon glimmered at the end of one street. Maura picked up her skirt and hurried in that direction. In moments she burst into what was a familiar open field.

The factory was engulfed in flames that licked from the base to high above its timbered walls.

Men with axes shattered windows, causing flames to billow out. The massive door she'd tried to open days before was a gaping hole. Men and women hauled out children in assembly lines as parents screamed for their little ones. Bucket after bucket of water passed from person to person in a long procession from the river to the factory. When the buckets drew near the fire, men grabbed them, tossed them into the building and grabbed another one. The inferno was untouched by their efforts.

A great crashing noise sounded as part of the roof collapsed.

"He's still inside!" A woman shrieked with such agony that Maura ran to the crowd near the entrance of the factory. She saw Aiden, his face lined with soot and sweat. A man drenched him with a bucket of water. He shook like a large dog, then ran toward the entrance that had once been a door.

"Aiden!" Maura shouted.

Aiden placed a dirty rag over his face and went inside the building that seemed to be crumbling from every side.

Maura tried to reach him but was caught in a mass of people. She called to a young man who had placed the child he carried into the arms of a woman. "Find Aiden. Please…"

She wasn't sure that the man had heard her. He glanced in her direction as he snatched a bucket of water. Pouring its contents over his head, he ran inside. Moments later, he emerged with Aiden on one side. Aiden held Rory in his arms.

Maura ran toward them until she tripped on something and fell to the ground.

A small foot extended in the middle of the chaos. She'd stumbled on a child who lay on the ground, his coarse trousers scorched, his face blackened by smoke. She flinched at his raw, blistered flesh but leaned over him and crooned softly.

The child's large brown eyes locked on hers. She had nothing to offer. Only the sound of her voice. The child's front teeth had fallen out, and a gaping hole waited for others to grow in. While the children near the Gunter home slept under downy comforters, this little one had gone to work. Lifting his head gently into her lap, she sang in a voice that first croaked, then rang clear.

When stars brush earth, we'll know, we'll know,
That they watch, they watch over you below.
In the darkness, they shine over you, over you,
In a place where dreams never die,
Never die for you.

Maura sang as smoldering ash descended like snowflakes, and the child shuddered and went limp. Still, she sang the blessing over and over through the crush of grief and anguish all around her. A hand rested on her shoulder. It was Aiden.

"Arson," he said, simply. "I saw someone at the back of the building. The factory was in flames minutes later."

He took the limp child into his arms.

Maura said, "Whoever it was left in a carriage." Her mind spun and she struggled to find words. "Why?"

Aiden cradled the boy, rocking him back and forth.

Maura had never felt so alone or helpless. She wanted to hold Aiden and the child, but she was afraid she'd hurt them. Afraid it wasn't enough. Afraid she didn't belong. The impenetrable wall of her dream had arrived to mock her. She struggled to connect thoughts until finally she blurted out. "I'll go. Get help."

Aiden didn't respond.

It was impossible to tell what time it was. The air was full of ash that obscured sunlight that had somehow risen to its peak, despite the pain below. The timber of the factory was gone. There was no more fuel to feed the blaze. The massive engine that powered its looms listed to one side, defeated.

Lilith had lied about Nona. She and Anton had influence in the city, though. They could gather resources. If only she could get her body to stand. Maura crawled to the nearest tree and leaned against its trunk. Gasping in ragged breaths, she willed her legs to hold her up as Aiden took the child to join others at the river's muddy shores.

After what felt like hours, Maura trudged up the

steep ascent to the Gunters' home. Carriages filled the streets. Vendors carted their wares to the shopping district beyond her host home. Children skipped down sidewalks dressed and ready for a school day. Mothers blew kisses, and nannies held small hands.

Unlike the tenement children, who worked despite their age and yet were somehow unworthy to be educated. Maura thought about Aiden's words. Poverty was a fearsome taskmaster. How many generations of children had been enslaved in its grasp? By the time the familiar porch of the Gunters appeared, sunlight blazed through the gloom and shone over the statue of Athena. Gold spilled off the end of the woman's gown, hiding the serpents that lurked behind her shield.

Wealth and privilege in one part of this city. Soul and body-crushing lack in the other. There was nothing in between. Maura scaled the steps to the lovely porch and stood at the front door to gather her thoughts. The gathering wasn't to be as the door opened. It was Lilith who stood at the threshold, holding a sheet of paper.

"There's been a fire at the factory," Maura said, struggling to speak as she caught her breath. "Children are injured. Rescuers need help. The fire was deliberately set."

The woman surveyed Maura's gown, now shredded, and streaked with ashes and mud. "You're wanted at the Hall. Now."

"But I…The fire…Didn't you hear me?"

"I'll contact Anton, and we'll send help. Tobias said it is urgent. Trust us."

She'd missed her interview with Tobias. "What time is it?"

Lilith answered. "It's noon. Adele prepared a light

meal for you in your room, and a carriage will be here in a half an hour."

Maura's stomach rumbled with hunger. Drained and sick with grief, she trudged up the stairs. She mustered enough strength to bathe, change clothes, and eat a few bites of her meal before the carriage arrived. The attendant—not Aiden, but Maura wasn't surprised—bowed and helped her into the plush seat. She held the door before he could close it.

"Sir, have you heard about the fire?" she asked.

"Aye, that I have. Terrible bad. It were cotton dust—like tinder itself. One spark from the loom, and it were up in flames. 'Tis a bad lot."

"I heard it might've been set on purpose."

The man seemed immediately guarded. "I ken't speak to that, miss."

"Do you know Aiden Garrett?"

"Good man. The best, I'd say."

If she'd had doubts about Aiden's courage, watching him carrying out child after child settled them.

By the time she arrived at the Hall, Tobias was waiting inside the great door. He bowed slightly. "Maura. We must speak privately." He led her past the tapestry of the griffin and closed the door of his office behind them. Motioning her to sit in the upholstered chair, he stood for a moment and studied a letter before taking a seat, not in the chair on the far side of the desk but beside her. "Where have you been?" His words came from a far-away place. "Why did it take so long to get here?"

"There was a fire at the factory. The one I told you about. Children died, along with some who tried to save them. I saw a person leaving the area right before the building was enveloped in flames. This must be investigated."

Her guardian's eyes widened, and his posture stiffened.

"I went this morning when I saw smoke above the tenements," she said, taking a deep breath. "I was worried about Nona and her grandson. And Aiden."

Tobias averted his face. When he turned back to Maura, the muscles around his eyes contracted, but he spoke evenly. "This is truly regrettable, of course. I went to the Gunters' to find you this morning and to remind you that your trial has been set for tomorrow morning. We had much to accomplish to seal your defense."

She wasn't ready. Tobias knew that. "Have you found Benjamin?"

He let out a long breath and shook his head. "I'd hoped for more time to prepare the strongest case possible. When you return home, every other issue will resolve. For now, you must be ready for what you'll face in the morning." His shoulders crumbled from their usual military bearing. "I wish…" He studied his hands for a moment before he spoke again. "You'll sit in the center of the amphitheater, facing the Council and Sir Taylor. Sir Taylor will call witnesses first."

Maura knew Tobias had given this speech to countless others. Maybe she wasn't any different from any of them. Except she knew that wasn't true. She didn't know how, or in what way, but Tobias cared.

He cleared his throat and took a breath. "You must listen and not respond, even if the testimony is incomplete, misleading, or an outright lie. You may not correct any witnesses. You won't be forced to testify, although you may if you choose to do so. I'll lead the questioning. You'll also be interrogated by Sir Taylor. I've been working day and night to understand this case, to break down every lie, every verbal assault Sir Taylor will make. For you, my friend."

Tobias glanced up, and she caught the sheen of moisture in his eyes. He rubbed them and kept going. "A carriage will come for you at first light. Don't go anywhere tonight."

"I have to check on Aiden and the others."

His gaze held hers. "I understand that your heart is drawn by compassion. Our city has protected and cared for you. Honor us by complying with what we ask of you."

What about his words reminded her of Lilith's speech only yesterday? "Compliance is not honor," Maura said, trying to keep anger from bubbling up over her words and spilling out.

"Compliance for you is life or death," Tobias said, undeterred. "Your heart is aching, that I understand. I'm trying to keep you alive."

"While you bind my hands?"

"I don't know how else to say this. Your trial is tomorrow. Let me help you."

Maura searched his face for anger and found none. "Tobias, I need to know what will happen..." She hadn't dared to ask, hadn't ventured to the place in her mind, where a question always lingered like a shadowy but certain predator. "If I'm found guilty."

Tobias held his hand out. "I've found nothing that would prove you to be anything less than a loving governess."

"But. If I am. How will I be executed?"

Tobias's body jerked as if someone had kicked him.

His eyes darted around the room, at anything except her. "Tell me."

Tobias sighed deeply. He arranged and rearranged his hands, then finally spoke. "The Council determines the manner of death after they make their judgment. We'll leave your case in their hands. Laws have been in place for generations and will continue to work for whoever complies with them. Don't leave the Gunters' today. Not for any reason. Your verdict is at stake."

Maura remembered what Aiden had said about the lies that insinuated the tenements were dangerous to enter. Surely, Tobias wasn't in on the ruse. "I'll stay. It's too late, though. I've seen the tenements. I know how people are oppressed there. Not that I understand. If I could, I'd make sure they were helped, that the refuge of the city was more than a thinly disguised lie." She stood and curtsied to Tobias. "I'll be ready in the morning." When she left, she hoped he'd follow her. He didn't.

It was still afternoon when the attendant drove her to the Gunters' home. Her body ached as if she'd been dragged through a week instead of one day.

Adele bobbed as she greeted Maura at the front door. "Mrs. Gunter requests your presence in her sitting room, miss," she said. "Supper will be brought to you there." She led Maura to a suite tucked away in a corner upstairs, where Lilith stood from a plush settee and welcomed Maura with a warm smile. "I'm glad you're back."

Adele pushed in a cart filled with shepherd's pie, steaming from slits in its golden crust. A custard tart and a pot of tea sat beside it. She dished up a generous portion of the meal onto a china plate and placed it on a small table between two plush armchairs.

"Come, sit." Lilith motioned her to one of the armchairs. "You must be famished."

Maura's empty belly rumbled as she took the seat beside Lilith. The ever-present emerald pendant draped around Lilith's neck. Their chairs faced a hearth, where a fire wavered inside. How different than the blaze she'd seen that morning. One warmed while the other consumed like a ravenous beast. Maura took a bite of the meat pie and felt its crust melt on her tongue.

Lilith delicately sipped her tea.

Maura was too tired for pleasantries. She dove into the questions that had pressed on her heart. She needed answers. "Did you talk to Anton about the fire? I saw someone leaving. Perhaps one who deliberately started it?"

"Oh, I doubt that."

A brass hall tree stood beyond a rich walnut desk where a velvet cloak the color of mountain ferns hung.

A memory pressed into the small room, into Maura's heart. An early morning glimpse out the window and a longing to be outside had called her as a child. No one could know. The air was crisp against her cheeks, and damp earth soaked her light slippers. A woman with raven hair had beckoned her in the meadow so many years before.

Maura stared at the woman in confusion. "Are you the one? The woman I saw in the meadow?"

Chapter 16

Lilith smiled as if Maura had discovered a hidden treasure while Maura struggled to swallow the bite of food she'd enjoyed only a moment before. She shivered, despite the fire, as she shifted into the long-forgotten memory.

"I remember you," Maura said. "I was a little girl. Dancing in the meadow. You called to me."

Lilith leaned back in her chair as if relishing the moment. "Why, yes, Star. That was me."

"Only Papa called me Star."

"That's what your name means, correct? Maura is a Celtic word for star."

Her daddy was Celtic. At least she thought so. A floral scent filled the room, though there were no bouquets in sight. Somehow, every question seemed to fall away in Lilith's presence. Maura entered a shadowland where hard edges of reality blurred into softness. One memory remained clear, though. It was how the woman's sweetness had lured Maura beyond Papa's boundaries.

"You haven't aged." She searched Lilith's face for wrinkles, scrutinized her frame for weakness. Lilith possessed timeless grace and beauty. "You're still so…perfect."

"Thank you." Lilith stroked the emerald pendant. "My eyes have been on you for many years."

All the times Maura had felt watched. At the chateau as she'd walked Nicolaus. The eagle sentinel at the hedge. Even the tiny glass-covered hole in her room. A shadow, a glimpse of movement. Her heart pounded with the realization.

Maura couldn't remember seeing Lilith since that morning in the meadow. She was certain she and Anton hadn't lived near their village. She ran through the small population she'd known so well, but Lilith's face didn't appear.

"Who are you?" Maura asked.

"I'm a friend."

Friend. That word meant many things in this city. Lilith had welcomed her when she arrived the first day. She'd included her in family meals and even taken time to prepare her for the trial.

She'd also fired Nona after promising to help her. And refused to be deterred when it came to Maura's meeting with Tobias, even though she was frantic with grief over the factory fire.

Lilith was not a friend like Aiden or Nona. Or Tobias, for that matter. Maura remembered the early morning chill and the winsome call of a woman wrapped in a robe the color of evergreens. "We met only by chance when I was a child," Maura said. "I never saw you again. That is, until I arrived in the city."

"You didn't know me," she said. "But I'm one who understands you. And knows the gift you carry."

Longing overtook Maura's reserve. It was what she'd felt as a child, warmth drawing her out of the cold. "Gift?"

"Oh, yes. You may not be aware of it, but others are."

Maura shifted in the chair, uncomfortable. "I don't understand."

"How could you?" Lilith shook her head with faint disapproval. "You were placed here for this very moment, so that I could extend an invitation."

A steady alarm grew in Maura's gut. "I'm here because of my trial."

"Yes, of course. An unfortunate incident brought you to us."

A childhood memory rushed back. She'd bent down to breathe in the fragrance of a perfect bloom when Papa had jerked her away. "Aye, 'tis pretty, lass," he'd said. "Only from the outside, though. You must never touch it or bring it home from the meadow. It's poisonous."

Maura had taken Papa's hand, and they'd walked away. The medicine sent for Nicolaus had the same scent. The one captured in the woman's gown and exhaled as Lilith spoke. Maura was exhausted and over-wrought. That was why it was difficult to speak, much less form thoughts that made any sense.

Lilith placed her teacup on the table and leaned closer. Her eyes never wavered, although Maura refused to peer into their depths. "Enter with me into an authority you've never experienced. One that can change the world. And save the children."

Maura fidgeted, trying to find a comfortable place to lean into, but felt only jabs and lumps against her tired body. She needed to stand, to stretch her legs, yet couldn't rise. A gentle slumber crept over her senses. She couldn't remember what they'd just talked about. The children. They'd been talking about the children, changing the world. "I'm sorry. My mind is foggy. I must be tired. Did you say save the children?"

Maura tried to take a deep breath in what had become stifling heat. She shook her head. "It's too late for that. Many were killed in a fire this morning. The one I tried to tell you about. It was at a factory where they worked." Maura peered into Lilith's sincere countenance. "Why were children there in the first place? And only those who live in the tenements."

Lilith's placid tone stayed constant. "Perhaps they're there so you can learn of an authority you've never known. One that can change their circumstances."

Maura shook her head, trying to clear it. Heat from the fire was as unrelenting as the intensity of Lilith's eyes. "I have no power," said Maura.

The woman's voice was direct, yet appealing. "So, you've believed. I, however, know differently. Let me teach you."

Maura had rehearsed Mama's words many times. They comforted her at night when she felt alone and afraid. *You'll teach others how the light of the stars burns bright in the darkest of times.* Perhaps Lilith had come into her life to help her fulfill those words. "I was pursued to this city because I was accused of murder. If I'd had any power for children, Nicolaus wouldn't have died."

Lilith took a sip of tea and returned the delicate cup to its saucer. "Some things are regrettable but serve to lead you to where you should have been all along."

Maura remembered Lilith's voice and how, as a child, she'd wanted to draw near. Even now, she tried to stand. How could rising from the comfortable armchair require such strength? She lingered for a moment. After all, Lilith offered her friendship. She'd opened her heart to Maura and extended an invitation. Still, something

157

inside stirred her to rise, to stand. She felt the almost forgotten pull of a puppet string that had once drawn her where Papa had warned never to go. Was it luring her to a place of danger?

The emerald pendant shifted around Lilith's slender neck as though by a silent breeze. Its golden chain shimmered in the same luminescent shades Maura had seen as a child. Gold and emerald melded into an undulating coil and became a serpent draped around Lilith's shoulders.

Terror launched Maura to her feet. "That's the snake I saw when I was in the meadow."

A flash of something Maura couldn't define crossed Lilith's eyes. Was it wrath? Or apprehension.

"My helper." Lilith resumed in a calm, measured tone. "He isn't apparent to all. You can see him?"

"Of course."

"This serpent is a symbol of creation, rebirth, and healing. One that teaches us to understand earth's cycles." Lilith smiled. "You are indeed a seer. Your eyes. Has no one told you? Not even Benjamin?"

Maura trembled. "How do you know Benjamin?"

"He's been a guardian of sorts. One who helped us find you."

"Us?" Maura's mind spun in confusion. "Who are you talking about?

Lilith stood as she removed the bright green serpent, exposing the yellow scales of its belly. Maura recognized it. She and Benjamin had studied the green mamba found in tropical climates, far from this cool, mountainous region. It was feared for its venom and its ambush from the cover of leafy foliage. She took a step back toward the door as the snake circled Lilith's arm, its onyx eyes never leaving Maura's.

"Benjamin never told me about you," Maura said, slowly backing away.

"Don't be afraid, child. It must obey me." Lilith walked to a covered basket near the fireplace. She opened the lid, and the serpent slithered inside. "As for Benjamin. Perhaps he wanted you for himself."

Maura watched the twitching basket. "I'm leaving. Now."

Lilith pointed a finger at the basket, and it stopped moving. "Please. Stay. We have much to share."

Maura longed to run, but an unseen weight kept her feet pinned to the ground. "What do you mean, to himself?" she asked, finding her voice had become a whisper. "Benjamin has only loved me all these years."

"He left you here alone. He could have come to offer his support."

Tobias had said he couldn't find Benjamin. That the cottage was locked, and he was nowhere to be found. Maura shook her head, trying to see through a fog that descended over her mind. Had Benjamin been able to come but chosen not to? "No. He was prevented from coming. He would never abandon me."

"Surely he would've come by now."

Benjamin had promised Papa he'd take care of her while he was gone. At least, that's what Benjamin had told her. Besides, she'd tested his vow in countless ways and given him plenty of reasons to want to be rid of her. Sometimes, her temper spewed out of control, and she was opinionated to a fault. Suspicion charged the atmosphere.

Maura protested in a small voice. "He directed me here. Taught me the stars. Loved and protected me when

I lost my parents." Her legs wobbled as if they resisted her will to stay calm and unafraid.

"You needed him as a child. But now. Where is he?"

The cover of the basket shuddered, then opened. The snake uncoiled itself and slipped to the floor.

Maura knew about the mamba's speed. She could never outrun it. There was a tiny flower in its mouth. An autumn crocus, the flower Papa had feared. Fragrant, lovely—and deadly. Its fragrance filled the room. A chill began in her belly and seeped into her limbs. As the snake neared, she cried out the words that had saved her in the meadow.

"I call upon the authority of the scroll!"

An ashen stream spewed from the serpent's mouth. As the snake whirled around Lilith in a graceful pirouette, Lilith's body twirled with it. The circle became a spin and rotated into an emerald funnel that hovered, then rose to the ceiling. Maura felt its sucking pressure and collapsed. It took all her strength to crawl toward the door.

When she did, the swirl took a sharp turn and blocked her exit.

In horror, Maura watched as the evil dance became a writhing mass of serpents, their green and yellow skin twisting in an unrelenting gyration. The stench of burning flesh and a bone-chilling cold filled the room. She had to run, had to escape.

A window stood open on the other side of the room. A burst of adrenalin propelled her away from the serpentine gale that now towered to the ceiling and inched toward her. She reached the floor below the window and shot one arm up, searching for the sill in darkness that had descended over the room. Yanking herself up in one pull, the warm light of a late afternoon beckoned overhead. Her fingers grasped smooth wood. Reality. She could feel it. Touch it. Take its escape.

Maura grappled its wooden frame and hoisted her body up until she crouched on the broad sill. Gulping in fresh air, she kept her eyes on the street below. Dusk was settling in the sky overhead. No carriages rattled by. There were no neighbors sauntering past with a friendly wave. Why was it so quiet? Had the supernatural behind her rushed in and shifted the real world below?

Furniture crashed, and wind roared that pulled her like a chain, threatening to yank her back into the room. She clenched her hands around the window frame, longing to jump but unable to let go.

A man's voice shouted over the din. "Chaos, stop! Wind, be still!"

The room quieted behind her, and a gentle breeze caressed her face. Maura clung to the broad sill. The brocade curtain brushed against her arms. Someone grasped her waist from behind with bandaged hands and pried her fingers from their grip.

"Let go, Maura."

Turning her head, she saw Aiden's curls and homespun tunic against blistered, swollen skin. He pried her fingers from the windowsill and led her to a small couch. Maura grabbed him in a tight embrace with her eyes clenched shut. When she finally opened them, the vapor had disappeared. Lilith was gone.

Maura buried her face into his chest and became small against him.

He repeated, "I'm here," as if she were a child awakened from a nightmare.

Maura took a deep breath and leaned back to peer

into his eyes. "How did you know?"

"I'll tell you later. We have to leave." He stood, keeping one hand on her arm. "Are you strong enough to walk if I help?"

She pushed to her feet, still unsteady. Aiden held her against his side as she hobbled out into the hallway. He pulled a familiar midnight blue case from inside his cloak. It was the scroll. And the pouch Mama had crafted with strands of silver and gold weaving stars set into constellations of the night sky.

"Be ready, Star."

He called her Star instead of Maura. She'd ask him about that another time. "Ready for what?"

Just ahead, a serpent slid from under the door of one of the rooms that lined the hallway. Another followed underneath a door across from it. One after another, a tangled mass of snakes, gathered and rushed toward them.

"Back," Aiden commanded, extending the scroll. The snakes formed an impassable barrier. Luminous in the gloom of the corridor, they glided closer. Aiden held the scroll out. "I command you to part, in the name and power of the scroll!"

Coiling their bodies, the snakes separated so that a narrow passageway appeared between them. Walk through a writhing nest of serpents? Couldn't he somehow spirit himself and Maura out into safety? "I can't," she begged, paralyzed with fear.

Aiden kept the scroll extended. "Don't be afraid. They must obey."

The serpents wove their way along the wall as if they had sticky skin. From time to time, one stuck out its head as if to sink its fangs into them. Maura cringed, but

Aiden led the way between them, holding out the scroll as if it were a flaming torch. Finally, the snakes disappeared as they approached the kitchen. There was an eerie quiet in the house. Where was everyone?

"We have to move fast," Aiden said, hurrying now. "She's regathering forces." Opening the kitchen door, he scanned the deserted room.

Maura expected Mrs. Ransbottom to charge out of her room at any moment. All was quiet, though. Constellations danced around the walls from Mama's pouch.

"This home is her domain," Aiden said. "We have to get out now."

A roar exploded from the hallway behind them. Maura turned to see dark shadows morph into a giant wave that towered from floor to ceiling. It rushed forward like a furious galloping steed. Maura slammed the kitchen door against it. They dashed to the back door, but Aiden tripped over a kitchen stool and fell headlong to the floor.

"Run!" he shouted.

Maura pulled him to his feet. They sprinted out the back door into the fresh air, free, but still pursued. Behind them, the doorway was full of dark clouds, writhing and pressing toward them.

"Follow me," said Aiden.

The wave rushed over paved sidewalks and billowed over carriages, intent only on Maura and Aiden.

The streets were deserted even though it was early evening. How could a supernatural wave overtake an ordinary world without a trace? Still, galloping waves followed them, obscuring vegetation, and pursuing them with alarming speed.

Where were the neighbors? Was a racing wave that pursued innocent people such an ordinary occurrence that they were unsurprised? Or did they merely peek from their windows at a safe distance at the sight of two people fleeing for their lives.

Aiden kept his hand in hers as they skipped over curbs, across streets, and through the city. A grove of trees appeared on one side of a residential area on the outskirts of the tenements. They veered into it, leaping around brush and exposed roots.

Still the wave plummeted toward them, mowing down dense undergrowth of the forest. It's fiery heat kept moving closer, undeterred, leaving a broad, scorched path behind it.

"Use the scroll," yelled Maura.

Aiden pointed at a tree several yards ahead and held her hand more tightly as they ran toward it. It was a towering pine with branches that extended in tiers that led up into the sky.

"Come, beloved pine," said Aiden. "Come to us now, in the name and power of the scroll."

Branches grew out of the trunk and became a leafy stairway that extended high above. The wave approached, closer and closer.

"Jump, Maura!"

****

SIR TAYLOR

She escaped. I don't understand how. Something about a fire at the factory. The attendant aided her flight. I was immediately aware of the danger he presented. Sadly, no one listened. The Gunters were away at an important Council meeting when she disappeared. Somehow the spies within the home were caught unaware. They should be fired. Promptly.

The woman left without a word of thanks for the kindness and care she'd received from gracious hosts. Worse, she stole a valuable scroll, one that she'd brought to the city to return to its rightful owners. That didn't surprise me. A murderer. A liar. A thief.

And now she's left the Gunter home, and probably the city. Foolish. At this point, even the conventions of this city agree that flight requires immediate retribution. She lost her right to a trial. She awaits certain execution. When we find her.

Many have been enlisted in her pursuit. Anton Gunter informed me that a battalion of soldiers have been deployed to track her down, as well as what he called extra reinforcements. Whatever that means. The Council has been seeking out enemies and doing what is necessary to remove their influence for generations. Those men wield power even I don't fully understand. What does that matter? We still work together toward a common goal.

It was reported that she'd spent time in the tenements and spoken with dissidents there. The Council seems concerned about that, but I am not. She's one woman. We won't allow even the glimmer of a potential platform. Reformer? I think not. Her uncle encouraged an allegiance to a Creator supposedly above the work of man on earth.

Impossible. Where was this supposed God when my wife and child died? Science is the only rational response to emptiness that shouts all around me.

Chapter 17

Maura grabbed one branch and hoisted herself up to clutch another. Aiden waited until she was safely perched, then grasped a bough and lifted himself. They climbed, branch after branch, until they were high in the magnificent tree. The smoldering wave curled along the base of the trunk as if it considered coming after them. It lifted beside the trunk, but instead of climbing, dissipated.

Taking a deep breath, Maura peered at the ground below. Everything on the ground shrank into miniatures. Aiden was behind her, closing the distance as she clung to the tree. Suddenly, she couldn't move, couldn't do anything but tighten exhausted arms around the trunk and hope they held. Time had suspended in the stillness of pine needles and branches. Somehow the shawl had survived the climb and still draped her shoulders.

"A few more branches," Aiden said, cheering her on. "Then we'll stop. I promise."

Maura thought about reaching up to find another branch, but it was hopeless. She couldn't move.

"Okay, we're good," Aiden said. "We'll stay here."

Maura snuck another peek below, where a wide canopy of branches spread out. All she had to do was sidle down the trunk until she could sit. But her arms refused to move. Aiden climbed onto the branch where she stood and wrapped his arms around her. She felt the warmth of his breath against her face. "It's okay to let go."

"You're crazy."

"Hey, I have the scroll. And we're in a good place. The branches will keep us from falling." His hands were bleeding against bandages now ragged and torn.

"How do you know we won't fall?"

"This from the woman who escaped a raging demon, a writhing horde of venomous snakes, and a noxious wave?"

"Nice adjectives. Like I said—how do you know?"

"You can't hang here all night. The sun is going down, and we need to get settled."

"In a tree?"

"We'll figure it out. For now, release one hand. Just a little. I'll be right here."

He *had* gotten them out of the Gunters'. And she'd watched him rescue children from the fire. She relaxed her hold with one hand and grabbed the trunk tighter with the other. Then lowered her hand, creeping it down the tree trunk until it rested near her side. Before she could protest, Aiden pulled himself under the arm she'd released and held her.

"Oh." That was all she could say. He pivoted away from the tree as she let go with the other hand. They sank along the trunk until a crook in the branch signaled their destination, and she settled on her bottom, landing in Aiden's lap. She flinched in sympathy at the raw skin that stretched from his neck to arms and hands. The arms and hands that had been injured when he'd saved others.

"Wait until you're sure," he said.

"Sure of what?"

"Sure you won't panic and wrestle me out of this

tree."

She laughed. And suddenly wanted to rest her head against his shoulder. Then remembered she was on his lap. She grabbed a branch and scooted over to another sturdy limb next to him. The shawl had slipped off her shoulders and lay on the branches in front of them. Somehow, it joined the branches and became a tiny, fragrant nook set apart for the two of them.

There was no end to the beauty and diversity of Hildegard's shawl. Soft needles curled around its fabric, supporting, and releasing a delightful scent. Maura even dared to gaze outside the sloping tree limbs to the world below. The wonder of the view from their perch almost overcame her fear of the dizzying height.

Aiden's red curls stuck out in wild freedom and his legs spread out on a branch as if he were an adventurous ten-year old. Except he was a grown man, handsome in a way that twisted her belly and made her flush at their closeness.

He followed her gaze over the city.

Maura couldn't decide whether to cry in relief, scream in fear, or laugh in giant belly guffaws. "Everything about this city has been mystifying and terrifying at the same time. Tobias couldn't explain why my uncle is gone. I don't know what happened to Nicolaus." Her breath quickened. "The fire, trying to get help—and my trial tomorrow. Then we were chased out of the Gunter home by the hostess turned demon." She stopped and realized… "Wait. The scroll obeyed you."

She studied him. He stopped bouncing one leg against the branches and became silent. His rakish exterior disguised a man with uncanny knowledge of the scroll. Who had taught him? The scroll, safe in the embroidered pouch, peeked out from under his tunic. He shifted it to one side and leaned back against the trunk, then hoisted his legs up to rest on a nearby branch.

"Where did you find my scroll?"

"In Lilith's room."

"I never realized it was gone. Or that Lilith had it."

A soft breeze whispered through the branches. Aiden kept his eyes on a squirrel that dashed from its nest onto a nearby branch, then dodged back near the trunk. "Did Benjamin ever tell you stories about the Magi?"

"Yes. My parents did, too. When I was a child." Maura felt her back scrape against the rough bark as she turned to face Aiden. "Wait. How do you know about Benjamin and Magi stories? And you called me Star at the Gunters' home. Only my family called me that." And Lilith, but she didn't mention that. "Did you grow up near our village?"

Aiden was the one who'd started this conversation, but again, he was silent. The longer she waited for his answer, the more she realized how much he was like her uncle. Even-tempered, wise. But other than a lowly carriage driver, who was he really?

Maura scanned her memory for early days when Benjamin had forced her to go to the village school. That hadn't lasted long. She'd refused to go back when children laughed at her strange eyes and giggled about her unchildlike love of the universe. Her dear uncle had conceded after more than a few impressive tantrums. He'd taught her more than she would've learned in school, anyway.

Aiden's gaze shifted into an interest in the sky above. Freckles and stubble met and formed a muddy jumble of auburn and copper. Ragged burns splotched his neck and hands. The climb against rough bark must've hurt. He'd said nothing about pain as he'd coaxed her down from her perch, paralyzed with terror.

She'd seen his strength with Sir Taylor. And his bravery when he'd rushed into the burning factory. He seemed to show up at the right time and didn't appear surprised to see her—except when he'd stared so intently at their first meeting.

She rubbed her temples, exhausted, and too confused to do anything but ask the question one more time. "Please. Tell me how you know Benjamin."

He was so close that she felt the rough texture of his tunic against her arm. He smelled like—well, like he'd finished a race against a diabolical wave. So unlike Tobias, who rarely had a hair out of place, much less ever broke into a sweat.

Aiden stared into the sky, now turning to rosy dusk. He fingered a loose pinecone and tossed it. Finally, after taking a deep breath, he let it out long and slow. "I was there," he said, simply.

She probably smelled as bad as he did. Her gown was torn and stained with tree sap and who knew what else. He could at least pretend to pay attention to her, though. Aiden seemed to love riddles. What a time to be obtuse.

"At the chateau." His expression didn't change.

Three words, but she drew back at them. Shocked. It couldn't be true. "No. I don't understand. Not the same…"

"When I was little."

Maura saw an image of a freckled face, scarlet in late afternoon heat. They'd raced, climbing flight after flight of narrow stairs to the watch tower. He'd won.

Again. He'd strut around like a fiery bantam rooster, taunting her and chortling with pure joy over his victory.

"Paddy?"

That crooked smile appeared, lighting his face.

"You knew my parents too." Her voice was barely a whisper. "Tell me. Tell me what happened. I've waited so long. My parents said they'd come, that they'd find me."

Aiden's body stiffened.

"Tell me!" Maura beat her hand against a nearby branch, which jumped up and down in protest.

Aiden lowered his head to his chest and closed his eyes. A leaf feathered his cheek in a small breeze.

"Please," she whispered.

"I hid when the soldiers came," he said, opening his eyes and staring into the clear evening air. "No one saw them approach. We'd said good-bye to you. There were suitcases and boxes of supplies by the front door so we could leave early the next day.

Maura remembered seeing the lights as she and Benjamin had driven away. Torches.

"They smashed windows with axes and burst through the doors. I heard the adults scream, 'Hide, little ones!' They formed a shield between us and the soldiers as we scattered. I ran upstairs with two of the smaller children and tried to get them to hide in the chimney, but they were too afraid. They ran."

Paddy. He'd stayed when she'd been safely spirited away. They'd all been taught to hide, to disappear at a moment's notice. He'd done that.

Maura held her ears and rocked back and forth. She imagined she could hear the stomping boots, frantic cries, and screams of pain. Had her parents been cut down protecting the children? She wanted to ask more but didn't. Instead, she considered the terrible knowledge of what she had escaped, but others hadn't.

Aiden was silent, but she didn't press him. Not now, not anymore.

"It must have been hours later," he said, after she'd given up hope of hearing any more. "I'd curled up so long against the blackened stone in the fireplace that my legs were almost frozen in place. Finally, the chateau was quiet. I climbed out, ran into the darkness. Until I arrived here."

All this time, she thought her parents would come for her, that they were out there, searching for her. Now, she wept with understanding. Aiden's grief and hers mingled in a web of sorrow that had no beginning or end. Tendril after tendril woven in unspeakable pain, face after face, hope after hope destroyed. She took him into her arms and held him as if he were still that little boy. Overtaken by what he never should have experienced.

They held each other through dusk and then darkness, when night creatures skittered nearby, and the great horned owl mourned with them. Then fell into an exhausted sleep, resting against soft branches that secured them by a power that held them against all odds, together.

Chapter 18

Maura opened her eyes to a chorus of chirping. Her head ached, and her eyes were crusty with tears. Still asleep, Aiden's arms were wound tightly around her waist. She felt his measured breathing, saw his eyelashes fringe swollen lids. The stranger was her friend.

The morning air was fresh, the sky brushed with light. Loosely wrapped by soft branches, Maura felt rested and oddly at peace. A mama bird and her babies in a nest below were the source of all the racket. She peered down to watch the mother stuff bits of worms into hungry mouths, then fly off, only to return. Maura's belly groaned. It had been a long time since the supper prepared for her in Lilith's home.

A raven soared to the end of the branch where they rested and veered so near that Maura squealed and Aiden woke up, startled. The bird took flight, back into the sky and out of sight. A loaf of bread sat on Aiden's lap.

"What? First the tree, and now the birds take care of you?" she asked.

Aiden rubbed his eyes and stretched against the tree trunk. His hair stuck out in shoots here and there, and his stomach rumbled at the sight of the bread. He tore the loaf in two and handed her one piece. Did he feel as awkward as she did? He'd been her best friend and staunchest opponent as a child. That didn't mean she knew him now.

Aiden stuffed a large chunk of bread into his mouth and chewed. He swallowed, wiped his mouth, and stifled a smile. "Extraordinary circumstances." He took another bite, then added, "And we do need breakfast."

The bread was warm. She held it to her nose and took a small bite. Nutty goodness filled her mouth. She took another bite, then another until her half was gone and she remembered a question she hadn't asked the night before.

"Who took care of you when you made it to Sanctuary? You were only a boy."

"Nona caught me stealing tomatoes from her garden." He yawned and wiped his hands on his pants. "She grabbed me by the ear and demanded to talk to my parents. I…couldn't speak. For almost a year. Don't know why she took me in, but she did. When my voice came back, she listened. And understood. She's Magi, after all."

"I haven't heard about Magi since I was a child. Benjamin told me a little, but I thought they were from the past. Legends, you know."

Aiden shrugged and tore off a piece of bread. "Not so much. They're all over Sanctuary. In the tenements, anyway."

"The people from the east who came for refuge? Stuck in poverty? You mean the people in the tenements are Magi? All of them?"

Aiden nodded.

"What have they done to deserve such treatment?" She studied welts of scarlet burns on his hands and arms. "What about the factory fire? The children. We both saw someone right before the fire. Who would've done something like that? And why?"

Aiden scanned the landscape below. "Remember all the kids at the chateau? With only a few adults? Your parents were protecting Magi children. Many of their parents had been killed, targeted by Gad El Glas."

"Gad El what?" Even as she said the word, she remembered. "A little girl sang in the forest outside the city. Something like, *Shine bright, O star of the morning...*"

"*Through me, your bonny lass. For you have come among us, our dear Gad El Glas,*" said Aiden, finishing the lyric. "Children learn that song from an early age. It's supposed to teach them that Sanctuary is a safe place." He picked a pinecone from a branch and studied it. "It isn't. Not for Magi. Gad El Glas is a demon that has despised and preyed upon Magi for generations. The political system it operates under changes, but not the source of its evil. Lilith is its emissary. She was the one responsible for the fire."

Maura recalled the cloaked figure and flash of green. It had been Lilith she'd seen near the factory. "She offered me power. Right before...I had no idea what she was talking about. I refused. That's when she and the serpent became one and twirled around until a tempest filled the room." She thought for a minute. "I think that was what happened. It seemed like a dream."

"If she offered you power, it was stolen. Or illegal in some way. I didn't know how she'd present herself," said Aiden. "She changes her appearance, although the demon has existed for centuries. I'm not surprised that she and the serpent became one. She was trained to rule in its power. No one knows how, but she submitted in some way. Either through fear or lust for dominion. Maybe both."

Aiden took another bite of bread.

Maura saw her friend with new eyes. And began to understand why, even now, he wasn't quick to speak. Unable to talk for a full year? It tore her gut even to imagine the kind of terror that had stolen a child's voice. Thank God for Nona. Lilith, on the other hand, seemed fearless. What had shaped *her* as a child?

"It's hard to believe Lilith has ever been afraid," she said. "Except when I called on the authority of the scroll. Like Papa did when we played hide and seek."

Now she understood why she and Paddy had been so good at hiding. Her parents had protected them from unexpected raids with a game. Until, for whatever reason, they couldn't shield them any longer. The scroll dangled from Aiden's shoulder.

"I still don't know how you found my scroll." she said.

"I sensed its presence."

"Did you ever have one of your own?"

Aiden seemed interested in a tiny beetle that crawled in and around the branches. It sure took patience to talk to this man. Patience she was glad Nona had, even years ago. Finally, he shifted long legs over the wide branch and spoke again. "My scroll is at the chateau. I'd been studying it with your father the day of the attack. I was too scared to go back for it."

If his body hadn't been so close, she wouldn't have seen a small tremor in his limbs. "You were so young... How could you have gone back?"

When he didn't answer she shifted gears. "I had a dream about a scroll one night."

She'd mostly meant to make conversation, to move them away from his painful memories. But Aiden sat up and turned to her. "Tell me."

She wasn't sure where to begin, but she started talking and hoped it made sense. "The scroll and I were pursued by horsemen," she began. "We became one and shone like a spotlight in the darkness. The enemy saw the light and captured us both."

Aiden stared at a spider ambling across its web along spindly twigs. "Do you know what your dream meant?"

"No." Maura immediately felt defensive. "I mean. No."

Aiden peered at her with those intense blue eyes. "You're the one who had the dream. You're the one to understand what it means."

"I don't know how to do that."

He stretched out his arms as if his lanky body had suddenly noticed it was perched on a tree limb. "You could ask for help."

Maura folded her arms and harrumphed. "I just did. I asked you."

Aiden remained unflappable. As usual. "Better to ask the Giver of dreams Himself."

Papa's quiet words as he said good-bye. "The One who set the stars in place and keeps our lives bundled into His," she said, repeating the phrase that comforted her at night when she couldn't sleep. Maybe Papa had said it many times and she hadn't noticed until that night. Besides, she knew the words. She didn't know the One.

"So, what is the scroll, anyway? I mean, Benjamin read from it. He taught me some of its principles. Like, you know—love never fails or whatever."

"It's like a carriage pulled by the strongest of horses, taking you where you need to go. Faster than on foot, and certainly faster than our own strength and devices."

"A carriage of truth. And wisdom. I like it. Except, we—the scroll and I—were captured by the ones who pursued us. Our light became so bright that the enemy used it to seize us." Maura adjusted her behind against the trunk. The gown she'd chosen for her meeting with Tobias bunched in uncomfortable places, and its delicate fabric didn't protect her from the tree's spiny needles. She resettled herself and glared at Aiden, who seemed to think her predicament was amusing.

What was behind those eyes the color of a summer sky? In her heart, she knew she'd been spoiled and protected by parents who adored her. She was sure they'd done their best to keep her childhood free from the fears they had borne for her and the other children. After all, hiding from the enemy had meant a game of hide and seek. But why was she the only one sent away into the night?

Glimpses of a hurried exit, whispered good-byes, and gut-wrenching heartache had become images she wasn't sure were real. Except for one other. Hurried packing amid worried glances. They'd been preparing to leave. In a moment she understood what her child's heart hadn't grasped. Her breathing quickened into shallow puffs. The pine needles kept stabbing her as a reminder there was no relief anywhere. Because after all these years, she knew.

"The attack came because Lilith saw me that morning." Her voice choked. "I caused the death of my parents. Of them all."

"You were only a child. You couldn't have known." Aiden reached for her hand, but she yanked it away.

"We had to leave because Lilith saw me."

Aiden's ruddy forehead crinkled with deep grooves that belied his youth. He shifted his weight beside her. Was he drawing closer or farther away? Suddenly, he bolted upright.

"What?" she asked.

"It's the interpretation of your dream. I should've known. You and the scroll become one. Light always conquers darkness, Maura. Maybe what you saw as capture was an opportunity to defeat your adversary."

She took a deep breath and let it out in one trembling puff. She knew what they had to do. Something she'd longed for since the night she'd left with Benjamin. "We have to go back. Back to the chateau."

Gentle Aiden's response was strangely brusque. "No."

"Benjamin may be there. And there are clues we need. Do you remember where it is?"

Aiden's eyes flitted around is if he were searching for some kind of escape. "We can't leave. You'll lose your protection against Sir Taylor."

Maura rolled her eyes and lifted her hands as if in surrender. "I've already lost it by leaving Sanctuary. You know that. Not only that, but we were also chased out of my host home by a demon. Another generation of Magi children is threatened. We can help them if… We can find your scroll. And you can teach me how to use mine."

Aiden sighed. "I can't."

"Okay. I'll go myself."

"Right. Be an idiot."

"We have to go back," Maura shouted. She lowered her voice to a grumble when she realized she could be heard by someone other than Aiden. "You are so stubborn."

As soon as she spit out her frustration, she regretted it. She'd been so dense. Of course, Aiden was afraid. She'd covered her own fear with anger and temper tantrums. But Benjamin had whisked her away that night. She hadn't heard marauding soldiers or the cries of loved ones as they lay dying.

She'd watched Aiden face down Sir Taylor, pull children out of a raging fire, and stop a demon intent on destroying her. And yet, Paddy, the child, was still ravaged by memories of what had happened one terrible night.

He lifted his head and spoke into his hands as if they held the terror a child had known. As if he wondered what to do with pain so deep it seemed bottomless. "I don't remember much," he said. "The nightmares stopped a few years ago. And I can talk again. Obviously," he said, with a wry smile.

"I'm sorry." Maura fumbled with her words, ashamed. "I…fly into action. And don't think."

He didn't rush to receive her apology. Instead, he peered into the sky at some unknown target in its expanse. "The bodies. There wasn't a burial."

Maura's stomach lurched. She grabbed onto a branch as a wave of dizziness washed over her. The ones they loved ravaged by wild beasts, decomposing without the honor of even earth over their remains. There was nothing to say. She touched Aiden's arm. When he didn't flinch or turn away, she reached for him with first one arm, then the other. "Hold me."

Suddenly, his breath was against her neck, his embrace tightened and drew her close. They stayed wrapped in a bundle as the sunshine of a new day grew warm and the forest teemed with squirrels jumping from tree to tree and birds trilling with happy abandon. Maura didn't speak. She had nothing left to cajole Aiden, to try to convince him to do what she wanted to do. She rested in his arms and waited.

"The adults were caught off guard for the first time." Aiden's voice was muffled by her hair. "We'd had raids before, but never like this one. Your father had trained me with the scroll. Maybe I could've…"

She held him tighter. The warmth of his skin and strength of his arms enfolded her. She'd loved him as a child. His confidence, the way he threw open his arms and crowed at the joy of being alive. How he'd irritated her—because he knew her. Now, his embrace stirred a heat in her body, and she didn't want to let go. Only draw closer. She buried her head against his heart. In a moment suspended in time, he brushed her forehead with his lips. Then her cheeks.

When his lips reached for hers, Maura straightened up so fast that she hit him in the nose.

He rubbed it with one hand and smoothed his tunic with the other as she scooted to another branch. She tried to speak, but her voice cracked. She cleared it and tried again, on a mission to hold back yet another tsunami. For now.

"My life has been filled with questions since that night," she said, her voice quivering. It was too late to hold anything back. "What if retrieving your scroll matters? And that we met again in Sanctuary. Nothing else makes sense. Except for who we were. And are. Together."

Maura leaned back against the trunk. Close, but not too close to the fire she'd felt between them. "This is part of my dream about the scroll, too. Our enemy pursues us to a place of light. A place that will help show us where to go from there."

The day had only begun, but a decision had to be made.

Aiden spoke into the space between them. "What kind of quest would take us back to such pain?"

Maura thought for a moment. Maybe that would become a habit someday. "One to prevent the pain of others. If we can."

Aiden's gaze searched the terrain below. She watched as emotion drained out of his countenance. His words were terse. "We need to leave now."

Chapter 19

"But how? It's daylight. Surely, we're being watched." Maura searched Aiden's face. She was the one who'd insisted they needed to go to the chateau. Aiden had been resourceful in impossible situations, but she had no idea how an escape from the pine tree would work in broad daylight.

Aiden moved from inaction to action faster than anyone she'd ever known. Just when she was sure he was lost in thought, he planned and acted.

"We need a distraction until we get out of the city. And a horse, as well as provisions. I know an innkeeper nearby. We can get what we need at the White Hart." He sized her up, as if she presented an intriguing puzzle. "You need a disguise. You're the one they seek. We'll go through the forest. It's dense enough that I think we can stay hidden."

"Wait a minute. Hildegard's shawl." Maura retrieved the shawl at her feet and studied the tree of life woven into its threads. She wasn't sure what other magical powers it carried. It had formed a nest for them in the tree limbs, keeping them secure and hidden. Hildegard said she'd need it. Maybe there was something else. She flipped the shawl out in front of them and studied the pattern. Sure enough, a fold was tucked away near an emerald vine of embroidered leaves. Turning it inside-out, she found an underside of mottled greens and browns and even a hood. When she draped the shawl over her head, it covered her completely.

Aiden laughed in amazement at her transformation. "Nice work, Hildegard."

Maura's bladder ached, and she longed for a bath. Hopefully the inn would provide at least an outhouse. She followed Aiden's lead as they crept down through pine branches. They were almost to the ground when Aiden held up his hand. He searched the perimeter, then signaled her to follow. With one graceful bound, he swung from a lower branch and landed on the ground. He held out his arms to her and caught her in another swoop. She'd evidently gone from circus freak to princess. Not a bad trade.

He took her hand in his, and they ran into the wooded area, zigzagging in a winding trek that seemed certain, even in its twists and turns. How he knew the way she wasn't sure. It was a noisy mid-morning in the forest. The sun peeped through the leafy canopy, casting streams of interrupted beams on the ground below.

A blue jay cawed overhead as a branch cracked behind them.

Aiden grabbed Maura and put his hand over her mouth. She turned and saw his face, now etched with a fiery alert. Wasn't it only the stirring of a hare?

Aiden peered up into the heights of a tree as if considering another climb. The sound of boots against woodland terrain became more distinct, and he pulled her against the trunk of a giant oak.

Footsteps gathered. They were being pursued. As they crouched to hide, Maura leaned against the tree for support and fell backward into what felt like a small cave.

Aiden ducked in behind her. It was a hollow in the tree, large enough for them to settle in together. He tucked his legs around her and shielded her with his body. She felt his heartbeat as she breathed against his back, able only to see an army of boots trampling vegetation. One set of those boots tripped on something ahead of them and cursed.

Maura pressed her body further back into the cavity. How could they not be discovered? Surely the hollow was big enough that they were visible, even with Aiden's dark clothes. She pulled Hildegard's shawl tightly around them.

"Find them," roared a deep voice. "They can't be far."

Aiden muttered quietly.

A hawk plummeted to the ground in front of one of the men, who cried out in fear.

"What's ye fearin'?" asked another, kicking the soldier in the butt. The man cursed in response. "Be moving now. No delays. Orders of the High Council."

The Council, under Lilith's direction. At least they'd sent a mortal army this time.

An owl swooped low in front of another soldier, and he yelped. "Ayeee."

"Damn it all," shouted the man who sounded like the leader. "Keep moving, ye bunch of suckling babes."

She and Aiden watched as the soldiers disappeared in the tangle of woods and brush ahead.

"Wait," Aiden said, in a voice so low Maura struggled to hear. He kept himself wrapped around her. It was hard to breathe, and she longed to stretch her legs but tried to relax into the shelter of Aiden's body. They waited a moment longer in the stillness. Then, they heard

185

another set of boots that stopped outside the tree.

Something whooshed through the treetops and swooped low. Maura caught sight of the wingspan, of the tawny colored feathers. This wasn't any bird. It was the eagle, Maximillian, she'd seen her first day at the hedge. How would they escape those piercing eyes? Again, it flew low across the ground near their hiding place. It wouldn't be long before it would pounce on them like prey.

Maura held her breath so long, she thought she'd pass out. Suddenly a roar sounded from above and a man yowled as he ran away. The eagle screeched in a mighty battle cry. Feathers flew, claws tore, and blood spewed over the forest floor. It was a clash like none she'd seen or heard before. Finally, the eagle lay on the ground, just beyond their hollow. Something trampled the ground outside of her field of vision as leaves and crackling branches scattered on the forest floor. It ascended into the trees, a certain but injured victor. What kind of creature had the power to overtake Maximillian?

Maura watched as the eagle lifted its head and struggled to rise. It rested against the dense undergrowth of leaves and limbs, then rose as if with titan will, flapped its wings, and flew away.

Something had defended them. Something larger, more powerful than the eagle. Maura sighed in relief for their unknown protector.

Aiden unraveled his arms and legs from around her and ducked out from the tree. He stayed low at its base, as if discerning the scent of unseen things. Finally, he reached in to take her hand. "Keep quiet."

Maura pulled herself up and out from her crouched position. Her limbs were stiff, and her lungs ached for fresh air. Fully out from the cover of the tree, she saw the trampled ground, the feathers, broken tree limbs and blood. The battle had taken place right outside of their shelter. Aiden pulled her close and whispered. "Follow me."

Maura welcomed every tree, every hollow that offered a hiding place. Aiden led them, once again, as if he knew where he was going. Maura's heart raced as they dodged obstacles. They were still prey, whether they recognized their predators or not.

Aiden pointed ahead to a weathered stone building. Its long narrow windows were dust-covered and dark even in the light of day. A scraggly row of rose bushes wound around one side. A wooden sign tilted over its entrance, announcing *White Hart Inn* with an emblem of a majestic stag rearing over a coat of arms. The inn seemed strangely deserted, except for a young livery boy who brushed a dappled mare with long even strokes outside the stable.

A man wearing a dirty apron drooping from his large belly stepped out the door and yelled. "Be done, will ye? Hunting party'll be arrivin' tonight, and yer wastin' time with that horse."

The young man hurried to lead the horse back to a rough corral.

Aiden nodded in his direction. "Stay here. Listen for my signal, then crawl through grass until you reach the inn."

"Crawl through the grass?"

Aiden rolled his eyes. "Just get there without being seen."

Maura sat under the cover of a dense line of bushes on the end of a field that faced the inn. She longed for their tree hollow. Wrapping her arms around bent legs, she scrunched herself into a tight ball under the camouflage of the shawl. A whippoorwill sounded, then another answered. She didn't know whether to stay crouched or position herself for a sprint. In minutes, though, Aiden appeared and beckoned.

She refused to belly-crawl. Okay, she would. By the time she reached Aiden, her dress was wet, and grass stained. She'd been like a large brown caterpillar with a blue belly inching toward him.

"There are facilities here," Aiden said in a low voice, pointing at a tottering, moss-covered outhouse. Maura wrinkled her nose. It was better than nothing.

"Leave the dress and put these on." Aiden handed her a pair of boy's pants and a shirt with boots that were too big. She'd keep her leather shoes and ditch the dress. A large, brimmed straw hat finished off her disguise. She wrapped the shawl over everything which, unlike the clothes, didn't smell like a smoky inn.

By the time she peeked out of the dank outhouse, Aiden was outside the corral on the back of the mare. She took his hand and hoisted herself onto its back. He carried a flask of water around one shoulder and handed her a cloth bag full of apples, bread, and cheese. At least they wouldn't starve. Maura had never ridden horseback, much less bare-back.

Tightening her legs against the animal's haunches, she tried to stay perched in the middle instead of listing from one side to the other. She hesitated to wrap her arms around Aiden's strong back. It wasn't as if she hadn't survived the towering pine tree by practically mauling him or enjoyed his body near hers as Hildegard's shawl made a nook just for them. Aiden solved the dilemma in one reach of his hands to hers, placing them around his waist. She tried not to snuggle. Resting in the warmth of his strength was too distracting.

Aiden scanned the surrounding area, alert to movement or anyone following them. Lilith wouldn't be easily deterred. Maura took a deep breath when they made it to open countryside. Then realized open meant easily seen, especially without the cover of forest. Maximillian, the mighty eagle, had been injured, but not killed. It could still pursue them. Daylight waned into late afternoon, and she wished for darkness.

A great owl plummeted from its perch with a mighty screech, and she shook so badly she almost fell off the horse. If only she could turn off her imagination. Or memory of the mountain lion's eyes that had never wavered from hers when she'd first arrived outside the city. And of course, tales of majestic griffins like the one she'd seen on the tapestry. As if real-life predators weren't scary enough.

Not only was Lilith hunting her, but she'd also missed her trial. Tobias had no way of knowing she'd been forced to run from the Gunter home. She'd betrayed him as her advocate. And as a friend. They weren't safe anywhere now. By leaving the city before her trial, Sir Taylor recovered unlimited rights of the blood avenger. Lilith knew that. She'd use that as an excuse—if she needed one—for speedy execution.

Aiden adjusted the strap that held the scroll around his chest. She hoped he could find his own at the chateau. She, on the other hand, wanted clues about her parents. She'd always longed to go back and had never understood why she and Benjamin hadn't returned.

"Please. Only for a visit," she'd begged him. Maybe

Papa and Mama were there, taking care of children as they always had. She'd stopped pressing Benjamin as she grew older. But she'd never stopped expecting them to come. Now she knew. They would've come if they could.

The weight of knowing why pressed on a hole in her heart. She wanted to ask Aiden about his parents but didn't dare. She couldn't remember them at the chateau, so maybe he'd already been orphaned when he arrived. Still, he had to remember her papa and mama.

"Do you...? Can you tell me anything about my parents?"

They continued to ride in and out of the protection of wooded areas. Aiden was so focused on the journey she wasn't sure he'd heard her question. He finally answered. "They spoke several languages. Children came from all over, and your parents could talk to them. We fought over your mother's bread when it came out of the oven. And I beat you in *every* contest—races, school projects, everything."

"My. Everything." She rolled her eyes.

Aiden held up one hand, as if solemnly swearing an oath. "Everything."

Maura felt a wall inside crumble in the darkness. He was Paddy, after all. All grown up, but still Paddy.

"It wasn't fair," she said, continuing the banter. "You were bigger. Besides, I could've beaten you. I was fast."

"Only not *as* fast."

"I can see that your ego is intact," she said, a little miffed. A soft breeze ruffled her hair, and she stuffed an unruly strand behind one ear. There was a question she had to ask. One that had been unspeakable before now.

"Were they all orphans?"

Aiden nudged the horse's side as they came to a hill. The forested terrain stretched into foothills at the base of towering peaks. She was tempted to grill him, but that hadn't worked. He was immune to her pressure.

"You were one of the few who had both parents," he finally answered. "Some had one family member. Most had none."

She'd been such a brat. No wonder Papa had been angry when she'd shoved that girl against a wall. She'd never thought about Aiden's parents. And why it was important for him to always win. She was silent so long his voice surprised her.

"What are you thinking?" he asked, clasping her arms tighter under his as they bounced over a rut in the dirt road.

Her question blurted out. "What about your parents?" When Aiden didn't answer, she longed to retrieve the question. "You don't need to tell me."

"It's okay," he said in a low voice. "I think about them every day."

Chapter 20

The sun was setting on the horizon with brilliant orange and rose hues. Maura had draped Hildegard's shawl over them both like a small, cozy tent, its warmth a comfort against the evening's chill. Every step of the horse that carried further from Sanctuary and nearer to the chateau. Aiden shifted again as the hill became steeper and secured Maura's arms around his waist. She waited for him to speak.

"They were regents of another kingdom, hundreds of miles east of here," he said in a low voice. "We were an arborist tribe of Magi—guardians of the trees. Have been for generations."

"I've never heard of Magi arborists. Did you live in the trees?"

She felt his belly move as he chuckled. She wished she could see his face. "No. Although we do understand their language."

"Trees talk?" Well, a tree *had* protected them. She hadn't heard it say anything, though.

"The stars have a voice, right?" asked Aiden, craning his neck to glance at her.

Maura nodded. "Day after day, they pour forth speech and night after night they reveal knowledge. There are no words, but in quiet evidence, their voice has gone out to the ends of the earth." She'd heard those words from Papa, and then from Benjamin, so often that she'd memorized them.

"Trees are like stars in that way. They don't use words, but their voice is heard by those who learn to hear. Like those beech trees." He led the horse closer to the pale, smooth bark of two massive trees. Their trunks were so close that they were almost connected. Maura peered up to see their crowns tower over the other trees in the moonlight, like kingly guardians.

"They're old friends," Aiden said. "They've shared the sunlight and root systems for many years. When one dies, the other one will, too. An underground web connects the trees of a forest. Even 'mother' trees feed tiny saplings so they survive until they can reach through the canopy for sunlight."

Aiden adjusted his position on the horse and pulled her arms tighter. "There are only a few of us left. I'd never known another life until the year I turned seven. A provincial governor arrived at our home one morning. His battalion had been hit heavily by snipers. He warned that an army was on its way.

"My parents gathered their people into the deepest forests, ones that had never been penetrated before. By subterfuge, our shelter was discovered. When the enemy arrived, they brought torches in one hand and axes in the other. They cut down and burned the largest trees. They knew that in doing so, the younger ones would die also. My nanny took me away by horseback. Her name was Gwen."

Gentle Gwen who always had a smile and a game for the children.

"My parents tucked their scroll into my belt as they kissed me good-bye. Gwen and I raced along the edge of the forest, the trees sheltering our escape while flames and smoke billowed behind us. She'd heard of a refuge for Magi children, but we'd given up hope finding it. One morning the chateau suddenly appeared through a thick stand of aspen. Your parents were there to meet us."

A young boy forced from his parents, with no news of their fate. They'd shared the same pain in many ways. Maura rested her head against his back. It was easier to ask hard questions without being distracted by those blue eyes. "You didn't you tell me who you were the morning I arrived in Sanctuary. I went to the Hall and to the Gunters without knowing. I felt so alone."

"I couldn't tell you. It was too dangerous. But I'd been…I knew it was you," he said.

"Knew it was me? How?"

"I'll explain later. We need sleep." Aiden found a sheltered place in a grove of sycamores, where he led the horse to a nearby stream and tied the lead around a branch. Maura was happy to stretch her aching legs. Together, they gathered kindling, and Aiden started a fire against the evening chill. They sat by the fire, eating, and drinking from their supplies. When they were done, Aiden gathered a soft cushion of pine needles, took off his jacket, and rolled it into a pillow for Maura's head.

"You'll get cold," she said, protesting. "Besides, I have the shawl."

"I have the fire. We'll sleep and be off in the morning."

Maura snuggled down into the pine needles. She was exhausted but had one more question. "How did you know I was in trouble at the Gunters?"

"I knew you and the scroll were being attacked."

"How?"

Aiden stooped to stir the fire. Flames waved, and

their warmth crept like a blanket over her. She couldn't go to sleep yet, though. She needed to hear his answer. Finally, he stopped tending the fire, leaned over, and pecked her on the cheek. "Maybe because we're connected like the trees." With that he curled up next to her and said no more.

Maura stared at his outline. Where was the child Paddy in grown-up Aiden? There were a few clues in that profile. She'd put so many people out of her mind since those days at the chateau. People with children who'd become only images of crooked smiles and fights over who got the last hot biscuit at dinner. They'd been treasures of her childhood. Friends who were never replaced. She hadn't planned never to open her heart again. It had just happened. Except with Benjamin and Nicolaus, of course.

Firelight wavered over Aiden's face. A mop of red curls fell over one side. She suddenly wanted to kiss the scorched cheek of the one who had saved her, had saved so many. But not tonight. She closed her eyes and slept.

It felt like minutes later when Maura's eyes opened to light rising on a gray horizon over mountains that loomed ahead. She was snug, wrapped in Hildegard's shawl. Temperatures had plummeted at the higher elevation, but she was warm. Sitting up, she watched Aiden snuff out the fire until the last of its embers died away into gentle puffs. Maura went to the stream and drank deeply. She lay the shawl over a branch, peeled away the shirt and pants long enough to relieve herself and wash in the icy water. When she walked back into the clearing, the horse neighed as if greeting her.

Aiden called out. "Climb on. We'll eat on the way." She did, and they started out. Maura was ready to talk, although Aiden seemed lost in his own thoughts. Climbing, rutted paths that wound around precipices were proof they neared the chateau. Unlike Aiden, Maura tried to sit still but couldn't keep from wiggling with anticipation. The terrain had become steep pitches with sharp turns and twisting curves. Before long, the high-pitched warble, *chur, chur* of a mountain blue bird sang in a tree nearby. Aspens along one side of the road stood like graceful watchmen. Tiny mountain aster dotted thick grass.

Suddenly, they came to a clearing, and she recognized her meadow. The one she'd claimed as her own, the one where she'd first met Lilith.

"Aiden, stop. I need to…" She wanted to feel the ground, to touch the stiff grass and breathe in its freshness. The sounds and smells hadn't changed. She tried to clamber off the horse, to run on the same path she'd taken countless times.

"Wait," Aiden said, pulling lightly on the reins.

He'd heard something. She half-expected to see Lilith standing in the open meadow, raven hair flowing over the velvet cloak. Nothing. The fear she'd felt on this journey—all throughout her time in Sanctuary—was gone. They'd been chased, hidden in various states of trees, and finally arrived at the destination that Aiden dreaded, and she longed for. It was as if the air around them had cast aside fear as an unseemly garment. She'd planned to locate the chateau first, but what filled the yard made her stare in disbelief.

Flowering trees and bushes dotted the lawn around its perimeter. Wisteria, crimson crepe myrtle, and butterfly bushes grew together in tangles of fragrant blossoms. Mountain phlox, shrub roses, and quince were positioned as if by an artist's eye. Even though warm summer temperatures filled every day in Sanctuary, here it was spring.

Aiden rested on the horse. It was all Maura could do not to scramble down and touch the beauty around them. Finally, he dismounted. Maura slipped off and ran to the entrance of the garden.

Aiden walked in behind her. Surely, like her, he'd revel in the wonder of an oasis that couldn't have just happened, stretching out before them like an invitation. Instead, he knelt on the ground and bowed his head. Maura forced herself to kneel beside him, feeling strangely awkward. She was afraid to touch his shoulder or disturb him in what seemed like a holy moment. Amid such opulent color and fragrant scents, two Hawthorn trees stood like guardians in front of them.

Maura gazed around in wonder. She had to speak. "I don't remember these trees. Even in spring, this rocky soil barely sprouted grass."

Aiden answered in a hushed tone. "My people have been here."

Arborists. Of course. They'd left their work of art outside the chateau.

Aiden wept quietly at her side.

Maura wrapped one arm around him and waited as mid-morning sun became warm against her back.

Rising to his feet, at last he found words. "They came to honor our dead."

Maura caught her breath. They'd honored their families with the gifts closest to their hearts. "It's more beautiful than any garden I've seen. Such artistry, although I don't recognize the design." In the next moment, she understood. Aiden spoke what she knew.

"Each tree represents a grave."

Chapter 21

Maura and Aiden stood as witnesses of a sacred garden planted in honor of those who'd died that night. The rosy saucers of a tulip tree waved in a slight breeze. A cherry tree's pink blooms filled the air with their fragrance. Which one carried the sweetness that embodied Mama?

Aiden seemed to read her thoughts. "Your parent's memorials are these two Hawthorns at the entrance. They speak of hope and enduring love."

Never had trees been so precious. She touched one and then the other, soaking in the beauty around them. She turned to Aiden. "Tell them. Tell them thank you."

They walked arm in arm through the garden toward the stone walls of the chateau. Brush and moss joined crumbling remains of giant slabs of limestone that had once been invincible walls. Vines and wild grasses grew unhindered, forcing Maura and Aiden to pick their way over timber and climb across the threshold of their old home.

Maura turned around to remind herself of the garden, and of the meadow just beyond it that still beckoned. All sense of place vanished as she faced the chateau. Where were the nooks she'd hidden behind countless times? What about her mother's rocking chair, where she snuggled as they read stories at night? Or her father's workbench, where he'd crafted their furniture.

She stumbled over a rotten plank, full of lichen. Maybe it had been the family table, where they'd spent so many hours together, sure that life would never change. Threading through debris, she fought to salvage memory after memory reduced to ash and soot. She'd imagined rushing into her parent's arms. Countless moments missed and grieved. Like when she'd learned to climb a tree or discovered an empty chrysalis and knew a butterfly had been born.

Falling to her knees, she threw her out her arms in the middle of what had once been the giant, sun-lit foyer. "Papa! You knew the power of the scroll." Her strong father had protected them and never wavered in his faith. Lifting her voice, she cried. "Why couldn't you save them?"

Maura had seen the terror in Lilith's eyes when she'd called upon the scroll. What power did that piece of parchment wield? Lilith Gunter wasn't one to be afraid, certainly not of an aged roll of paper. Benjamin had taught her some of its tenets, but she'd never sought them out for herself. Still, those written words carried power that made a tangle of snakes divide so she and Aiden could pass through. Yet for all its power, Papa hadn't been able to wield it against the ones who'd come against them that night.

And then, she remembered. Papa had tucked the scroll under her arm before she and Benjamin left. He'd given her his best, even to the end. With enormous cost.

Maura bowed her head and wept. "Why did you send the scroll with me? I wasn't worth it, Papa. I've done nothing to deserve the authority it carries. Why did you entrust it to me, a child?" She wept and wept, gushing the pain of that moment relived.

Aiden hung one arm around her shoulders and drew her close. "Maybe he knew something you don't."

Maura wiped away her tears. It didn't feel like an answer, but comfort came anyway.

"I'll be back," he said and ducked through a hallway with charred walls. Maura knew where he was going. He knew exactly where he'd left the scroll, despite the debris-filled hallways he had to navigate. Instead of following him, Maura scaled a staircase that wound its way up to a splintered second floor, where the library had once been.

She wanted to climb as high as she could, to get her perspective back. It was the room where they'd played with Gwen, and where she'd heard stories of the Magi. Light cast weird prisms through its cracked windows. She peered outside over the flowering trees to the meadow. There had to be proof that her parents still spoke—even from the grave.

Maura skirted a nest of field mice on the patchwork floor. A board creaked, made a mighty groan, and broke away. She fell into a crevasse that swallowed one leg and left the other trapped above. Crying out in pain, she tried to crawl out of the hole surrounded by rotting timbers that opened to the entry below.

Aiden ran up the stairs. "Easy. I'll help." He lifted her into his arms, carried her out of the pile, and set her gingerly in one corner. Then tore a part of his shirt to bandage the quickly swelling lump on her ankle bone.

He smelled like the mountain. Fresh, unhurried, safe. What about this man brought him on the scene so quickly when people were in need? Maybe a compass had been etched inside his quiet heart that drew him to the place where his compassion was needed.

"Did you find your scroll?" she asked.

Aiden shook his head.

A door dangled on a rusty hinge over a small closet, where a sliver of brass glimmered in the light between rotting wood and plaster. Mama's trunk. She'd said it came from a life before she was married and collected all those children. Wiping away the dirt with one hand, Maura recognized faded initials JO that had almost disappeared from their metal plaque. Judith O'Donnell. A pang of loss pressed against Maura's heart at the sight of her mother's full name.

Aiden hauled a heavy wooden trunk to Maura's side. He leveraged a narrow limb into the lid and leaned on it with all his weight until it opened with a thwack and the scent of an ancient library.

Maura expected to see its contents decayed into shreds. Instead, the papers were strangely intact. The top sheet was a letter written in script she didn't recognize. She read it out loud to Aiden, who peered over her shoulder.

Though an enemy builds its shelters on high and sets its nests among the stars, she who carries the light of stars will find and bring them down.

"You know it?" Aiden asked.

"Papa spoke it over me, many times." She studied one after another of the yellowed parchments. These letters and prophecies declared things Maura had never heard.

Listen, O daughter, give attention and incline your ear. Forget your people and your father's house...for your beauty is more than a golden crown and your mantle more than embroidered silk. Your kingdom calls in the hearts of children. The stars will affirm, they will acknowledge what others have not seen.

Another parchment was rolled like a scroll and sealed with wax. The seal had been broken and its wax was a faded red stain. This one was addressed to Judith. Maura carefully rolled it open and held it out to catch sunlight from the window overhead.

Beloved Judith,

Your mother and I send greetings. I've sent trusted emissaries with this letter, which comes with the most urgent of pleas. We miss you more than life itself. The kingdom totters on my aged legs, and our enemies know I am weakened. The army remains strong, but of what use is a kingdom without its royal lineage?

Your sister hasn't been found after all these years. We'll never stop searching. You know your sister. She would've gladly ruled over your mother and me, even from the womb. We fear someone recognized her royalty, even lusted for her extraordinary beauty.

Return to us, daughter. Even though time and distance separate us, you cannot deny the crown in your heart. You'll rule wherever you are, and you'll rule well.

Remember your sister. Someday, she'll be found, and when she is, she'll need you. Always be allies, for in each other you will find strength.

We love you forever and always,

Father and Mother

"A royal stamp. Aiden, do you know it?"

Aiden shook his head.

The parchment was dated years before Maura was born. Mysteries rose one after the other in this image painted of a mother she hadn't known. Mama was a princess, in line to rule a kingdom. She had a sister. And yet, she'd given up that throne. As far as Maura knew, she'd never found her sister or returned to her parents. "Mama was royalty?"

Aiden's eyes filled with tears.

"What? What do you know?"

"A principle in the scroll. The seed buried in the ground."

Maura caught her breath. Benjamin had taught her the same thing as they'd worked in the garden. She spoke his words out loud in the silence, their memory rising from a deep well inside.

"Unless a grain of wheat falls into the earth and dies, it remains alone. But if it dies, it bears much fruit." She covered her ears as if she could erase what she knew to be true. "No. I won't believe that."

Aiden tried to gather her into his arms, but she yanked herself out of his embrace. "This is wrong," she cried. And yet, Benjamin had repeated those words many times as they'd put tiny seeds into the ground. As always, she was full of questions.

"How does the seed find its way out?" she'd asked her beloved uncle.

"It always does. You know that." He'd take another and cover it with the dark, moist soil.

"Don't cover it, Uncle. It'll die."

"Only the hull around it dies, little one. When it falls away, the life inside that seed is free. Free to become a plant that feeds others."

She'd struggled with that thought. What could grow hidden away in dirt? Even now, she shook her head and cried out to the ceiling overhead. "Mama, why did you choose this life?"

Then terrible rage billowed up from her gut. Aiden had told her what happened while they were in the tree.

They'd talked on their journey to the chateau. But losing Mama, Papa, and her friends had been like a story told from the lips of a stranger. Now, she understood the truth.

Lilith had searched them out. She'd hidden in wait like a venomous serpent ready to strike at the most vulnerable moment. With hate so terrible it burned everything in its wake like a pillaging fire.

Maura tried to stand and fell back down. She picked up a stray doorknob, long fallen from its frame, and threw it as hard as she could. "I'll kill her." She picked up shards of wood, rocks, whatever she could find and hurled then through the towering windows. Glass shattered like gunshots as a rock hit its target. Others catapulted through already broken glass. "I hate you. I hate you," she screamed.

Aiden dodged the missiles of hurled debris but didn't leave her side.

"Mama. You laid down your life to raise the children. You were hidden, like that seed. An evil woman destroyed you. I know her. And I'll make her pay. Somehow."

Maura shuddered once and fell to the floor, exhausted, body trembling. She wept now, soundless tears, hands over her head, feeling rough timbers on her checks, shivering in the cold that drifted up through the rafters from the first floor.

Aiden crept over and pulled her into his arms. She smelled the forest, its damp earth, its shelter. Finally, as he held her, his strength stilling her body, he spoke. "Your mother was a true queen over her kingdom. She had no storehouses of gold and jewels, and yet she was a keeper of treasure. Somehow, she knew she belonged here, at the chateau.

Maura nestled her head against Aiden's neck. After moments of silence, he kissed her on the forehead and settled her beside him. "There's more. When you're ready."

This trunk had given her glimpses to her mother she'd never known. What else did it hold? She reached back in, fingering other parchments, hoping to find more about her mother. But the papers that filled the rest of the chest were all childish drawings. She picked one up, careful not to let it disintegrate in her hands. *Star* was scrawled on the back.

That was like her mama. She'd saved the drawings Maura'd etched on cold winter days or when they weren't allowed to go outside. As Maura pulled out one sheet after another, the images improved. Stick figures fleshed out into faces and limbs and smiles—or frowns. They were caricatures of her parents, other children, and adults. Of Paddy.

Further into the trunk, she discovered pictures of constellations, etched like intricately crafted lace against blue paint. The Archer, the Big and Little Dipper, even the great Taurus, were drawn in precise detail, far beyond the ability of a five-year old. One picture lay tucked away in a corner of the chest. Unlike the other images, it was drawn in charcoal. A towering castle stood in darkness with yellow light streaming from each window. Outside the building, twisted gargoyle faces glared out from dark shrouds with torches in hand.

Aiden studied the picture. "This is the chateau. Before the attack."

Maura remembered the sinister figures and their lights. She'd seen them the night she and Benjamin had ridden away. "I remember the torches," she said. "I couldn't have drawn this picture, though. I was already gone."

"Unless you saw it before it happened."

"That's impossible." She handed the picture to Aiden.

Aiden's eyes were tender, almost pleading. "You were a child. Maybe your gift worked when you didn't know it yourself."

"Lilith talked about my gift. And now you. Explain."

"It's your ability to see the unseen."

"You're making fun of my eyes again."

"I've never made fun of your eyes. They were the reason I recognized you that first morning in Sanctuary."

"Oh. Well." She straightened and tried to stand. Then yelped in pain and sat back down across from him. "I could've saved myself a lot of trouble over the years if I'd been able to see the invisible. I could've stopped…"

Aiden shook his head as he wrapped her ankle in the strips of fabric. "You were a child. Like me."

The touch of his hand brought a warm flush that covered her face. She pushed hair out of her face and stared at the ancient trunk, then around them. She imagined the happy squeals of ball games in this room, so filled with light it had been almost like being outside. "What good was a gift that didn't protect the ones I loved?"

Aiden lifted her leg gently and placed it on the floor. "Have you ever heard of a seer?" he asked.

"Lilith called me that. She said not everyone saw the emerald pendant on her neck become a snake. Then again, she and truth parted company in more ways than I knew. She may have only been manipulating me. Or trying to bring me into her confidence."

"Benjamin never said anything about it?"

"Not that I remember."

"Your eyes may signal your gift, but there's much more. A seer perceives beyond the natural. It's like having a peephole in a door, offering vision when life is hard and people need courage. Or warning of things to come. It's the kind of treasure that must be protected— and fought for."

"Papa told me we're equally precious. Equally valuable."

"True. Although seeing the unseen is essential when you have an enemy. And crucial to possess if you *are* the enemy. You were too young to understand it then. You can now. When you comprehend your gift, you'll understand why Gad-El-Glas fears you."

"Not likely. You're the one who rescued me from Lilith. Even at the fire, I couldn't stop…anything." Maura fingered her sore ankle and brushed against Aiden's hand. He touched it lightly, and she wished she was in his arms again.

"It's a mystery. Like the stars we don't fully know or comprehend. But we know the One who put them in place. The same One who placed the ability to see the unseen in you."

Words whispered in quiet urgency stirred inside. They had been Papa's. *We aren't afraid. For we know the One who set the stars in place. And keeps our lives bundled into His.*

"I don't know where to begin, how to…besides, a chest of pictures is no proof that I'm a seer."

"Let's go outside." Aiden led her back through the chateau and over the threshold. She leaned against him, hobbling on the injured ankle. They made their way to the hawthorn trees, and Aiden gently lowered her to sit as he retrieved apples from their sack of provisions.

"We hid at a moment's notice," he said, taking a giant bite of apple and reminding her of what she knew. The rat-a-tat of a woodpecker sounded above them. "One signal from the adults, and we'd sprint into places that couldn't be seen. Places of safety. Until they weren't safe any longer."

Aiden pointed at a leafy bush beside them. A delicate katydid hid in plain sight on a leaf. Its color mimicked the leaves around it, a perfect camouflage. "The Creator designed it to blend into its surroundings for protection. Like we were taught to do. Only now, it's time to make an appearance."

Many details had become hazy over the years, but she knew hiding had become second nature. Had she buried those memories of being hunted in their own home?

"There was a reason your parents sent you away alone," he said, tossing the apple core and watching a squirrel stop by to give it a taste.

"I've always wondered why. None of it made sense."

"Think again. You were young, but you shared a lineage with them. Do you remember any clues?"

"Papa was wise. He had foresight. Mama had…vision. She imprinted constellations on my scroll's pouch. She wove what she saw into fabric. Those lights helped Benjamin and me escape from Sir Taylor the night Nicolaus died. What does that have to do with me?

"Wisdom and the ability to see—to translate what you see as light that conquers darkness. You're a Magi seer. The best part of both."

"A seer? And now Magi?

It wasn't fair. She barely knew her parents. She'd struggled to understand who she was all her life. "My eyes are bizarre. We found a picture I drew as a child. Neither of them proves anything. I was spared—the least worthy, so unlike the Magi I loved in stories. And I don't know why."

The air around them was full of life. Squirrels rustled branches as they dashed around in the canopy overhead. A hawk screeched and then plummeted to the ground for its prey.

"Close your eyes," said Aiden. "Tell me what you see."

"Fine. I'll prove you're wrong." She closed her eyes tightly, willing herself to see only the darkness behind her eyelids. Immediately, Rory's face came into her mind's eye. His brilliant eyes were locked in fear. She shot up off the ground in alarm.

"Rory! He's in danger."

Aiden nodded. "What should we do?"

"Find him."

Chapter 22

They rode away from the chateau and its holy grounds. She wanted more time there. So much more. She'd wanted to bring the trunk somehow, to keep its link to her mother close to her side. Of course, that was impossible on horseback. Aiden had finally convinced her to tuck it away in a safe place. It would be the promise of their return. After a hurried meal, they were on the road again.

She and Aiden were returning to Sanctuary, traveling only because of what she'd seen. The image of Rory's frightened eyes pulled her out of the past and plummeted her into the present of a small boy. One very much like her.

Maura wondered if Mama's sister had ever been found. Surely, Maura would have met her if she'd been discovered. Her mama had left her parents and lost her sister. Maybe that explained her pensive stares out the window on cold winter days.

Maura's ankle ached, but she pressed her legs around the horse's wide haunches as tightly as she could. The horse had begun its steep descent, and the chateau disappeared. The way was so steep that she expected to hurtle over the edge as Aiden helped the mare navigate a narrow path that hugged the edge of the mountain. She held her breath at every turn where the vista became endless sky.

Trees towered above, shielding them from the bright afternoon sunlight. They'd been busy with their own thoughts for the first hour. She couldn't take much more silence. She still had questions. The horse maneuvered around a deep rut, and she swayed, holding tighter to Aiden's back. "Tell me why the pine tree obeyed you."

"My people are arborists. I told you about them."

"What about the tree we climbed?'

"It was a bristlecone pine tree, the oldest living tree. It recognized me—and welcomed us. We've protected them, nurtured and cared for trees like it for centuries."

Wind shifted through the trees, and sunlight mottled the floor of the forest as they rode alongside it. "Anything else about this gift—or you—I need to know?"

"Our people understand root systems that give life to the tree. If the root is diseased, the tree dies. The motives of people's hearts work in the same way. They're hidden, though not forever."

"Roots are underground. They can't be seen."

"You've heard the old saying, 'A seed hidden in an apple is an orchard invisible'? Truth is a seed. So is a lie. Both become a tree, even an orchard with the right time and care. Depending on whether the lie is believed—or if the truth is nurtured."

"Slow down. You're telling me that you see what makes people do what they do."

He hugged her arms to his waist. His laugh sounded like young Paddy, a joyful chuckle that rumbled in his belly. "Not when I'm...distracted."

"Then explain to me why Lilith is so powerful."

"Maybe her lie became an orchard."

Maura felt the scroll bump against her leg,

reminding her that Aiden hadn't found his own. She hated that for him but was glad he had hers. "It isn't hard to see that you love the scroll."

"Every time I discovered one of its truths, I knew my parents were speaking to me. Gwen helped, but your father was the expert. He spent hours training me in its mysteries. I learned its authority from him."

"You got to learn, and I didn't. That's not fair." Maura felt like a jilted teenager, jealous of Papa's attention.

"You weren't old enough," Aiden said with a chuckle. "Surely you had the opportunity with Benjamin. He's skilled in the scroll."

Maura remembered how Benjamin had suffered the brunt of anger that hid her grief. "At first, I missed my parents too much to listen. Benjamin didn't press me. Maybe he waited for—for me to be open." She was ashamed. Talk about root issues. This man…

"Your parents paid the price for the lineage they knew and chose to act upon. Benjamin was afraid to lose you if he pushed too hard." Aiden took a long breath and suddenly was done talking.

"What?" she asked, recognizing now when something whirled about in his mind. He'd wait until the words came together before he spoke. She was the one to blurt it out and hope the tangles sorted along the way.

"I need to tell you something," he said. "About what happened at the chateau."

The afternoon sun had started its descent in the western sky, taking her courage with it. She dreaded the journey back to the city they'd have to navigate again in darkness. Besides, she wanted to forget, not learn more.

A rustling sounded in the woods. Was it a rabbit? Or

a stealthy scout from Lilith? Maura readjusted her grip around Aiden's belly.

Aiden seemed intent on a train of thought. "They came for Magi children that night. To do that, they targeted every child at the chateau." Aiden's hands on the reins tensed. His words seemed to come from his core, studied and certain. "It begins with a sign or wonder, often in the night sky. One that catches the attention of those who're alert to what's happening overhead. Gad El Glas and its cohorts notice."

"Strange that our enemies believe the heavens speak." How could an evil so given to guile and deception acknowledge truth? Unless it recognized what was true only to overpower it.

"They know the signs are infallible," he continued, "unless the plan those events signal is thwarted. A sign points the way to a new generation arising. One that threatens the rule of Gad El Glas. The people of the tenements are on the alert right now for that very reason."

Maura's head spun. Mama was a princess. Maura shared her lineage. Her mind raced as she tried to connect what she'd learned at the chateau to what lay before them. "You said a sign had to appear. One that all could see."

Aiden studied to road ahead as if he searched for a landmark. Or wanted to avoid an answer. After a moment, he said, "Yes," then was silent as the horse jostled up a small rise. "Only this time it wasn't in the sky."

Mourning doves tucked unseen cooed a low murmur that filled the air.

Aiden rubbed his chin and combed back tangled

hair. Red curls scattered this way and that through the brimmed hat he'd jammed over them. His eyes stared intently ahead. Once again, he'd slowed the conversation to a halt.

Finally, he cleared his throat. "What if the sign is you? Remember the prophecy? You, your mother, her sister were the ones to bring the enemy down from its high places."

Maura's arms became rigid around Aiden's waist. She started to speak, then stopped.

"Just listen. Everything shifted when you came to Sanctuary." He patted her hands as if he comforted a child.

"The Council made sure you were pursued into the city," he said. "You were placed in the Gunter home. A refugee has never stayed in a Council home. And you, daughter of a kingly lineage, landed in a house with another queen."

"Queen?"

"Lilith. The high priestess of Gad El Glas."

Maura didn't know what to say. "It would've helped to know this at the beginning."

"It wasn't time. Not when you were afraid and in a new city, not knowing what to expect."

She pressed her hands against the mare's haunches. "You didn't say anything, even after I'd seen the factory, after Nona wouldn't talk to me."

"Your presence attracted attention from powerful people—people who have ears in many places. Of course, you were known among Magi in Sanctuary also."

"For so many people supposedly recognizing me, I sure felt alone."

"All I know is this. When no refuge exists, we must

become one. There's stirring in the people of Sanctuary. Maybe only in the tenements. But the stirring is felt by the enemy. And Gad El Glas *will* respond."

Movement crackled against dry leaves amid a stand of trees. Had Aiden heard it? Or was he so lost in thought that he'd forgotten their danger. That wasn't likely for the man who seemed to have internal ears.

"Our enemy already has a plan," he said, reaching back and taking Maura's hands back into his. "One designed to extinguish hope for the future. All of us, like the stars, carry a message," he said. "You aren't the only sign. But the eyes of Gad El Glas are trained upon you because of your lineage. That demon will act on your greatest fear, hoping to you never realize that what you carry inside has the power to defeat it."

Maura tried to pinpoint her worst fear. She'd had so many since that night when she'd held Nicolaus' lifeless body. Her courage had been pummeled in countless ways. She wanted to argue, but Aiden pointed at something on a ledge above them and reached for the scroll. "Shh. Stay here."

Maura froze, remembering the mountain lion she'd seen her first morning in Sanctuary. Aiden climbed off the horse, scroll extended.

"Be careful!" she said in a shrill whisper as he scaled a ledge several yards away near something that dangled above. Images blurred in fading light of a large cat lying in grassy stubble on a rocky plateau. Aiden crept closer until finally he stood over its dark shadow.

"He can't hurt us. He's dead," he said, motioning her over.

Maura climbed off the horse, tied its lead to the trunk of a young maple, and scurried up the rocky crag.

It was the carcass of a mountain lion with a long incision that began at the cat's throat and extended down its midsection. Something had ripped its body open from neck to belly.

"Not the work of any predator I've seen," he said, lightly fingering the precise cut. "Must've been something huge."

"A grizzly?"

"Too clean." He peered around at the sun now setting on the western horizon. "At least the cat won't be coming after us."

Maura shuddered and drew back. "It was stalking us."

His eyes scanned the ground around them, then the hill leading back in the direction they'd come from. After a moment, he said, "Can't be sure, but probably." He pointed out broken branches and trampled grass near its perch on the ledge.

She trembled even though it was warm. As they walked back to the horse, Maura stuck close to Aiden's side, wishing they could climb on and gallop far away. Far from beasts and demons and shadowy, yet all too real, threats.

They'd ridden a short way when she heard a melancholy hum, almost a melody that sounded above the canopy of trees. Maura chilled at its haunting tone. Suddenly, the horse reared. If Maura's hands hadn't already clenched Aiden's belly, she would've fallen off.

"Whoa, boy," Aiden murmured as the animal pranced nervously. He kept his voice low and gripped the reins as the horse whinnied and strained against his hold.

An enormous, winged creature soared overhead. Its

jagged talons stretched out from huge paws like knives. Power rippled across its lion-like chest and haunches.

The horse reared again and took off into a full gallop.

Aiden struggled to slow the breakneck charge to the plains ahead.

Maura held on with all her strength as they careened forward. She sneaked another look overhead and sucked in a breath. "It's a griffin!" she yelled.

"Hang on. We're getting out of here." Aiden let the horse run freely into open range.

The griffin rose and flew away. When it disappeared, the horse slowed to a stop and pawed the ground, calming only a little at Aiden's gentle command.

Maura trembled, her hands still in a death grip around his waist. "It doesn't matter that it's flown away. A griffin has the vision of an eagle. It's seen us."

Aiden guided the horse to the canopy of a towering oak. They watched with awe under its shelter as the griffin circled above a nearby gorge, then dove into a crevice in the mountain's granite wall. It emerged on a narrow cliff and scrutinized the horizon with a keen gaze. Then turned to them with unflinching eyes.

Would the griffin tear them to pieces with his immense talons? She'd heard tales of riddles offered to travelers—and certain death if they were unable to answer. The griffin made no move in their direction. It watched them, as if guarding treasure inside that crevice. Its giant hind legs were motionless.

"There must be gold nearby," she said, unable to take her eyes from its majestic form. "Griffins can spot veins of ore. Benjamin told me they mine it from rocky places using strong beaks and claws."

Aiden gripped the reins as the horse pranced in fear, then continued along the cover of dense forest. The griffin was in flight again. Its shadow swooped low, staying just behind them as the sun set. They traveled closer and closer to Sanctuary, and the danger it held. There should've been evidence of Lilith, especially now as they neared her domain.

No one snuck through the trees, no arrows sped from the woods beside them. What had killed the mountain lion that had stalked them for miles? And yet, wherever they stopped, ate a quick bite, or let the horse graze, the griffin was in sight. Not too close, but near enough that Maura wondered if it was protecting instead of pursuing.

****

SIR TAYLOR

Finally. The woman and her companion are in sight, proving their stupidity by riding back toward Sanctuary. Much has been going on in the city since their ill-fated flight. There are rumblings of an uprising that stem from disgruntled occupants of the tenements. An unlikely analogy occurs to me, especially considering the Council's intended response to these two rebels.

Maura O'Donnell's uncle once explained gardening as the work of an artist. His canvas was on the earth with living plants as his brush. I understood that in my inventions. Each one began with a thought, then grew in detail as I gave it time and attention. The finished work became far more than I envisioned in the beginning.

There's another parallel in gardening that I've seen in Sanctuary. An uprising of discontent can result in much needed pruning. Broken, diseased branches must be removed. Their weakness is expunged for the good of all. Even healthy limbs must be severed to make room for the most growth possible. Pruning is nature's way to ensure plentiful growth and abundant profit.

If an insurrection arises, some will die. The city will grow, however, and continue to flourish. The more time I spend here, the more I'm in awe of Anton and Lilith Gunter. Their gracious wisdom, strength of purpose, and unyielding devotion to the tenets of Sanctuary are nothing short of heroic. Let no one be deceived, though. This city will surpass its archaic structure as a refuge. And become so much more.

Maura O'Donnell isn't a demon. I know that. Her death won't be enough to fill the gaping hole of my loss. But it is necessary. Her execution will serve justice, as well as an order of the universe that requires judgment without mercy.

Chapter 23

It was mid-morning when they finally approached Sanctuary's borders and headed in the direction of the tenements. Maura leaned her cheek against Aiden's back as they passed the burned-out hollow that had been the factory. A blackened spire of the once towering chimney stood askance against a pile of scorched bricks. Tiny crosses lined the river's shoreline, crafted out of scraps of timber from the building that had taken young lives. One of the enormous gears that propelled yard after yard of cotton thread stood alone.

The factory would be re-built. Its location was perfect, near a river that powered its machinery and endless spindles of fiber. The crosses reminded anyone who passed by that innocent blood was its foundation. Young lives would not be forgotten. Maura had watched the set of a father's jaw, his clenched fists and the anguish of a mother rocking the still body of her child. Rebellion smoldered beneath those ashes.

Maura and Aiden had only ridden a short distance from the ruins when they heard singing in the air and the voices of children at play. She remembered Rory's face and the fear etched in his starburst eyes. Maybe she'd only imagined what she'd seen. As they rode nearer, unmistakable sounds and sights of a festival appeared.

Towering poles with ribbons of shimmering fabric rippling in the breeze stood in the market square, now bustling with vendors. With all that had been happening, she'd forgotten it was May Day, the holiday she'd celebrated in the village every year she could remember.

They dismounted, and Aiden secured the horse to a post and watering trough. He waved at friends who'd gathered in the marketplace. Children weaved in and out each other's arms in a festive dance. But something was wrong. This wasn't like any May Day she'd ever enjoyed. Adults appeared to be standing guard instead of enjoying a party. There were no cozy groups of friends who chatted. No one sat on nearby benches. Instead, most stood with crossed arms and grim faces. Now and then, a parent stole furtive glances toward the area of the crowd closest to the children.

One of the bystanders looked familiar.

Maura had seen him before. He was a guard at the Hall of Justice. She recognized another who stood across the square. Neither was dressed in uniform but in the simple homespun of tenement dwellers. Maura clutched Aiden's arm.

"Those two are Council guards."

"I know. Stay close."

A small straggler from the group of children chased a mongrel puppy down the street and into an alley. The little girl screamed as one of the guards grabbed her and carried her away. Her mother ran after them, shouting. "Stop him!

The woman's scream seemed to charge the atmosphere.

Soldiers appeared from alleys, from abandoned buildings, and from behind storefronts.

Caged wagons barreled down the main road and from side paths. Men with no identifying marks as

Council guards grabbed children and tossed them inside, then fought off parents who chased after the wagons with desperate cries.

This was no celebration. It was a set-up. Lilith had used the holiday to target the children. And to bring Maura out of hiding.

Aiden ran to a small rise in the center of the crowd and shouted commands.

Suddenly, an army of tenement dwellers came into formation. No longer a wailing rabble, adult after adult stood side by side, ready to take back the children who belonged to them.

"Don't fear them," Aiden said, shouting above the chaos. "You aren't alone! Your friends and families are here. Take your places. This attack won't go unanswered."

Maura watched in amazement as Aiden directed small groups of men and women to rush toward the carts of children. They'd been preparing for this. With Aiden at the helm.

Team after team overwhelmed caged wagons.

One of the drivers slowed to push away the crowd that swarmed his perch. Two men overtook him, tossed away his weapon, and dragged him off the cart. Others wielded metal bars that broke the lock and forced the cage door open, releasing the children, who scurried away and were whisked into nearby homes.

Ahead, other carts were overtaken, and their drivers bound and hauled away. Men scaled the cages of children, who jumped up and down, cheering them on as more locks were broken and doors opened.

Maura watched as the army of parents and friends united in a common goal. And it was working. Cart after cart was plundered of its precious cargo, and children ran into the arms of loved ones. She jumped in to help them. Maura had just handed another child into the arms of a woman when a fresh surge of guards pressed in from behind.

Aiden didn't notice them. He'd taken a stand on a large rock on one side of the road, and examined the scene like a general overseeing his ranks. He lifted his hand and pointed in one direction, then shouted to another group of men, alerting them to children still locked inside a cart.

Maura ran toward him, fighting the crush of people. She had to warn him.

The soldiers advanced closer, but Aiden remained unaware of their presence.

"Aiden! Behind you," Maura shouted, pushing through bodies and side-stepping fistfights that had broken out.

A soldier intent on retaking his wagon stuck his boot out and tripped her. She tumbled and crashed against the cobbled stones. Brushing herself off, she rose, determined to get to Aiden, even if she had to crawl.

She'd almost made it to the side of pavement outside the central conflict. Hiking up her pant legs she prepared to sprint the final yards between her and Aiden. To her horror, she watched as soldiers came from behind Aiden and hurled a metal net over his tall frame, dragging him to the ground. He fought to loose himself, but couldn't.

Someone grabbed Maura from behind. She'd twirled around to fight when a hard blow smacked the back of her head. Her legs tottered, and she fell to the hard pavement where darkness overtook vision and she fought to stay conscious.

Minutes later, Maura peered up from the pavement and rubbed her eyes She searched the perimeter for any trace of Aiden's red curls or rallying voice.

Commotion in an alley tucked away from the chaos yards away caught her attention. There he was, fighting a contingent of soldiers who tossed him, struggling, into one of the armored wagons.

The driver snapped his whip, and the horse charged away.

She dashed after them. "Stop! Stop that wagon!"

The bedlam that raged around her swallowed her words. The wagon angled through alleys and connected to the main road far above the center of warfare.

Maura sprinted after plumes of dust that rose behind the wagon. It took a sharp turn toward the glittering dome of the Hall of Justice and disappeared. She fell to the ground in despair. And heard someone call her name.

"Maura. Maura O'Donnell." It was the same voice that had chased a crow like vermin from her shop. She was only a few feet from the apothecary shop and her friend, Hildegard.

The little woman beckoned, waving her arms like a small bird trying to take flight. "Oi, beloved. Hurry."

How could Maura bring her aged friend into this catastrophe?

"*Now!*" Hildegard said, hands on her hips.

Maura forced herself upright. She checked her surroundings to be sure there no soldiers who watched nearby. Then ran toward her tiny friend.

Hildegard hurried her inside and bolted the door shut. Familiar peace of this orderly universe greeted her as soon as she crossed the threshold. The old woman wrapped wiry arms around Maura as she melted into her embrace.

"Aiden. He was taken." Maura stared at the door in terror. "And I can't stay. I'll only put you in danger."

"Nonsense. Were the shawl a help for ye?" Hildegard helped her take a seat on a tottering stool, then dragged another one over for herself.

"It's been a blessing over and over. It can't hide me from what's to come, though. I have to confront Lilith. Alone."

"Why alone, my dear?" Hildegard stood to prepare tea in the ancient china teapot. She added biscuits from a metal container on a small plate. "Ye must be starvin'."

Maura's head ached, and her belly was empty. The stink of her clothing surely drifted over to her friend, but Hildegard seemed not to notice as she laid the plate of biscuits in front of her.

Maura's breathing slowed a little, and she took the cup of tea with a nod of thanks. "I can't endanger anyone else. She's searching for me." Taking a biscuit, she was tempted to stuff it all in her mouth. She forced herself to take a bite, chew, then finish before she reached for another.

Hildegard sang a lilting tune, crooning softly with her hands extended to Maura.

"Though an enemy builds its shelters on high and sets its nests among the stars, she who carries the light of stars will find and bring them down."

Maura cried as she recognized the words of her prophecy, set to a tune in her tiny friend's quivering voice. "You know the prophecy?"

"Aye, me dear." Hildegard took a seat beside her.

"Why didn't you tell me?"

"Ye carry its heart. Except ye can't do it alone. We

who love you don't make you smaller. We be part of help when helpin's needed." Hildegard took a sip of her own tea, as if they had all the time in the world for this quiet moment together. "What do ye have that Lilith fears?" she asked simply. "Will ye face an enemy with no weapons? Think. Receive peace and think."

Even though Aiden didn't have his own scroll, he understood it. Her scroll in his hands had rescued them from Lilith. It was a treasure, even though she didn't know how to use it. Hildegard's shawl had been a shelter, too, except it wasn't hers. They were both mystical pieces of ordinary that became supernatural help.

"I don't understand. I've had help from you and Aiden. Which weapon truly belongs to me?"

Hildegard stood and pulled a linen gown out of a closet tucked away in one wall and placed it on a nearby table. Maura sighed with relief at the sight of a clean dress. Hildegard placed a withered hand on her shoulder. "Are not your eyes meant to see?"

Rory's eyes had been a warning. She'd seen correctly. If she hadn't been aggravated at Aiden and closed her own eyes only to prove him wrong, she wouldn't have seen the fear in Rory's. She and Aiden would still be at the chateau. Her foresight and Aiden's quick action had averted the worst of Lilith's attack against the children.

One question haunted her. Why hadn't she gotten to Aiden in time? Once again, her gift had failed one she loved. She took a sip of tea, grateful for its warm comfort and gazed into Hildegard's eyes. The little woman sat expectantly, as if she knew what Maura was about to discover. An image danced in those piercing eyes. It was the picture of a little girl.

"Who is she, Hildegard? The one I see."

"Aye, ye see well. She be me own daughter. T'were the fever that took her. Me shop—it were me, seekin' fer answers to a mystery. Now 'tis a weapon in me hands. Not fer evil, but fer good."

No wonder Maura saw worlds in the woman's eyes. "You are Magi?"

"Indeed. And I be watchin' for ye."

"You knew I'd come?"

"I hoped ye'd come. Mysteries, they don't stop a person. Fear, anger, they be like bile in yer belly. They be tying a rope around ye, keepin' ye from bloomin'. Be free, child. Be free to go with eyes that see. Not perfect. But enough to guide others."

She handed Maura the fresh gown and led her to a room at the back of the shop where, a basin of water and a towel rested on a small table. Maura peeled off the foul-smelling clothing and laid Hildegard's shawl carefully on a cot. By the time she'd washed and changed, her strength had returned.

She walked back into the shop and draped the shawl carefully over the shoulders of her dear friend. Its threads glimmered with a myriad of vibrant streams, alive with light. Maura wasn't surprised. The shawl shone as it was intended on the one called to carry its gift.

Somehow, Maura's gift would shine too. It had been prepared for her, as certainly as the shawl had been designed for Hildegard's thin shoulders. It had waited for its owner, and then swirled with delight that it was home again. If soldiers came to question Hildegard, the shawl would find a way to protect her.

And of course, there was the broom.

"Good-bye for now." Maura wrapped her arms

around Hildegard and kissed her cheek. "I'm returning the shawl to its owner, for I know my weapon. And will use it."

Hildegard held her tightly for a moment. "Be keepin' our girl, Abba. Be keepin' her safe," she said, whispering a prayer.

After another quick squeeze, Maura headed outside, onto the main road she knew so well. She sprinted up the steep incline just beyond the tenements. A group of soldiers blocked the road with drawn swords. One of them saw her and shouted.

"Stop there. Now."

She couldn't run. They were too close, and there were too many of them. She'd have to figure something out. "I was held against my will," she said as one of the men approached. "I'm a refugee, a friend of the Gunter's."

The soldier studied her with a bewildered gaze. "You're like no refugee I've seen."

Although she'd changed into the clean, homespun dress, she was hardly a picture of gentility.

Another guard pulled her aside and searched her face. "Aye, she's the one. She lives with the Gunters. Seize her." Swords enclosed her in a tight circle. One soldier reached out to grab her, but she dodged through a tiny opening at his side.

The whistle of a sword sounded behind her. Thankful for the gown's ample room to move, she scaled a neighbor's fence and landed in his manicured backyard. Standing, Maura studied the surroundings.

A stone wall ran along the back of the yard with a thatch of woods beyond it. She'd duck back into the cover of forest and escape the guards. The area was deserted. She crouched on top of the broad stones and jumped to the ground, ready to sprint.

Soldiers rushed from a line of dense shrubbery, where they'd been hiding. Rough hands grasped her arms, her waist. They half-carried, half dragged her to a familiar wraparound porch with wicker chairs that was only a block away.

Lilith stood at the door dressed in a deep violet silk gown. The emerald pendant around her neck glistened in the sunlight. She smiled broadly, as if welcoming Maura home after a long absence.

"Why attack the children?" Maura cried. "I'm the one you want."

Lilith's beauty was marred only by a look of mocking conquest. "You're in no position to ask anything, dearest." The woman motioned her inside. "Come. We'll have tea. Guards, leave us. Now."

The guards untangled Maura from their grasp and backed away.

Maura stood upright, refusing to cower to Lilith. They walked into the parlor, where Lilith had welcomed her that first day. The same place she and Tobias had made plans for the trial. And become friends. Memories of what the Gunters offered as shelter filtered through her mind. Sweet, but only fantasy. This home had never been a refuge. Only a trap.

Lilith sat primly in the velvet settee and motioned Maura to take the other, as if this were an ordinary teatime. "You could've joined me, avoided all this." As she extended her hands, a vision of Rory huddled with other children, caged, and crying, appeared on the wall.

Maura stared at the image. Was it true or only a subterfuge of the dark arts to shatter her courage? Nona would be in anguish without Rory. The children were alone and afraid. Her heart filled with bitter anger. "You brought me here to use me. Why?"

"I've demonstrated my love for you in countless ways." Lilith spoke as if she appealed to Maura's better reasoning. Or corrected an errant child. "Why did you turn against us? If you had only cooperated."

"Fie! You remember that day at the park when we met the woman and her child. That child had my eyes. He was a Magi child. Like me when you raided our chateau home. Turn against you? I've learned who you are. And what you've done."

"Have you now." Lilith settled her tea on its saucer and placed her hands on her lap. "It was *your* disobedience that brought you to this place and to your fate—so unlike the one I'd prepared for you."

"*You* only prepared a trap."

"Indeed. You have a rebellious streak. If you'd obeyed your father instead of appearing in the meadow against his warning…"

Maura stopped short. Lilith had no way of knowing about her father's edict to never go outside alone. What else had the woman divined about her?

"It was your fault that your parents and friends were killed," Lilith said. "You defied orders. Even as you have since you arrived here by ignoring small requests we asked of you in our home. We warned you to stay within our protection."

"If I'd stayed in your home, I'd never have seen the tenements or how the children suffer." Maura's body shook. "Or known that it was you who killed my parents, along with all the others at the chateau."

"*You* brought about their destruction," Lilith said,

unmoved. "*You* set forces of the universe in motion. Even the stars you claim to love remain in the place ordained for them. Once those laws are violated, all the universe suffers."

Guilt crept over Maura like a blanket soaked and prepared to suffocate her.

Mottled sunlight flickered through a towering window. How could it shine on such an evil day? *Not enough*. The words screamed in her ears and banged on her heart. Not enough knowledge, not enough strength, not enough time to stop Lilith intent on destroying another generation of Magi children.

"Mama said I'd teach others to live by the light of the stars," Maura said, pressing against the shadow of guilt. "Those words weren't platitudes. They were spoken by a mother as she said good-bye to me, her daughter."

"You're certainly one to teach others. You who are accused of murdering your young charge by neglect—a fine nanny you turned out to be." Lilith mocked her with each accusation, jabbing Maura's heart over and over. "How will you teach anyone? Besides, your mother sent you away. Wouldn't a loving mother accompany her child? And your father. Where was he?" Lilith's chin jutted up. "They sent you packing, unwilling to risk the others' lives. They placed children who weren't their own above you. You were too much trouble. You'd brought all this calamity to their doorstep."

"No. They…"

An ebony spired temple appeared in Maura's mind. Its darkness was broken only by jagged torchlight that beamed on a jewel-encrusted throne where a demon sat, leering at something.

She sought out the focus of those glittering yellow eyes. A young girl dressed in a purple dress with a dingy white sash, torn and ragged. Her eyes were wide in terror, but she straightened her back and lifted her chin. Her small hands clenched into fists, and ebony curls bounced with nervous energy. Planting small feet on the stone ground, she refused to budge until a man who stood nearby struck her with a blow that hurtled her to the floor. She felt into a crumpled heap, head bouncing off the ground.

A dark figure dressed in ceremonial robes and a turban walked toward her and the man with a pouch of golden coins extended. The man grabbed them and ran out, slamming gigantic doors with a crash.

Maura watched as the child became a woman dressed in a scarlet gown, her slender neck and head lifted proudly. Raven hair circled her head like a crown. Charcoal rimmed her dark eyes, and crimson stained her lips. She bowed, arms outstretched, to the fiend on its throne. A blaze shot from tentacled fingers, and an emerald pendant circled her slender neck in an unbroken interchange.

Ghoulish imps squealed and howled with glee as she took her place on a throne beside the demon.

Maura's tears flowed at the images. She'd seen vision of Lilith as a child. And what led to the woman she'd become. She trembled in pity. "You were…sold."

Chapter 24

Lilith's body twitched—only a little. Her lips pressed against her teeth. She adjusted her posture. "I was purchased. As a prize."

"You were sold." Maura tasted her own tears. She wondered if that moment in the temple was the last time Lilith had cried.

"I was prepared," she said simply.

"By terror and abuse?"

"You wouldn't know, would you, precious Maura? Loved all your life. Born, not initiated into your destiny. So pure, so innocent—so blind. You who should see."

Maura knew Lilith was right. She'd never treasured her own gift. Until now. "Your power is fueled by the fiend that captured you as an innocent little girl. Is that why you're always after children? Acting in behalf of the one you represent?"

"Not just any children." Lilith sneered with chilling certainty. "Magi children. Undefiled—and full of power yet to be unveiled. Like treasure waiting to be discovered. Like this scroll that arrived many years ago."

Lilith held up a rolled parchment like a trophy. It wasn't Maura's. Its cover wasn't the shade of midnight when the stars shone brightest. This one, wrapped in simple linen, emanated warmth that reached Maura and melted what had begun as a slow freeze around her heart.

"Whose…?" There was only one other she knew of.

It was Aiden's. "Stolen," she said, outraged. "Taken from the chateau after the massacre *you* led. You're a murderer *and* a thief. Were you hoping it would work for you? That its magic would become yours."

"I am a collector of sorts. I recognize what is often unnoticed or unused by others and take them as my own. That collection has made me very rich and powerful. Too bad you didn't know your mother. Or yourself. It's too late, of course. Always too late. Besides, I don't have to hope. The scroll is mine."

"Surely you don't need a scroll," Maura said, railing back. "You already offered yourself to that monster. And for what?"

"Power you've never known. Although you could. You have the capacity." Lilith straightened her shoulders and smirked. "Some are born into what they never receive. I, however, paid for my place. Admit it. You have what you never worked for. And therefore despise. I earned the power I carry. It was a high price but worth its cost."

What had seemed free for most of Maura's life had come with the incalculable cost of her parents and their loved ones at the chateau.

"I was willing to share my command," Lilith said. "You refused it."

"You don't need me under your dominion." Maura felt courage rise. "Or perhaps you want me to become like you, powerless against those who lust for my gift."

Lilith drew back her arm and then extended it. A blade shot from her hand into the wall in front of them. "I'll show you power."

Maura saw Benjamin, propelled by an invisible arm, and pinned against a wall beside the children. She struggled to keep her body still and refused to react with the horror Lilith watched for, expectantly. Was it really him or only an apparition? His skin hung in yellow pallor. But his loving eyes—it was Benjamin.

"Don't bow, Maura," he pleaded. "Her authority is fueled by your fear. The scroll won't operate in her hands. Trust it."

She turned to Lilith and straightened her shoulders. "You've lied to me. Over and over. What do you want?"

"I want your ability to see. You don't use it."

"It isn't mine to give."

"Then watch him die." Lilith shot both hands forward, and a metal band gripped Benjamin's neck. He contorted in pain, struggled, then slumped against the wall.

"No!" Maura lunged at Lilith as guards burst into the room.

****

SIR TAYLOR

Apprehended. The woman went to Lilith Gunter herself, according to Anton. Returned to the home that had coddled her as she'd awaited a trial she didn't deserve. Of course, she was speedily dispatched to prison. Now, her end will come.

Anton kept me abreast of a seditious uprising that recently occurred in the tenements. People died. Children were taken. Unfortunate, but as I said earlier, necessary pruning in a culture that is called to move into a new identity.

I've waited so long to face Maura O'Donnell, to see justice finally overtake the injustice of her actions. A certain amount of dread has crept in now that her execution is imminent, of course. Abigail would not have wanted to witness this event. I'm built of stronger stuff.

It will be a spectacle, they say. Always effective for teaching purposes. Band people together in a common hatred, even in supposed fear, and they'll rise as a force to accomplish whatever is desired. Reason is not required. A few people filled with indignant rage move like wildfire to become a force for change.

Nicolaus will finally be avenged. I can't anticipate how that will feel. Abigail once told me that forgiveness was more powerful than revenge. Untrue. Payment must be required when something is stolen. Even though no recompense exists that will bring back my son.

Chapter 25

The Hall's dome glittered in midday sun. Instead of escorting Maura up the long flight of stairs, the guards led her to a timbered doorway in the back of the building. Two soldiers waited at the entrance with torches as another unlocked the door, which creaked open to darkness. Only light from outside revealed cells that lined both sides of a long corridor.

On one side, an old man squinted, his weathered hands grasping metal bars of a cell. Stench hit Maura's belly, and she knelt to vomit on the dirt floor. One of the soldiers cursed and jerked her back to her feet as she wiped her mouth with one hand. Jagged splotches of torchlight lit the hallway as she searched for Aiden. Instead, a gathering of small faces appeared in one of the cells. Children who hadn't been rescued by his ragtag army of heroes. They were strangely quiet, their eyes wide and afraid. She reached out to them, but strong hands grasped her tighter and dragged her away.

Was Aiden here, hidden somewhere? Would he know she was a prisoner like himself? Metal doors clacked open, and she was pushed into a cell, where she landed hard on the floor. The solitary lights bounced away and were snuffed out when the door clamped shut.

Darkness became a thick mantle that overtook Maura's senses. She struggled to breathe. No light. No sky. Only the tiny scurrying of unseen creatures and a deafening heartbeat in her ears that shouted she was dying. Sweat poured from her body despite the dank cell, and she panted for breath. A pinpoint in her vision grew into a tunnel and swallowed her, squeezing life out of her chest. "Papa! Help me."

The prison cell became a closet hidden behind a wall in her childhood bedroom. Once again Papa had bundled her into a faded blanket and placed her inside the narrow cupboard, where she couldn't move and struggled to breathe. Once again, terror screamed in her gut as she remembered the sound of boots pounding the wooden floor of her room. Time suspended as she slipped in and out of consciousness, struggling to hang on to the reality that she was no longer a child.

After what could have been minutes or hours, the doors of her cell flung open, and a light quivered overhead. She tried to muster strength to fight but was too weak. Defeat made her cower against the wall. A man with black hair that gleamed in the light of another torch walked toward her. He spoke softly as he approached, as though he came to tend a wounded animal.

"Beautiful Maura."

Tobias placed the torch on a ledge and lowered himself in his immaculate suit to the floor that reeked of pain and captivity. "My chair misses you, sweet friend," he said. "Your feet, that is." He wrapped his arm around her shoulders and drew her close. "You know why I was so angry now. I wanted to protect you from this." She felt his breath against her forehead, smelled the familiar scent that, unlike his appearance, was somehow wild and unfettered.

"I have answers to your questions. Finally." He

settled against the wall behind them. "Are the tenements dangerous? No. Those who feared what you discovered there were the real threat. The Council knew you. So did Lilith. I hoped to shield you, to come to trial and see you returned home safely. Once home, I believed you'd find for yourself what happened to Nicolaus." He sighed. "Instead, I failed miserably."

"No, no," she said, her voice small as if she were still that child in Papa's cupboard. She tried again. "You've been a true advocate. And friend. This wasn't your fault." Her terror slinked away in his presence. Her breathing calmed, and the chill that had overtaken her core retreated.

Tobias crooned to her softly, as if cajoling an injured bird to rise despite a broken wing. "You've been my light in the darkness, Maura O'Donnell. I'm still your guardian." He let out a strangled cough but stayed crouched in the filth beside her.

"You've been my advocate in the finest way." She mustered the strength to utter one word. "Benjamin?"

Tobias shook his head and looked away.

"What will happen to me?" she asked.

In the flickering light from above, his slender manicured hands covered his face. Lifting his head, he spoke with a low voice. "An exhibition by Council standards and for its purposes. One that will enthrall their audience with its pomp and pageantry."

"How will I die?"

Tobias bowed his head, his chest heaving.

Maura placed her hand on his arm. "Sometimes refuge appears where we least expect it," she said, reaching up to touch the scar on his perfect face. He'd been hurt, too. "You've been a shelter for me. One with the face of Orion."

Tobias tightened his hold on her, and she rested against the impeccable black suit and the tender heart it concealed. They sat together until a soldier appeared and commanded him to leave. Tobias squeezed her arm one more time. "I'll be there, Maura O'Donnell. Remember what you said about flying free? I'm planning to do just that. Not in the way you've known me, but in a form that was taken from me. One that might surprise you at first. It won't take long, though. You'll recognize me as you remember our journey.

"Then again, you'll know me. I'm your friend. And remain your guardian, no matter what the cost."

He left as quickly as he'd arrived. Another figure carrying a torch took his place and something brushed her arm. Maura jerked away, surprised to see gauzy white fabric flutter to the ground beside her. Adele, the maid from the Gunter home, stood next to one of the guards.

Maura tried to rise to her feet and greet the young woman. "Adele," she said in a voice that wavered with a thread of hope.

Adele was dressed in finery. No longer in servant's garb, she wore an elaborate gown the color of rubies. Multicolored streamers flowed from each sleeve, and a garland rested on her blond curls, which were no longer hidden by a prim scarf. "Put the dress on," she said, pointing at the gown beside Maura. Timid Adele was gone. This young woman had only scorn in her voice. "If ye knows what's good fer ye."

Maura touched the dress, lingering on the softness of its fabric. It was clean. Too clean for a ravaged body like hers. She recognized it, though. It was the one Lilith had pulled out of her closet when she'd offered to prepare Maura for trial. The gown was sent to mock her, to remind Maura of her defeat. It didn't matter how she presented herself. She would still die.

"I sed put it on. And be quick." Adele kicked a daintily shod toe into her thigh, and Maura yelped. She pulled herself to her knees, clutching the dress. Then stood to face the wall as she removed the linen gown that Hildegard had given her and slipped the white one over her head. It drifted to the ground over her worn shoes.

Adele's hand yanked her around so hard that Maura's neck whipped backward. She led her behind the guards and down the corridor where she'd entered only hours before. This time, her fellow prisoners weren't silent as she passed their cells. Little voices chimed in with the croaking voices of men who'd been held in the darkness for who knew how long.

One said, "Arise, Maura O'Donnell, you who carry the light of stars."

A guard smashed the cell bars with a metal baton. "Silence!"

When the door opened to daylight, Maura winced. Her eyes gradually adjusted to see hundreds of people gathered outside the amphitheater. Guards parted the thickly packed crowd as Adele paraded Maura through the middle of them. "Child murderer, conspirator, fugitive from the law of High Council," she yelled in a shrill voice.

A boot shot out and bashed Maura's calf. Brown, gooey spittle landed on one of the pristine sleeves of her gown. When she finally made it through an entrance, Adele thrust her into the arms of guards, who hauled her down ragged granite steps into the amphitheater.

A festival was in full swing, with revelry all around. Jugglers in scarlet leggings tossed balls into the air amid the happy squeals of children. Young women danced in slow circles waving emerald flags. A choir of children's voices lilted in a song she'd heard her first morning in Sanctuary, *Shine bright, Oh, Star of the Morning*. Aiden had said they learned it on the laps of their mamas, little knowing their song touted a demon that lusted for their young lives.

Buglers marched in and lined upper rows of the seats, sounding their trumpets. Their call signaled the opening of entrances around the perimeter of the massive stadium. Maura glanced into the faces of spectators who poured in from every passage. Some spewed abuse, although most ignored her while activities spun around them like a carnival merry-go-round. Had Colonel Perry and his wife already taken their seats, prepared to enjoy the show?

Adele led the way to the center of the arena, head lifted high and hips swinging in an exaggerated sashay that announced her newfound importance. The soldiers half-carried, half-dragged Maura between them. Her feet trailed along sandy soil in a circular arena, where a stage had been designed for the big event—her execution. Her legs were limp, and she tried to lean against one of the guards for support. He shoved her toward a metal stake in the middle while another tied her hands around it with stiff rope that chafed her broken skin.

Maura faced the ornate thrones that had been placed in a semi-circle with a dais in the middle. Between the thrones and herself, she saw a well. Its stone walls extended in a circular lip above the ground. A massive serpent engraved in bronze covered its opening. Raised as if ready to strike, the brazen serpentine head stared at Maura through onyx eyes. Wisps of dark smoke twirled around its edges.

A battalion of men uniformed in crimson marched in to beating drums that signaled a shift in the pageantry. The festivities, which were indeed a dazzling spectacle, only caused Maura to tremble, wondering how she would soon become its featured entertainment. She tried to stretch her arms but was able to move only a few inches. Peering around the arena, she searched for Tobias.

Instead of her advocate, white-robed Council members led by Anton Gunter filed in and took seats at the thrones. Sir Taylor arrived with great pomp in his scarlet cloak and sat next to Anton, proving what she'd already known, that her accuser had a place of influence with the Council. He'd even been promoted to a throne for the occasion.

Tobias walked in last, alone, noble and distinguished, as always. He nodded to her as he stood to one side of the thrones.

The crowd quieted as Anton Gunter rose from his throne. Thrusting his chest forward, he strode toward the center of the stage, his bulldog countenance full of bravado. He pointed at Maura and made a broad twirl as he gestured to the masses of people. "We're here in what would have been a trial determining the innocence or guilt of Maura O'Donnell. That question has been answered by her behavior. She ran, like a coward, from the home and family who sheltered her. She was a fugitive from a law set in place for generations, a law promising sanctuary until a fair trial can be offered.

"Miss O'Donnell refused this noble system. She

betrayed her host family and slandered our fair city, accusing us of abusing children we so diligently protect. She is therefore sentenced by the Council to die."

Maura's thoughts felt like a line of yarn, frayed, and tangled. She'd known the rules of Sanctuary. She knew she'd die if she was caught, especially after she and Aiden fled the city. Now, death had become a certain reality with no more delay.

Nothing in her mind could grasp it. She feared the pain of dying. Even worse was the loss of those she'd leave behind. Benjamin, the only father she'd really known. Aiden, or Paddy, her childhood friend who had become so much more. Nona, Rory, Hildegard. No good-bye, no thanks for all they'd been to her. And Tobias. She'd never see him fly free, whatever that meant. An end stood before her. And she had no idea what that meant.

The crowd stomped their feet, shook their fists, and applauded in such unity that they appeared to have been trained to do so. The towering waterfall spilled miles away like a spectacular backdrop.

Anton gestured broadly toward an entrance laden with flowers, where a company of young women dressed in silken dresses waved emerald banners emblazoned with a writhing serpent. "Welcome our beloved benefactor, Star of Darkness and choice representative of the divine presence, Gad El Glas," he called. "She reigns as queen—not only of this city, but over our known world. Bow before her."

Lilith made a triumphant entrance wearing a white gown overlaid with lace and pearls. A glittering crown rested on raven curls, and the emerald pendant circled her neck.

A sea of dancers parted, and the celebration paused again as she walked to Maura with the smile of a predator approaching its prey. The whole crowd, as if on cue, bowed when she came to a stop in front of Maura.

One of the guards slashed the ropes that tied Maura to the stake. "Bow," he said, slapping his sword against her back. Maura collapsed in pain. She tottered once as she rose and stood, feet planted, refusing to bow.

The squadron drew their weapons.

Lilith held up her hand. "I'll deal with her." As the soldiers withdrew, she turned toward Council members, swept her hand toward the vast arena of spectators, and pointed to Maura. "I've heard it said that our fugitive has supernatural powers."

A murmur of anticipation sounded from the crowd.

"In the true spirit of Gad El Glas, I've determined that we'll hold a special exposition. One reserved for a sworn enemy of this city and all we represent."

Shouts of approval and applause roared around them. Lilith whirled her gown and bent to whisper in Maura's ear. "You're forgotten, my dear," she hissed. "With only death as your shining moment."

Lilith backed away and gestured toward the circular well, where a half a dozen soldiers struggled to lift the heavy bronze cover, uncovering a pit lined in obsidian and frothing with plumes of dense smoke.

Lilith's lips spread into a victorious smile. "In holes you have hidden. In a hole you will die."

Chapter 26

Maura shuddered as she stared into the narrow pit. Abandoned to inky blackness, alone, as her life ebbed away. Lilith knew her greatest fear. She'd fueled it with every night-time raid against Maura's childhood home at the chateau. The terror of being encased in tomb-like darkness had been etched into her very being. This execution was designed just for her. In doing so, Gad El Glas provided a lesson for all to witness.

Unexplainable courage rose inside her. "Are your own children safe?" Maura shouted to the crowd, her voice almost swallowed in the din. "Will the lust of Gad El Glas be satisfied with Magi blood alone?"

There was no response, only distracted glances as the ceremony took on new furor. Dancers whirled, their colorful skirts spinning reds, yellows, and gold. Trumpets blew again, and Anton bowed to Lilith.

A company of black-robed priests stood at the entrance where Lilith had appeared. Two young boys dressed in white togas held censers in front of them as the priests stood as if they waited. Hall of Justice soldiers appeared from another doorway and walked into the amphitheater. Two of the men carried a child, who struggled against their grasp. Priests joined the soldiers and together, they walked toward Lilith.

A long, terrible wail came from someone in the crowd. A woman pushed and shoved her way from the spectators to the arena below. It was Nona, crying as she ran. "Rory! I'm coming."

People tried to restrain her, but she yanked herself out of each grasp and clambered over the dividing wall that separated her from the arena. Her feet barely touched the ground as she sprinted toward Rory. First two, then three, then ten soldiers tried to grapple her into the dirt, finally succeeding.

Lilith bent in a long, languid bow as the priests and soldiers approached with the boy. Agony flooded Maura's being and spilled out in a scream. "No!"

Rory's normally open and unafraid eyes were wide in fear. Just like the vision that had propelled her and Aiden back to Sanctuary. She'd thought the child's face had alerted them to the purge. Instead, it was for this moment. Lilith's timing was strategic, for now Maura was powerless to save him.

Rory tugged his small body against his captors and tried to reach out to her. She lunged toward him, but guards immediately dragged her away.

Anton Gunter bowed his stout torso and received Rory from the soldiers.

Lilith ascended a small platform that overlooked the pit and peered down in scorn at her husband.

Small and ugly, he trembled as he held the child's shoulders. His voice squeaked, then lowered in an obsequious tone as if prepared to lick her feet. "We present our best to Gad El Glas, and to you, Star of Darkness, his chosen."

Anton handed Rory to two soldiers, who positioned him near the pit and in front of Lilith. Lilith gazed at Rory with hungry eyes.

When the priests sounded a chant that rose and fell

with a haunting wail, Maura hurled herself toward them. "Stop! Now!"

One of the soldiers smacked her to the ground and jammed his boot into her back. A line of clouds passed over the sun. The sky darkened and the air chilled as a wind blew from the north.

Maura lifted her head and cried, "You can't do this. Let him go."

Fiendish delight covered Lilith's face. "Bring our enemy out of the dust to face me."

Maura felt the soldier's boot brush against her back, as if he hoped to bash her one more time. Rough hands pulled her upright.

"Not that it matters how you grovel, dear," Lilith said. "The child is mine. Why would I let him go?"

Maura reached for Rory again. Again, the guards yanked her away.

Lilith held out her hands as if hugging the air, mocking her. "Would you comfort him? Hold him, protect him from the inevitable? You've failed. In the ways you always knew you would."

Rory tried to appear brave, even through tears streaked his ruddy cheeks. He kept up his struggle against the soldiers' grasp. "Don't be afraid, miss. Don't be afraid, my Nona says."

Desperation flooded Maura at the sound of the child's courage. She held out her hands to Lilith. "Please. I'll do anything."

"Anything, you say? Wonderful." Lilith gestured before the priests, who'd formed a circle around the pit as if in wait for their sacrifice. "Bow before Gad El Glas. Offer your gift as a token of your worship.

"I won't. I'll never bow to it. Ever."

"As I expected. You may watch the child die—in your place." Lilith gestured toward the smoldering darkness of the pit. Her eyes were trained on Maura. "You should've kept hiding, you know. Should've stayed in the holes of your own making. Now, it's too late. Like it was for your mother."

"My mother?"

"Ah, she never told you about me. Never mind. Only know this. I saw her the night you were whisked away as a child into safety. I told her I'd find you. And I did."

Maura trembled.

Silence filled the amphitheater, as if everyone wanted to listen. Even Council members leaned in.

"I offered you an invitation. You ran, instead," Lilith said, shrugging. "Took the path of least resistance, like the mother who spawned you. You could've been part of us, shared in our power. This was so unnecessary."

"Share in this?" Maura pointed at Rory, whose chin quivered as he kept his head erect. "What kind of fiend makes a child pay for your hate?"

"One who understands what he carries."

Maura straightened her shoulders and took a step toward Lilith. "Take me. Take me, instead."

"That would be far too small a retribution. Besides, Star, are you not called to shine?" Lilith faced the audience with a flourish of her graceful arms. "She spouts her lies, hoping to delay our display of justice. Should we allow her to hinder the inevitable any longer?"

The *no* sounded in hundreds of voices, becoming a roar.

In a burst of strength, Maura wrested free of the guards, ran to Rory, and wrapped her arms around him, shielding his small body with her own.

The guards rushed forward, but Lilith motioned them away. Her laugh sounded like the cackling of a hen. "Let her comfort him now, while she can."

Lilith gestured toward Maura. "I've offered our enemy a choice. The child may live if she bows in reverence to Gad El Glas. If not, he must die. What kind of woman would sacrifice a child when she has the power to save him?" She faced Maura and pointed at the pit. "What is your answer, my dear?"

In the mass of nameless faces in the stands, Maura noticed a woman who held a child against one hip. She pumped one arm into the air, her mouth contorting with rage as the little one peered silently at his mother, caressing her face with tiny fingers. Another generation, another stream of sewage flowing into pristine waters. She searched for Tobias but couldn't find him near the Council members. She was alone.

"Where does this vile hatred come from?" Maura asked, crying out.

As if in answer, a picture rose in Maura's mind. Sunshine glistened on dewy grass near an ancient oak tree. Two sisters played with their parents in the courtyard of a magnificent castle. The older child had raven curls and wore a purple satin dress with a white sash tied in a perfect bow. She twirled with wild abandon. The other little girl, with a dimpled smile and hair the color of spun honey, was barely a toddler.

The older sister grappled one of the oak's low-hanging branches and swung back and forth, legs pumping against a breeze that ruffled leaves around her. She reached up to scale one tree limb, then another, climbing until she reached a granite wall around the courtyard. She scrambled onto the wall and crowed. "I am queen! Queen of the universe!"

There was something in the set of her chin. Maura searched Lilith with a question. "I saw a castle. And a family. Are you the child on the wall?"

Lilith sneered. "What else do you see, Star? Surely you won't miss the best part."

The crowd continued to howl, and Rory leaned into her body. He reached up to wipe her tears with a ragged sleeve. The sweetness of his gesture tore at her heart. She had to see, had to know for his sake. She closed her eyes, and the image returned.

As if not to be outdone, the toddler in her vision shook pudgy fingers free from her mother's grasp and staggered toward her father.

"Oliver! Judith is walking," said the mother, in delight.

The older sister crossed her arms and yelled down from her perch. "She can't climb a tree. She can't do this." With that, her raven curls along with the purple dress flipped upside down like a curtain, and her fingers splayed out on the wall in a perfect handstand.

Her parents missed the taunt, as well as the handstand. They were caught up with the little one's wobbly first steps. In a moment, the older sister no longer preened like a peacock from the courtyard wall. She was gone.

Maura shook her head in disbelief. The ebony hair and eyes, the set of her shoulders and tilt of her chin were a picture of a young Lilith. With a little sister named Judith. A royal family. She remembered the letter at the chateau addressed to her mother and the plea from her father, the king.

She whispered, her eyes wide. "It can't be. Not my sweet mother. How could you…?" Maura shivered at loathing that spewed, now unveiled from Lilith's eyes. "Why did you leave your family?"

The circle of black garbed priests hovered around the pit, chanting and scattering incense. Occasionally a blast of fire emanated from their hands.

"Why would I leave the family who so cherished me?" Lilith sputtered. Her lips quivered before the veneer of contempt reappeared. "I didn't leave. I was taken."

Maura remembered the temple with ebony spires and fiery altar. Lilith was the child she'd seen tossed at the feet of the priest. Now it was clear how she'd arrived there. Lilith had been lusted after, stolen away, and hidden beyond her family's earnest search. No one knew where she'd gone. Or why. Until she returned to exact revenge on the only family member left from that glorious morning turned to tragedy—her sister.

"No one came. Did you hear me?" Lilith words chilled the atmosphere around them. "No. One. Came."

"They tried. They never stopped trying to find you."

"No matter. Precious Judith. Jewel of our parents' eyes. Bearer of prophecy—like me. Only none of that mattered. Not when I was taken to the temple for *service*. Service, indeed. Until Gad El Glas chose me as standard bearer. It was worth the exchange."

The chanting of priests grew louder, and flames leapt from their censers. The crowd mimicked their frenzy, shouting and pounding their feet.

Rory stared up at Maura. His starburst eyes signaled another generation of Magi seers. What had Lilith said about an exchange? Suddenly, she understood. Turning to Lilith, she spoke what she'd never have believed before. "You're Magi, too."

Lilith lifted her chin and held up one hand as if to ward off Maura's declaration. "I renounced that disappointing lineage years ago." She turned toward the priests and bowed slightly. "I serve one who chose me instead of those who abandoned me. I received its power to rule over those who were too weak to save me or their own. I stand by Gad El Glas and against those who deserted me. The prophecy became mine in the end, anyway." Lilith held her arms to the sky and recited. "*Though an enemy builds its shelters on high and sets its nests among the stars, she who carries the light of stars will find and bring them down.*

"I searched for my enemy in a shelter built on high. Your family tucked you away there, hoping to keep you hidden. It wasn't hard to find my sister, though. Discover a refuge for children, and Judith wouldn't be far. What better way to make her suffer than to steal away the delight of her eyes—her own daughter? Like the sister her family never cared to pursue."

Council members sat on their thrones, intent on her and Lilith. Tobias was nowhere in sight. Maura wondered if they could hear their conversation. Were Lilith's revelations a surprise to them as well?

The priests increased their chants and whirled like frenetic crows in their black robes, inviting the presence of Gad El Glas.

Maura and Lilith remained locked in a world of the past through the eyes of a child who believed she'd been abandoned.

"My mother would never have harmed you," Maura said. "She laid down her place in the kingdom she was called to rule—with you. Instead, she took care of Magi children. The very ones you threaten. Why?"

"You. I wanted you, her greatest treasure. Nothing less." Lilith's eyes glittered with such venom that Maura quaked inside. "I made sure she knew. That night. I offered her a place by my side. She, being pathetic and stupid, refused it. I promised I'd find you and when I did, I'd corrupt her pure Magi blood and end that lineage forever. That's why you came to Sanctuary. It was my plan. And it worked."

"You killed Nicolaus with autumn crocus—a flower you knew I'd recognize." So many questions answered, in a scheme more evil than Maura had imagined.

"Sacrifices must be made," Lilith said, simply.

Sir Taylor shot up from his throne.

Lilith's face turned ashen. She must've forgotten how close the Council sat to the interchange between and her and Maura. Lilith spun around to face Sir Taylor who had risen to his feet and stood, frozen in place. She backed up a step, almost tripped, and righted herself.

Sir Taylor's gaze never left hers. His hands quivered, then clenched into fists at his sides. He turned to first one, then another of the Council members who sat nearby.

Maura couldn't hear the words he spoke to them, but no one responded.

The man turned back to Lilith and spoke in a low voice. "You killed my son?"

Lilith pointed at Maura. "Your enemy. She's the one."

"You said…" Sir Taylor strode toward Lilith.

Anton jumped up to stop him, but Sir Taylor pushed him away like a bear tossing aside a barking dog. Picking up his steps, he charged. In seconds, he was so close that Lilith drew back in fear.

Soldiers rushed to grapple the huge man before he was able to wrap burly hands around the woman's neck. More guards were summoned and joined the pile in their attempt to subdue the man who kicked and punched in every direction. He howled from under the tussled heap of uniforms. "You killed my son! Why? Was he merely a sacrifice like this child?"

"Lies!" Lilith's voice rose until it became a screech. "Lies from a woman who attempts to dissuade Gad El Glas from its vengeance. She's the one. She's the true enemy."

Soldiers dragged Sir Taylor back and tied his chest, arms, and legs to the throne where he'd been sitting. One of them slapped the man's proud face. Anything to silence his voice that kept shouting, "Villainy!"

People from the crowd had stopped their racket and looked at Sir Taylor in confusion.

Lilith whirled to Maura and hissed in a low voice. "Don't think this will stop me. Don't think for a minute you won't watch this child die. And know it was your fault. What will it kill in your heart—never to rise again?"

"My heart is *not* in your hands. Not today. Or ever." It was time to believe. She held Rory closer and cried out in a loud voice. "Power of the scroll, come. Reveal yourself in me. May your light invade this darkness. Now!"

"Are you hoping your beloved scroll appears out of nowhere?" Lilith asked. Her voice wavered for an instant.

A calm that defied reason washed over Maura's

heart.

"I don't have to carry it. It carries me."

A stream of light flowed out of her belly and surrounded her and Rory, rising like a tower and settling over them as a shield.

Lilith took several steps back. If there was a crack in the stone that covered her heart, Maura couldn't see it.

The priest's incantations and waving of censers came into full fervor, although no one around them stirred or made a sound.

"Light? A contest, is it?" Lilith asked, with a sneer. She lifted her arms and called out in a thunderous voice. "Gad El Glas we acknowledge you, Prince of Darkness. Come!"

Chapter 27

Murky gloom appeared first at the four entrances at the arena floor, creeping in like smoke that grew denser and denser. It filled the arena as if Lilith had bidden it to come for a visit. Circling the perimeter, it rose into the sky and covered spectators. In minutes, thick, impenetrable blackness settled over the entire amphitheater like a heavy blanket. It rose, obscuring daylight and ushering in an untimely, starless midnight.

Silence arrived with it.

As if to mock the evil darkness, radiance that covered Maura and Rory suddenly multiplied. Luminous towers formed around first one person, then another and another. They appeared as spotlights throughout the crowd, each one clothed in a glowing shelter. Magi were there. They'd come.

Lilith commanded the priests to continue their dark arts. Her rant grew desperate when fire that once blazed in the censers smoldered as though doused in water. Solitary columns of light appeared throughout the stadium, signaling a greater Magi presence. Had they been there all along? Or had some unseen communication drawn them.

Maura held Rory tightly and scanned the arena, longing for Aiden. It felt like she was peering from a fully lit room into a night illumined by countless stars.

Rory pointed at something that moved toward them

from the dividing wall. Moments later, Nona sprinted, swerving in and out among the luminaries until she reached them.

Maura released Rory, and he ran into Nona's open arms. The boy whispered in his grandmother's ear and ran back to Maura. He reached up and kissed her forehead.

He returned to Nona, and together they angled back through the amphitheater amid gleaming Magi.

At least he was safe. At least Maura had done that.

While she'd been ensuring Rory was safe, Lilith had gathered her entourage, though her bravado was gone. So was the scorn that made her refuse to have anyone at her side. Now, she was flanked by Anton, the Council members, and the priests.

Maura was an open target. The light she carried made her visible to the enemy. Just like in her dream.

"Enough! Enough of your incompetence." Lilith screamed.

The priests formed a tight battalion around the pit. Anton and the Council members followed Lilith in formation toward Maura.

"No Rory? Ah, well, then you will have to do," she said through clenched teeth. "You and I knew all along that this pit was prepared for you, Maura O'Donnell."

At her words, Magi became a shimmering wave that rushed to Maura's side.

Priests scattered, and Council members froze.

From his throne-turned-prison, Sir Taylor watched.

"Kill them," Lilith shouted in a shrill command. "Extinguish their light."

The priest's magical arts stopped working, as though their fuel was gone. Their hoods fell away in a gust of wind, exposing fear etched on each face. Like wind that separated chaff from wheat, it swirled around their robes, pulling away and exposing them as old, frail and all alone.

Magi stood firm as everyone around them struggled against what became a gale-force wind.

Wispy black smoke formed at the base of Lilith's gown, reminding Maura of when Lilith had joined the serpent in a devilish twirl. Only this time, the tendrils whirled madly and spun around her feet. A smoldering cloud lifted the woman into the air. Shadows engulfed her body and grew into an ebony wall cloud that boiled and spewed stabs of lightning.

Torrential rain stung Maura's skin and drenched her clothing.

Council members drew ceremonial hoods over their heads against fierce winds.

Spectators covered themselves with arms, clothing, whatever they could find.

Lightning slashed from the storm cloud and struck the earth with such intensity that Maura felt electricity buzz throughout her body.

An inverted cone-shaped cloud dropped from the storm. It grew wider, larger, as it snaked above, then descended as a funnel to the amphitheater. Except for Magi who stood as solitary candles, the crowd became a jumble of bodies that pressed together, crushing each other in the narrow exits. Doors that should have opened appeared to be locked. Like animals, the people turned on each other. Piles of trampled bodies lay near the exits, and cries became howls as people realized there was no escape.

The funnel churned downward, hurling debris—tree

branches, carriage wheels, and shards of this and that stripped from the area around the Hall of Justice. A child's toy was held aloft and twirled as if by a puppet's wire. Rain turned to icy hail that peppered Maura's skin. A voice cried out of thunder, resounding with earth-shaking force.

"Forsaken no more. Forsaken no more."

Chapter 28

Maura peered into the whirling chaos and saw Lilith's face, pale and stone-like, her arms extended as she directed the storm.

Maura understood now that Papa and Mama had protected her until they couldn't any longer. What happened when love's arm wasn't long enough? For Lilith, it became bitterness that blinded her to all except vengeance.

Pandemonium ruled in the arena and in the stands, but stillness encircled Maura and the other Magi. Sir Taylor watched the storm from his throne, refusing to bow in fear.

The guards, along with priests and Council members, were nowhere to be seen.

Maura had a decision to make.

Lilith wanted her ability to see the unseen. Exactly what her enemy needed. Would she take the chance like Benjamin did with seed after seed planted in dirt, believing that life would arise when only death beckoned? Maura could offer her gift, knowing it was a seed of light to be sown in darkness. She could trust it would do what it was designed to do—bring sight to the blind.

Maura shouted at Lilith as the tornado rushed in her direction. "You were loved. You were a daughter, cherished by your parents. Adored by the sister you were called to rule alongside."

The tornado stalled, then continued its advance.

Maura hadn't been the thief, but she'd give what she had. Running toward the funnel cloud, she threw open her arms. "It's yours, Lilith. The gift of our lineage. The one you refused when you bowed your knee to vengeance. See what you've been blind to and be free!"

"You never belonged to them," Maura cried. "You belong to us, your family. You belong to love." Maura flung her body toward the tornado. She felt the sucking pressure and heard the roar. Her feet lifted from the ground, and wind smashed her back down. She fought to stand. "It's yours! I give it to you—my mother's sister."

A breeze stirred inside Maura, gentle yet somehow stronger than the tornado. She held her belly as it shifted. She'd thought her ability to see was her own, one to use or to ignore as she chose. Reality spun like a funnel cloud at the core of her being. She realized what she hadn't until that moment.

She belonged to the gift. Her very life joined it in a dance unbroken since birth. Until now.

The essence of something more real than she'd known before churned from her belly, moved to her chest, and flowed out of her mouth. As it left, Maura collapsed to the ground, weakness overtaking the place where strength had been.

Light spiraled upward like a silver blast leaving Maura behind.

Lilith held out her arms, hunger visible in her eyes as cold began in Maura's gut and spread out like ice with every breath.

The rain lost its earthy scent. She could no longer feel it pelting her skin or coursing in rivulets down her face and into her eyes. Warmth retreated and flowed out of her extremities, leaving only a frozen tundra of emptiness inside. She was too tired to feel sad or even afraid. Her lids fluttered over eyes too exhausted to care about all that twisted in the clouds above. Fatigue she couldn't resist crept over her body as a welcome friend. There was no reason to struggle any longer. Rory was fine. She couldn't think of anyone else who needed her.

Until a voice sounded from far away. "Get up, Maura. Fight."

Aiden?

Maura opened her eyes. She had no ability to lift her head or turn in any direction. It was too late.

"Wake up! Now!" This time Paddy's freckled face appeared, hot and flushed with the heat of a race that wasn't quite over. She smelled the pungent scent of his sweat as he shook her shoulders. "Don't leave me, Maura."

"Go away, smelly boy," she said, irritated and unable to swat his hands away.

Still, he kept shaking her and commanding her to stay.

The blast of light out of her mouth had penetrated the storm cloud overhead. It entered Lilith and became a mix of light and dark that coiled together. With every rotation, the light became brighter, and darkness diminished. Still the tornado advanced.

Maura's heart pounded in a rhythm that pulsed, then hesitated, as if unsure how to keep beating. She watched helpless from the ground as the funnel veered away from her and toward the Council thrones, where Sir Taylor was bound.

The tornado descended, targeting Council members

who had huddled behind the thrones. Each man leaped to his feet and ran, with Anton in the lead. White robes sprayed out behind them. In the next moment, the same robes and bodies spun upward into the roaring cloud and disappeared. The funnel stalled, perhaps gathering strength to consume everyone who remained.

But no. It dissipated.

Lilith hovered over the storm that began an unhurried retreat. She reached slender fingers to her neck. With one determined wrench, the emerald pendant tumbled through the air and became dark matter that fled away like a startled raven. Brilliant sunshine splayed out behind it.

Lilith descended in a slow spiral to the muddy ground. Her gown, once pristine, lay in tatters against her pale skin. She crawled to Maura and laid her hands on her belly.

Maura took a shuddering breath as warmth rushed into her core, and the ice inside began to fade. "Forgive me, niece. Forgive me," she said, repeating the words over and over.

A rumbling growl emerged from the midst of the semi-circle of thrones.

Tobias strode into the center of the arena with the magnificence of a Grecian god. His gait wasn't the one of her genteel friend and advocate. He stalked out of the shadows with fierce resolve. Maura watched in alarm as his handsome face morphed from man to eagle. Sharp beak and glittering black eyes overtook his sculpted face. The arms he extended became gigantic wings, and muscular haunches of a lion replaced his body.

It couldn't be true. Except somehow, she knew. Tobias was the griffin. He'd been protecting her all along.

She remembered when she and Aiden laid in the hollow of the tree, the ruckus of the battle outside, feathers and fur flying. Tobias had defeated Maximillian, the eagle, before they were discovered by Hall of Justice soldiers. He was the griffin they'd seen as they'd hurried down the mountain. He'd killed the mountain lion that stalked them. He'd frightened away soldiers with his presence. And now he'd arrived at the amphitheater for one reason—to defend her.

The griffin soared up and down throughout the amphitheater. His majestic form swooped over the arena. Magi bowed in respect. Other people ran wildly, seeking hiding places in corners and doorways.

Lilith cowered at Maura's side as he flew across the arena, wings and talons extended, letting out a mighty roar.

With a powerful dive, Tobias landed on the ground beside her and Lilith. Crouching, his hind legs were tensed and ready to spring. Piercing eyes glared at Lilith, and he spoke in a human voice. "'Tis me, little Toby, milady." Stalking around her prostrate form, he spoke in a thundering voice for all to hear.

"I was a child you captured from my people. You forced me to comply with your evil rituals, your attempts to mold me as your puppet. You thought you owned me and my race. Yet now I ascend in the fullness of who I am and who you were never able to conquer, finally set free when you renounced Gad El Glas. How kind of you. Though far too late." He reached for Lilith with long talons extended.

"Guardian," he said, snarling. "Is that what you called me? Indeed, for protector of treasure I am. She is the one you accuse, the one you despised for what you could not steal from her." His eagle-eyes found Maura then returned to Lilith. "Maura O'Donnell is the gem I've come to protect. She's the one worthy of my care."

Maura faced Tobias, fighting terror at the massive beast her friend had become. "Don't. Please."

Tobias turned from her and charged toward Sir Taylor. With razor-sharp swipes of massive paws, he severed the ropes that bound the man. In another long stride, he pulled the brazen cover back over the pit. When it settled with a clank, he sprang into flight again. This time, he hovered over the few remaining Council members, who cowered against each other. "Fiends. You twisted my heart. Made me a monster like you. Did you notice that I locked the doors against your escape? Just as you did for me as a child when I cried for release."

Maura hated to think of what he'd endured. And what kind of dark covenant the scar had signified.

Tobias cried out to the crowd. "I disavow the Council and its evil rites. Who's with me?" Spectators ducked against each other as they looked on in panic.

"Tobias. My friend," Maura said, calling to him.

In a moment he'd rushed to her side. She pleaded with the man who'd been a true guardian. "Don't let them win, Tobias. Don't let them defeat you with their hate."

"Defeat me? Your true advocate?" The griffin laughed, though there was no humor in the sound. "How do you think they brought you to this city? They framed you for a murder *they* committed."

Sir Taylor walked toward Tobias, now a free man.

"Oh, yes." Tobias acknowledged his presence. "You've been a puppet. Nothing else. They needed your inventions and the wealth they produced to line their pockets. They poisoned your child to bring Maura here, knowing her gift. Unlike you, who was blind and witless, who pride yourself in your intellect." Tobias snorted in disgust. "They promised power and wealth. Did you know their price would be the life of your son?"

Sir Taylor's once proud shoulders slumped. The arrogant stance was gone, when only hours before, he'd sat enthroned with other Council members. The very ones who'd betrayed his allegiance.

The griffin turned again to Maura. "They lusted for you as their prize. No life was too precious. No child safe in their grasp. They didn't know they couldn't possess you. That you were of rare value."

Maura saw shadows move from near the entrances. Soldiers armed with bows and arrows took aim. "Watch out!" she cried.

An arrow embedded in the griffin's side, and he bellowed in pain. With a powerful jaw he dislodged it and flew toward the soldiers, who kept shooting, even though their arrows barely matched the griffin's speed and agility.

Tobias uttered the piercing shriek of an eagle in pursuit of prey and dove over the soldiers, who scattered in every direction. He grabbed one by the nape of his neck, flew over the arena walls, and dropped him from sky.

Maura screamed, horrified.

Behind her, Lilith said, "It's too late, too late."

Maura spun and watched as Lilith pulled a dagger out of her white gown and held it into the air.

Sir Taylor pounced on her and wrestled it out of her hand.

Maura rushed to them, but Sir Taylor pushed her away. With wild fury, he plunged the knife into Lilith's chest.

"No!" Maura charged the hulking man, pounding his back with her fists. "It wasn't too late. It wasn't," she said, throwing herself to the ground next to Lilith, trying to protect her and knowing it wasn't enough. She rested her head against the woman's neck and drenched it with tears.

"Ah, but it is, my dear." Lilith touched Maura's face.

Maura saw a smile play on her aunt's face, now tender.

"It is enough. I go to your mother. Free." Blood gurgled from one side of her mouth and ran down her porcelain jaw.

"Don't go. Please. I need you," Maura pleaded.

Lilith shook her head slightly, her eyes almost closed. "No. There's someone else. You need him more."

Aiden knelt beside Maura with a protective arm around her as they bent low over Lilith.

"Take care of her," Lilith said in a faint voice.

"Don't leave me." Maura stroked Lilith's ebony hair. "Please."

Lilith gasped once for a breath of air, gathered her strength, and spoke again. This time it was with queenly authority. Not of a tyrant, but of royalty. "You're needed here, Star. To rule well where I failed. I bid you…"

Maura leaned in to listen, longing to hear. But Lilith's eyes went vacant, and she was gone.

Maura fell over her, sobbing.

A rush of wings swooshed behind her, and she turned to see Aiden bow to Tobias.

Maura pulled herself from Lilith's lifeless body and ran into the downy under-feathers of wings, which held her close. She smelled the musty scent that had always signaled Tobias's identity and leaned into strength that had been contained in human form.

When he spoke, it was her friend whispering comfort. "I pledged to protect you with my life, Maura O'Donnell. You only saw a glimpse of me in a wrapping that was not my own."

"It's been you. All along. You were there when I didn't recognize you. What happened to you as a child? Why did they hurt you?"

Tobias, the griffin, lowered his head. "Magi weren't the only targets of Gad El Glas. My race, the griffins, were renowned guardians of priceless possessions. Lilith knew our gifting and lusted after it. Did you know a griffin's claw carries medicinal properties? Or that one of our feathers restores sight to the blind?"

Maura only shook her head, unable to find words or reason to understand the incomprehensible.

"Lilith knew. She sent her vile minions to capture me as a young griffin. My parents pursued, but she hid me in the darkness, far from sight. My captors understood that if I was allowed outside, even for a moment, my family would find me. I ached for my loved ones, for the smell of mountains in springtime and all that I'd known. I imagined flying again, soaring freely and without fetters.

"All of that had been stolen. Her magic bound me in human form. When I was a man, it didn't matter where my family searched, they'd never recognize me. She marked me with a token of her ownership. With every descent into black magic, the scar on my face grew. It didn't take long before her abuse shattered my heart as surely as my body.

"I could never return home. My race is pure and called to protect. They wouldn't understand the defilement I'd been forced to endure. I couldn't remember how to fly, even if I were able to salvage who I was as a griffin.

Tobias took a breath, as if gathering strength to go on. "Then you arrived, Maura O'Donnell. You stood on my chair, pointed your finger in my face, and demanded my attention. It took time, but my power returned as I carried out my role as your guardian. In the past, my nature only emerged in fits of rage. You witnessed part of that one day in my office. I was so afraid of losing you.

"No one should be allowed to steal something as precious as an identity. I decided to protect you as only I could. When I made that choice, the real *me* returned. You couldn't know my joy as I soared overhead in the mountains when you and your friend returned from the chateau. Knowing that you were safe in my care, despite Lilith Gunter's foul hate, only made me stronger."

Tobias backed away on muscular hind legs and bowed. "You, Maura O'Donnell, gave me courage to take back who I was. You're the one I love, the one I pledge my life to. Come with me. Rule with me in my kingdom."

Maura held a hand to her heart. She curtsied in honor of her true advocate. "Somehow I knew you," she began. "The real Tobias."

She knew what she had to do. She walked to an overturned throne and pushed it upright. Holding her tattered skirt in one hand, she climbed onto its seat and stood. She lifted her voice with a declaration, loud and strong. "This I vow, Tobias Fitch. Even without your chair as my perch."

She spoke to her guardian as if he alone stood in the arena. "I offer myself and all I am to you in true friendship."

She held on to the back of the throne as she tottered once, then straightened her shoulders and held her head high. "You honor me with your request. Understand that my calling won't allow me to accept. But know this. Together, we receive back the place we were born for. And in that knowledge, we remain aligned forever."

Aiden stepped forward and held his hand out. Maura took it and climbed down from the throne. Together, they walked back to the griffin and bowed low.

Aiden spoke in a low voice that trembled only once. "By your leave, Tobias. I'll take care of her now."

The griffin nodded his large head and wavered as more arrows penetrated the ground at his side. "Go then, in the fullness of who you are, Maura. Go, knowing my heart will continue to keep you and yours, whatever the future may hold."

He flapped giant wings and ascended above the low-lying clouds, farther and farther until he vanished amid the mountainous peaks beyond.

Maura and Aiden scanned the amphitheater, stunned amid devastation all around. People huddled in corners around the entrances, still too frightened to move. Sir Taylor knelt on the ground beside Lilith's body, shuddering.

Maura paused for a moment and then walked to stand at his side. "She knew what you'd do when she pulled out the dagger." Her plan had worked. Sir Taylor was truly the blood avenger. Only it wasn't Maura he killed to avenge Nicolaus's murder. It was Lilith.

Only hours before, Sir Taylor had anticipated Maura's execution. Her death was supposed to be a triumphant ending to a story that required payment for his son. But Gad El Glas had used him, even as it had Lilith. Like a strategic move in chess, Nicolaus had been a pawn.

Sir Taylor quaked with huge sobs.

Maura placed her hand on his shoulder. She recognized what had been there all along, hidden by greed and arrogance. It was a shattered heart. She reached out her hand, but he refused it.

Instead, he fell at her feet, his body still shaking. "You loved him too."

Maura knelt beside him, and they wept together. There were no words. Not after this day.

Moments later, Aiden drew her up from the ground and held her. She felt the familiar refuge of his strong arms. "She wasn't trying to kill me. She was turning the dagger on herself."

"I know, I know," Aiden whispered.

"How did you get free?" She gazed rested in those blue eyes.

"I was at the prison and knew when you arrived. They muzzled me so I couldn't speak."

Maura saw the agony of that cruelty in his eyes. She caressed his freckled cheek.

He took a deep breath. "The guards left us as the festival began. Suddenly, the prison doors opened. All of them. I made sure the children were safely in Nona's hands. Mrs. Ransbottom led the others out."

"Mrs. Ransbottom?"

"She trooped the rest of the prisoners to the Gunter's home. Carriage after carriage of prisoners, now free and dining at the home of their former oppressors."

The doors had swung open when Lilith renounced the hold of Gad El Glas. What other captivity had bowed when she'd refused to let the demon control her any longer?

"Let's go home," he said, taking her hand in his. She didn't protest, even though she wasn't sure where home was. Then again, anywhere with Aiden was where she belonged.

****

SIR TAYLOR

I'd had one desire. Avenge the death of my son.

And I did.

My hands wrested the dagger out of hers, the person I'd counted as friend and ally. My fingers held burnished metal and thrust it into her flesh. How can I erase that feeling? My hands. How they could be mine?

But they are.

Surprise covered Lilith in the instant I held the dagger over her heart. Terror came next, then a scream of agony as it stabbed through bone and pierced her heart. Dazed and confused, she reached to touch the wound as if to make sure it was real. I watched as her life streamed away with every pulse.

I knelt alone, at the feet of Lilith Gunter, feeling small fists pound my back. Maura O'Donnell kept yelling, "It wasn't too late."

It was. And too late for me, as well. Nothing I do, no amount of washing, will cleanse these hands. Or this heart.

I've seen the truth. Maura O'Donnell loved my son.

She did her best to care for him. I thought vengeance would diminish my grief. It only twisted it and made me as venomous as the woman who poisoned Nicolaus.

When I saw Maura O'Donnell on her knees beside Lilith Gunter, I understood. I'd been blind and witless, even as Tobias declared. I believed the Council, trusted them—not because they were trustworthy, but because of my greed. I served myself in the guise of avenging Nicolaus.

I became what I accused Maura O'Donnell of being. A liar. A thief. And a murderer.

God, have mercy on my soul.

Chapter 29

One Year Later

The waterfall tumbled ahead like a gossamer veil as she and Aiden traveled to the amphitheater, where Sir Taylor waited. After weeks of talks and gathering Magi wisdom, they'd come to this morning. Even the granite-lined stadium was clean and ready for a fresh start. Sanctuary was reclaiming itself through the hands of those who honored its role as a refuge.

Lilith had received her sight. And in doing so, had loosed the hold of the demon that controlled her. Gad El Glas fell away from her and, thanks to the Magi, was forced to relinquish its hold on the city itself.

The very atmosphere had changed as the earth responded to peace as it returned. Magi friends and counselors gathered from throughout the countryside. Stately arborists joined Aiden, going to the root of things, and upending a belief system entrenched in tyranny. Those who refused to reject the greed and subterfuge of Gad El Glas were imprisoned or banned from the city. The Magi would make sure they never returned.

Even Hildegard had come, wrapped in her brilliant shawl. "Aye, there be much healin' to be done."

Aiden opened the main floor of the Hall of Justice for her to do just that. She and other Magi healers received the broken who'd come for refuge. She'd brought her herbs and medicines with her. And the broom, of course. "Oi! It be keeping them crows out, now."

Sir Hugh Taylor had been elected as the new regent. Who better than one who'd learned vengeance was a never-ending spiral that robbed everyone? The man who'd never understood refuge had finally turned his heart to receive and defend it.

Children had strewn garlands of roses and morning glory over the dais and over two rows of chairs waiting for Sir Taylor, Maura, and Aiden. Rising to greet the people, Sir Taylor bowed to the audience, then extended a hand toward Aiden and Maura.

Maura smiled at her former boss and adversary.

"We're here today to celebrate the birth of a new city," Sir Taylor said. "Not one renovated by merely good ideas, but one truly new in spirit. For this we thank our friends Maura O'Donnell and Aiden Garrett. This is the peace of Sanctuary—a land that embraces the fearful and pursued. The city no longer corrupted but restored to its original intent. We're finding our way back. We stand together that it may endure."

Maura and Aiden rose to stand beside Sir Taylor. A swell of applause and shouts of joy sounded among the people.

Aiden bowed slightly and spoke in a voice that carried in the arena. "This is a new day for Sanctuary. From now on, this city will be one that receives wisdom of the Magi. Even now it thrives under the leadership of the honorable man you chose in a free election, Sir Hugh Taylor."

Aiden turned and bowed to the older man, who

grasped his hand and pulled him into a hug. The regent struggled to keep his composure. His face crumpled into something that vacillated between grief and joyous abandon. Straightening his shoulders as he adjusted the collar on his robe, he turned to the crowd again.

"This man and woman demonstrated courage against a wicked foe," Sir Taylor said. "Their bravery went unnoticed in countless ways before this time. Aiden Garrett, trusted attendant of the Hall, led an organized resistance that fought against the evil regime of Gad El Glas." Sir Taylor cleared his throat. His face flushed, and he struggled to speak. "Maura O'Donnell was falsely accused...She stood alone in the arena against our enemy, offering what she had to defeat it. We honor them both. And release them to do what is in their hearts—to train the next generation of Magi children."

Sir Taylor paused to let the audience cheer. When they quieted, he continued. "And now, my friend, Rory." Sir Taylor searched for and found the boy standing beside his grandmother. "We have an announcement to make." Rory bounded up the stairs two at a time with a huge smile. He hugged Sir Taylor's legs and then waved to the people.

The crowd cheered as if he were a pint-sized victor returning from battle.

And maybe he was.

Sir Taylor bent over to receive Rory's hug. The child almost throttled the man with his energy, then wiped tears from the man's face with grubby fingers. A grimy stream commenced down Sir Taylor's cheeks and into his beard. "Rory, my friend," he said, finally standing and motioning to the audience. "It's your turn."

"Aye." Rory stood on tiptoes and inspected the

crowd until he spotted familiar faces. "It'll be schoolin' for me now. And you, and you, and you," he said, pointing to one child after another.

Sir Taylor beamed with pride at his small friend. "A fine woman, a Magi by the way, is constructing a model for children's education in the region. Her name is…"

"It's me granny!" Rory jumped in, shouting, and dancing a jig on the stage.

"Exactly." Sir Taylor bowed to Nona. "Her name is Nona Grisham, Magi and new Minister of Education."

Nona rose like a queen over her kingdom.

Children rushed her from every side. She would've fallen into a happy jumble if Sir Taylor hadn't held up his hand to still the commotion.

Maura peered over faces in the crowd. Someone was missing in the midst of all this joy. It was a glorious day. Almost perfect, but not quite. Her heart jumped when she glimpsed a man in a tattered brown hat. When she struggled to get closer, he gathered a small child in his arms and walked away. The tiny sliver of hope vanished as quickly as it appeared.

It was Benjamin she missed. Fresh grief pricked her heart. How she longed to share this moment with him.

Sir Taylor continued speaking to the people with Aiden and Rory at his side. The sun shone brilliantly around gray-blue mountains in the distance. The hint of a rainbow crested over the plunging stream of the waterfall. She heard Sir Taylor's voice as if from far away. He was a changed man. One who stood without fanfare, extending hope to a people who'd had none.

"A true refuge city for the generations begins with our children," he said, checking his notes, then stacking them in a neat file on the podium. "Thus, we end this time together, knowing that it is only a beginning. Before we leave, I have something to present to Miss O'Donnell."

Had she heard her name? The crowd roared with approval. Aiden nudged her with his elbow. "They're cheering for you, Maura."

She tilted and would've lost her footing without Aiden's firm grasp on around her waist. Sir Taylor extended something to her. It was a navy-blue cylindrical pouch. The scroll Papa had laid into her arms the night he'd said good-bye. She and its light had been discovered by darkness, so that darkness would flee by the light that conquered it. Maura hesitated to reach for it, awed for a moment by its presence.

Sir Taylor seemed uncertain, as if he feared he'd crossed a line.

Maura took his hand that held the scroll and lifted it in her own. Together they stood, arms extended, scroll lifted high. As a reminder that wherever its wisdom ruled, refuge would be secure.

The crowd erupted in cheers. It was Maura's time to speak.

"We present to you the new city of Sanctuary. May we honor its tenets of safe haven for all."

Music broke out with songs and fiddles, which led to dancing amid thunderous applause. The celebration had only begun.

****

SIR TAYLOR

A new beginning. Could anything be sweeter? I've been forgiven. Pardoned by those who had no reason to extend that mercy to me, a sworn enemy and murderer.

Aiden and Maura pointed my attention to the stars.

They've spoken of a Creator who set the constellations in place. And has room for me. Why such riches would be offered to one like myself, I'm not sure. I've decided, though, to receive such grace as a gift. One that came just in time.

The place set apart for me in the city wasn't one I expected, even though the reasoning behind it becomes clearer with each day. I was actually elected regent of Sanctuary. Not regent with a capital R. Not this time. I'm merely servant of a people and friend of refuge restored.

Who would've thought? Me, the inventor who thought he knew it all. Turns out, I knew nothing. I once believed that humility was weakness. Instead, it alone had the power to open my heart to truth.

Then there was the peace that came like a gentle rain over my mind. I began to sleep at night. Yes, all night. That restful slumber released dreams for mechanisms that will help keep children out of the factories.

My purpose on earth is unveiling in a way I never expected. For I'm called to serve a people who were lightly esteemed. Worse, persecuted for no other reason other than fear and jealousy over the treasure they carried. Now, I'll govern in a way that their gifts will be restored. This city will continue to prosper, and the world will once again witness a true Sanctuary.

I'm free. And happy. For the first time. I've pledged my support to Aiden and Maura, as well as to Magi leaders who've gathered to rebuild this city. My heart still aches for the precious family I've lost. One thing I'm certain of, though.

Abigail and Nicolaus would be proud to see the man I've become.

For now, that is enough.

Chapter 30

Mountain Chateau—Six Months Later

Morning light was hours away, but Maura slipped out of bed and dressed, careful not to wake Aiden. Restoring the chateau to its former glory had taken all the strength they could muster. Even though the vestiges of the horror that had taken place there had been swept away, memories spoke to her in countless voices in the night. Sometimes she just had to get up and face them.

She tiptoed down the dark hall and followed a glimmer of moonlight from the kitchen window. The room where they'd worked so hard the day before was lit in pale shadows. She rubbed sore arms, a reminder of the hours they'd spent clearing cobwebs and scrubbing the massive iron stove. They were determined to get it into working order, especially since hungry bellies of boisterous children were short on patience.

The chair where Papa had waited for her that morning so long before stood in one corner. She'd rubbed the soot away and re-oiled its finish until her fingers were raw. The sting of his absence pierced more sharply in places where his presence lingered. She longed for one more hug.

Lost friends and loved ones reappeared in bits and pieces all around her. She imagined the creak of Mama's sewing chair in the bedroom she and Aiden had claimed as their own. When afternoon sun sent prisms of light dancing across the library, she remembered tiny bumps of terror that rose on her skin as Benjamin wove his stories.

It had taken weeks to return to the chateau. She and Aiden stayed in Sanctuary after that fateful day at the amphitheater. No one had seen Tobias since he'd revealed himself as a griffin and exacted vengeance on Lilith. He'd truly been Maura's guardian in ways she still struggled to understand.

And now Maura was at the chateau she'd loved. She pushed open the heavy door and walked outside. She searched the dark sky, where she knew she'd find the constellation Orion, the Hunter. The one whose name meant *He Who Comes Forth as Light.* Its brightest star, Betelgeuse, meant *Branch Extended.*

The Creator of the heavens had extended a branch to her that carried her through the impossible and brought her safely home. His message was a reminder to see. A certainty that light always overcame darkness. Lilith had died, but not until she came to know that love had never given up its hope for her.

It wasn't only the heavens that declared the glory of God. His glory danced in the hearts of people too. That was easy to see in Aiden. As it had been in Benjamin and her parents. It was harder to recognize in herself. She finally understood that unseen hands had placed their light in her eyes—an encoded message, just like the stars.

She and Aiden had adopted Alessandra Gunter, Lilith and Anton's daughter. A strong-willed, active child, she reminded Maura of another little girl who'd always tested the boundaries Papa had set. Although

Aless wasn't their own, her light curls were more like her Aunt Judith than her own mother, Lilith.

That was where the similarity ended. Aless crowed like a rooster with every race she won and climbed trees with the most agile. She tested Maura's patience every day. Of course, Aiden wasn't moved by a child who was so much like the woman he loved.

Shaking her head to clear away the rush of thoughts, Maura picked up her skirt and ran to the meadow. She closed her eyes and twirled in the gray dawn, singing the choruses of her childhood. Ones she'd teach other little ones.

Finally, the sun rose, and she heard a little one's voice calling from the chateau.

"Wait for me!" Alessandra rushed into the meadow, arms flapping and legs skipping over dewy grass and wildflowers. Pulling her into a hug, Maura whirled her around as together they greeted a new day.

Movement stirred near the aspen. She instinctively held the child closer as a brown hat bobbed through the tall grass. It was attached to familiar head with hair spewing out in wild shoots. A smile crinkled his eyes, and his crooked gait became an awkward gallop.

Benjamin. Could it be?

Maura placed Aless down on a thatch of grass and ran to him. They hugged until they fell to the ground in a jumbled pile of happiness.

"But I thought…" she said. "I saw her…"

"It was only an image, dear heart." He brushed hair from her face and studied her appearance. "I was on my way after Lilith died—when I knew she was free of Gad El Glas. But I was delayed the village."

Maura had too many questions to choose just one.

Benjamin seemed to understand. "That's a story for another time," he said, smoothing her hair with his weathered hand.

Maura peered over him from head to toe. "Did they hurt you? Why did it take so long to get here?" Her questions longed to escape like water from a floodgate.

Benjamin held up his hand to quiet her. "Lilith thought that if you believed she'd murdered me, you'd surrender to her without a fight. Then she'd swiftly dispatch you in sight of everyone at the amphitheater." His shoulders were thin and stooped. Stubble on his cheeks had become gray.

The last time she'd seen him was the day she'd watched Lilith murder him. Tears rushed to her eyes, and she bowed her head. "I'm sorry. I tried to…"

Benjamin chuckled. "The will of the scroll was stronger than Lilith. It kept me safe. And has a mind of its own. One even stronger than yours." His brown eyes shone with joy. "I'm proud of you, Star. You did rise up. As will the little one you carry in your womb."

Maura gasped and pretended to be appalled. Then giggled as she touched her belly.

Aless joined them, stretching up on tiptoes to come closer. Benjamin held his hands out, and the girl tumbled into them.

"Who told you?" Maura asked. "You don't even know… Aiden and I married here, in this very meadow. And Aiden is…"

"Paddy. I know. I have my sources." He pointed in the direction of the aspens.

Aiden burst into the meadow, his curls a burnished copper in the sunlight. He picked up Alessandra in one arm and embraced Maura in the other. Those long arms were coming in handy with the tribe of children they'd inherited.

Suddenly, a shadow appeared over the trees. Aiden instinctively pushed Maura and Aless into a cover of nearby bushes. Maura struggled out of the tangle of branches and pointed toward the sky.

"It's Tobias!"

Maura and her family stood together, hands extended into the air to greet the griffin, who soared once more over the aspen grove. His majestic form dipped low, then spiraled upward, as if to approve of their gathering. Or perhaps as a reminder that he was still guardian of treasure.

Chapter 31

Later that day Maura sat at the worn desk, its lovely, scarred grain polished to a gleam. Aiden had pulled it from the ruins after they'd arrived, determined to salvage its beauty. Pretty much like he'd done for her, although she wouldn't tell him that part. At least for now.

The tiny nook where she sat had been Mama's sewing room. Her trunk sat in a corner of the room. It was a perfect hideaway from the noisy activity of children who shouted nearby. Warmth of the sun on a chilly day made it even sweeter. A kiss tickled the back of her neck, and she turned to see Aiden, holding something behind his back.

"You're spying on me." She peered around his slender waist and tried to grab whatever he was hiding.

"No, no, no," he said, holding a yellowed sheet of parchment in both hands overhead.

"It's old. Another ancient drawing of mine?"

"Not exactly. Although, it *is* another jewel. Besides me, of course." He laid the paper on her desk and lifted her into his arms.

They'd married soon after they'd arrived at the chateau. Friends and family gathered in the meadow as deer peered through the aspen grove like shy visitors and a great horned owl stared silently overhead from a giant pine tree. Truly home at last, they'd lain under the stars and talked for hours. Well, Aiden answered her questions. One after the other.

"How did you know you'd see me again?" she'd asked, peering over at the outline of his dear face in the darkness. "You wouldn't have found me, not…not apart from Nicolaus's death."

"I can't explain how I knew you'd arrive or that we'd meet again. Or that this moment would come. I took a job with the Hall as an attendant so that I could watch for you. In case you were ever forced to seek refuge. You didn't understand why I was there when you needed me. But I'd been waiting for you. I promised the One who holds the stars in place I'd protect you and be your faithful friend."

Maura breathed against his chest and whispered. "Maybe that's why He always let you win."

Aiden had laughed and grabbed her into an embrace that took her breath away. There had been a lot of those moments. Even now, Maura's heart pounded with the closeness of her husband's body against hers.

"*Another* surprise?" she asked, nuzzling her head under his chin. Since her first day in Sanctuary, he'd arrived as her deliverer with the oddest regularity. He ducked his head as if suddenly embarrassed.

"It's a letter," he said quietly. "From your mother."

Her gaze jerked to his face, then to the letter he'd placed on the desk. Suddenly, its fragile parchment became like gold. Graceful script flowed from sentence to sentence on the page. It was what she'd longed for so long. One last word from her mama.

"How did you find it?" she asked, afraid to touch it.

"It was…near where she lay," he said. "I tucked it under my jacket as I ran. Then kept it safe at Nona's house." He winked. "I do have secrets, you know." He hoisted her into the air and kissed her one more time before he turned to leave. She watched his retreating figure for a moment, then sat and carefully fingered the last gift from her mama.

Dearest Star,

"Though an enemy builds its shelters on high and sets its nests among the stars, she who carries the light of stars will find and bring them down."

We made sure you knew this prophecy even as a child. I couldn't tell you about my sister, Lilith. You were so little and wouldn't understand how life twisted what was meant to be precious. An enemy captured her when she was a child and, although we kept searching, we never found her.

You share our lineage. Live with mercy, beloved. Understand that when terrible things happen, you have a choice. Will you believe that the light inside is enough? Will you offer that light even when your heart is broken?

Your ability to see the unseen is heralded not only by your unusual eyes, but also by what you carry in your heart. You were born as a Magi seer, not to lord your gift over your people, but to protect them. To deliver them, if necessary. And to help them take their place in this world as the kingmakers and nation-changers they were called to be.

If I bring this letter to you, my heart will rejoice. If someone else carries it, know that you're greatly loved. All we desired for you, and all you were created to accomplish, we placed into Benjamin's safe arms.

There will be others. Discover them with the eyes of your heart, with wisdom that sustains the universe itself.

Laurel Thomas

We love you until the end of time, in a place where dreams never die.
Mama

A word about the author...

A former high school English teacher, Laurel Thomas loves words and their power to convey remarkable stories. She's written for inspirational magazines including *Guideposts* and *Mysterious Ways*, as well as ghosted nonfiction. Her novel, award-winning *River's Call*, published by Wild Rose Press, boasts five-star reviews.

Laurel is general administrator of WriterCon in Oklahoma City, OK where she teaches and supports other multi-published industry professionals who equip writers for success through national conferences and weekend intensives.

https://www.laurelannthomas.org/

Thank you for purchasing
this publication of The Wild Rose Press, Inc.

For questions or more information
contact us at
info@thewildrosepress.com.

The Wild Rose Press, Inc.

Printed in the USA
CPSIA information can be obtained
at www.ICGtesting.com
JSHW050440280723
45520JS00004B/112